SQUARE AFFAIR

by

Timmothy J Holt

Square Affair
by: Timmothy J. Holt

Copyright © 2014 by Timmothy J. Holt

Published by
Christine F. Anderson Publishing & Media, Madison VA, 22727
www.publishwithcfa.com

CHRISTINE F. ANDERSON
PUBLISHING & MEDIA

ISBN: 978-0692350645

Printed in the United States of America

Author Note

All Biblical references are from the King James Version

Square Affair is a work of fiction. Names, characters, places, and incidents either are the product of the author's imagination or are used fictitiously. Any resemblance to actual person, living or dead, or locales is entirely coincidental. Where real-life historical or public figures appear, the situations, incidents, and dialogues concerning those persons are entirely fictional and are not intended to depict actual events or to change the entirely fictional nature of the work.

ACKNOWLEDGMENTS

Numerous individuals helped to make *Square Affair* a reality. To all of them, thank you. I should mention specifically the North Side and Evanston Writing Group who helped bring my original draft to what it is now. Without their suggestion Clara May and Frieda would have remained unknown. Christine Anderson took a chance on me and made *Square Affair* a reality. Thank you Christian F. Anderson Publishing and Media. I send a big thanks to my partner, Dan. He carried on without me while I disappeared into the office.

SQUARE AFFAIR

TABLE OF CONTENTS

Introduction

The five men might as well be walking The Square with a big scarlet "A" on their foreheads. Every time they're spotted on The Square the town folk stare, turn away, or grab their children and duck into a store. I told Frieda the other day, "This affair is *The Scarlet Letter* of *Our Town*."

Frieda huffed like a steam locomotive, and then responded, "An English teacher until your dying day. Maybe the town would be satisfied if the men involved in this affair had to wear a big scarlet letter A. They are adulterers, after all."

I looked at Frieda and tried not to laugh, but those words fell from her mouth like dead, brown leaves in autumn. Through my chuckles I said, "You're sweeter than Millie's sweet tea." She wasn't laughing.

You can call me Clara May. This year, 1969, Frieda and I are 70. We both like living in a small farming community and Dewers fits the bill. It's a small, rural town in Illinois, the land of Lincoln. Here people call me Clara May. My mother's name was Clara June, and I had to use my middle name to avoid confusion. My family has lived in Dewers since obtaining a United States Military land warrant in 1850. So you see, I'm well qualified to tell you about The Square affair that's been the talk of this community for the past year. Look, if you want to know anything about Dewers or the people who live there, you talk to me. If I don't know, it's not worth knowing.

Four of the five men accused in this affair were students of mine in high school: Bob, Thomas, Danny, and James. I also taught their parents. Gary is the fifth. He moved to Dewers from Chicago to run an insurance agency. Danny lives just down the road from me in the house he inherited from his granddad. I know him best.

You need to know some things about me and the town of Dewers. It will make it easier to understand the story.

They call me a spinster because I've never married. To me it's a disparaging label. I'm not some crabby old maid who spends her life being bitter because life has passed her by. It was my choice to remain single. I had many offers of marriage but turned them all down. And life has not passed me by.

Out of all that I have experienced, my views on life are formed from regular church attendance, the easy-living life of the roaring 1920s, the scarcity of the Great Depression, friends and neighbors who never came home from wars, and the fight for the right of women to vote. While this Square affair has the town riled, it's far from a disaster. Worse things have happened and will again. Dewers is experiencing growing pains. It is hard for the city to move out of its complacent morality and into the new worldview that is being shaped now by the emerging war in Vietnam and the beginnings of a sexual revolution. Dewers does not yet understand sit-ins, flower children, love children, or war protests. And contrary to the opinion of Pastor Jenkins, the changes taking place will not cause the moral decay of Dewers.

What you need to know about Dewers is that it doesn't try to be any more than what it is: a conservative, God-fearing farming community. You'll find straight roads, Victorian-style farmhouses with steep roofs, corncribs, fenced-in pastures, cattle, silos, red barns, and laundry hanging on clotheslines. In spring farmers are in the fields, and the smell of fresh dirt permeates the breezes. By early summer the land is green with corn, oats, wheat, soybeans, and clover. In late summer and fall, I am always amazed at how the land is transformed to shades of gold. We understand the meaning of a bountiful harvest.

The focus of activity in this community is The Square with its stores, restaurants, and banks. In the middle of The Square is our county courthouse. Saturdays are the busiest time, especially when it's not planting or harvesting season. Everyone gathers on The Square to shop, to visit, and to catch up on gossip. Men frequent Marty's hardware store, Jim's barbershop, Squeaky's Tavern, or, for a seedier atmosphere, they go to the Washington Street Inn. The men discuss weather, crops, cattle, market prices, and their sex lives. Town gossip seeps in but they'd never admit it.

Women are upfront. They gossip or if you're more refined, they catch up on the news. As for me, I gossip. We catch a Coke or coffee at the counter in Rexall Drugs. You may find us chatting over hats in Nellie's hat store or among the dresses at Montgomery Ward. We are also more apt to find a friend sitting in his or her car and join them for a good chat. When I am on The Square, my preference is to gossip while shopping. But I play bridge every Monday night, and I get some juicy tidbits from that group too. Little goes unnoticed in the town of Dewers.

Dewers is a place where neighbors help neighbors and where there are few secrets. Morality is a topic of daily discussion. The most common sin: not loving your neighbor as yourself, or doing unto others as you'd have them do unto you. We try to live in the presence of God, and as long as a person works toward that goal, regardless of their belief, they are attempting repentance and their sins are forgiven.

I'm old in years, but don't call me an old lady. Most people my age are lost in fear of the world becoming unfamiliar. So they run to hide in their history, forgetting that they're still alive. But they'll run up against the ultimate unfamiliar: death. I remember the past but I don't live there.

You've never seen me in a pair of pants and probably won't. I can't say never because I may surprise you one day. I wear sturdy black oxford shoes with a Cuban heel, white in summer. I never liked spike heels or pointed toes. They make your calves look great, but I don't need to impress any man. People like me for who I am or they don't. You'll see me in dresses, usually floral and always just below the knee. On Sundays in the summer it's a white or light-colored dress with a lace collar and in the winter black or brown with a lace collar. At church I wear a hat and veil. They are small and unassuming, except on Easter Sunday, when they're grand.

I've often been asked for my secret on aging. The answer I want to give them is, *I've made it this far because I've not had a husband to drag me down,* but I don't, unless I'm with the bridge club. I believe the secret of aging well is to laugh a lot, a daily gin and tonic, and never saying *if only* or *remember when.* And remember you can't stop change. Even death won't get you out of it.

That's enough about Dewers and me. It's time to get on with the story. I've verified all the relevant facts, so go grab your favorite drink. I'm going to have a gin and tonic. Make sure the dog's been out. Turn the phone off. Find a comfortable chair. I've got a story to tell that's better than any in all my years in Dewers. We'll have a piece of my lemon pound cake when I'm done.

Chapter 1

Clara May on Bob Thompson

Frieda is coming over this morning for tea, so I baked a pound cake. I used my grandma's recipe, and when I eat it, I reminisce back to the times she'd bake for me. I'd tell her, "Grandma, this makes me feel good inside."

I can still picture Grandma: hair up in a bun, wearing an apron made from a flour sack, and a broad smile. She'd say, "Honey, that's what it's supposed to do."

Looking out the kitchen window, I see Frieda driving up. It appears as if a light snow is falling. After waving to Frieda to come in, I turn to set the table for our tea. Frieda never knocks. She just comes in, a habit we've had for as long as I can remember. "Whew. It's cold out there. Is that pound cake I smell?"

"Yes, it is. I need to feel good today."

After hanging her coat in the hallway, Frieda takes a seat at the kitchen table. "Well, today is it. Trial starts today. Heard anything yet?"

She asks about the trial of The Square affair five, and today Bobby Thompson goes on trial. "Goodness gracious, I never thought I'd see the day when our Bobby would be on trial. I need to get at this cake because I need something to make me feel good."

I pour a cup of tea for Frieda, coffee for me, and place two slices of pound cake on the table. Frieda fixes her tea with cream and sugar before speaking. "Bobby always knew how to get his dad's goat, but I imagine this really gets under William's skin."

William is Bobby's dad. I respond to Frieda, "He never got along with his dad. Remember in high school how I'd have to intervene."

Frieda had been the principal's assistant at Dewers High School, where I taught English. "Oh, lordy, I remember the time you were counseling him on his career and college. Mr. Thompson called and insisted I get you from class. He was mad."

It all started when I asked Bobby what he wanted to do for a living. Without hesitation he said, "Miss Clara May, I want to be a writer or an artist."

This was not a surprise to me. I had him in my English class and he loved writing. Next we talked about college. "Have you thought about college?"

Bobby said, "I'm not sure. I haven't researched it much. Dad wants me to go to his alma mater and pledge his fraternity. He wants a legacy."

I was pretty sure this was not what Bobby wanted. "A legacy?"

Bobby's eyes narrowed and his grin became a fine, tight line. I could hardly see his lips until he spoke. "Yeah, he wants me to take over managing the bank after I graduate."

Frieda cut in, saying, "And the next day is when Mr. Thompson called, all hot under the collar."

Many parents had called me during my teaching but usually to thank me for keeping their kid in line. William Thompson wasn't calling to thank me. "Miss Clara May, I want to have a word with you. My son says you've been helping him to find a college so he can major in writing and art. I'll have none of that. What kind of a career can he have with that foolish degree? I will not pay for college if that's what he decides to do."

Frieda takes a sip of tea, and then says, "As I overheard you talking, I recall you were having none of William's high falutin behavior."

"No, I wasn't. I told him if he insisted on talking to me in that tone of voice, I'd take all my money from his bank and make sure all my friends did the same. It wouldn't have amounted to a whole lot, but it would have made him look bad. I said, 'Billy, you leave that son of yours alone, and he just might amount to something'. I told Billy I remembered when he was but a whippersnapper with similar feelings for his dad."

Frieda started laughing. "Remembering what happened in school makes me wish I was still working. I do miss those days. What would you tell Bobby today?"

"I'd tell him to shut up. Listen to the judge and his attorney. Speak only if he has something important to say. And I'd tell him the same as I did in high school. There's nothing wrong with you."

Frieda tilts her head to the left, scrunches her eyes until her eyebrows wrinkle, and asks, "What do you mean, what you told him in high school?"

"I don't tell you everything. He came into my room all flustered one day in his senior year. He asked me if there was something wrong with him, because he'd rather read than be with the boys on The Square. He said he only dated because his friends were. He didn't want to be the odd man out."

Again Frieda sits poised for a question. "But didn't he give his class ring to Mary?"

"He did. The football players were all talking about getting to the bases with their girls and, as the quarterback, he felt left out. He gave Mary his ring so he could have bragging rights."

Frieda points a shaking finger at me. "Mr. Thomas was none too excited about that relationship when it led to a marriage proposal."

"No, he wasn't." I pause to look at the kitchen clock. "It's about noon. Let's turn on the radio and see if there's any word about the trial on the midday news."

Chapter 2

Bob Thompson

As I exit the courthouse and descend the steps with my attorney, he turns to me and speaks. "Bobby, I think we did okay today."

We walk on together. There is no response from me. If he says we did okay, we did okay. I look at The Square and Halloween is everywhere. Children are trick-or-treating. Ghosts, cowboys, witches, and spacemen walk the streets on The Square, seeking favors from the stores. There is an especially large group peering into the windows of Montgomery Ward, where a window-decorating contest is taking place. Children and parents are gathered, voting for their favorite decoration. One vote, one dime, all proceeds go to UNICEF. For most, the day provides an opportunity to pretend to be someone else, to live a fantasy, to be a different personality. Even adults enjoy a good disguise. How I long to be behind a mask, in a costume, anything not to be the person descending the courthouse stairs into the nucleus of my town.

The morning weather report indicated a possible freeze and an early snow. With my heavy overcoat I'm shivering, but it isn't the cold causing me to shake. A coat cannot replace the loss of a town's affectionate warmth. Most saw me as an honorable man with two small children, as an Elder in the church, as an educator with a successful teaching career and member of the school board, while others now see me as an object of lust. Like the trees on my friend's farm stripped of their leaves, the bark left exposed and dying by the spring tornado, my personal tornado leaves me naked, cold, and wondering if I'll survive the winter.

The town of Dewers is in the heart of Lincoln-land. A statue on the north side of The Square honors Abraham Lincoln and his legacy. It's the location where Lincoln gave his speech about not being able to fool all the people all the time. The speech is an accurate depiction of me. I fooled some of the people all the time. I fooled all the people some of the time. The day's court proceedings did not change the adage. Now I am fooling no one but myself. I'll have to deal with the person I have become, not the person I pretend to be.

The wind catches my overcoat, blowing it open to expose me and all I think of is a flasher exposing himself to an unsuspecting victim. Tightening the belt and buttoning my collar, I attempt to keep out the cold world that has now seen me naked. Thanking my attorney for his defense, he departs on foot for his office off The Square, and I walk alone to my car, parked at the bank on the opposite side of The Square.

My walk takes me past parents who, at the sight of me, tighten the grip on their children and turn their faces away from me. They try to avoid looking in my direction but cannot resist a sidelong glance as I pass. I sense their piercing stares and pull my hat low, raise my collar further in an attempt to hide my identity, but to no avail. An active, successful life in a small town carries many benefits, which I enjoy, or should I say previously enjoyed. My opinions are sought. I'm asked to serve on prestigious boards. I share my legal savvy at Rotary meetings. I am a member of the Elks. I coach a Little League baseball team and never miss a high school football or basketball game. I doubt if anyone will seek me for anything now, with the exception of a divorce attorney seeking new business or the child welfare office investigating the safety and moral upbringing of my children and those with whom I come into contact.

Luckily I pass the Montgomery Ward without notice. The kids and parents gathered are focusing their attention on the decorated windows. I long to stop at Squeaky's, the bar on the corner of The Square, for a drink. It's the place where it all started. I had no idea a vodka tonic and a game of pool would lead me here. The drinks, games of pool, and conversation changed my life and set me on this unplanned journey -- a one-way trip -- its destination imagined only in the fringes of my thoughts.

I need a drink so I keep walking, off The Square, behind the bank, to the town's skid row. Clapboard siding on the apartment house is in bad need of paint. I think the first house was red, but it's now a pale shade of fading pink. One of its wooden steps is missing. The three-story apartment building next to it has missing bricks on the corner. What appears to be copper molding around the roof is coming loose and flopping in the wind. The iron handrail is resting in the weeds of an unmown lawn. At the corner, a skeleton of a house is being torn down for a parking lot. Will one of these be my new home? If my wife divorces me, I'm sure she will try to take all the money she can for her and the kids. One of these houses will be all I can afford.

Across the street is the old butcher shop and locker building. As a kid I'd go there with my sister and father to collect meat we had stored in the locker freezers. They had a soda fountain, and Dad could be counted on to buy us a soda, my sister a Green River and me a Swamp Water. I'm not sure what was in them. I think it was ginger ale and lime. Their green color was not appetizing, but the flavor I can still remember. Next to the locker was the penny candy store where we picked up the Sunday paper and spent what we had left of our quarter allowance. How I long for a row of candy dots and a Swamp Water. It was nice to be innocent in those simple times.

I stop to peer into the cracked windows of the abandoned bakery. No more aroma of baking, only the smell of stale urine where the drunks have pissed in the gutter. There are no long johns, glazed donuts, or cinnamon rolls, only anonymity and a cold beer in the bar.

I walk on past other abandoned buildings where only those seeking solitude can be found. One of the only businesses left -- the Washington Street Bar -- at the corner, is a place where everyone has skeletons that they're hiding in a closet somewhere. Shots of liquor and beer help to keep that closet door locked. There's an unspoken rule: secrets never leave the bar's front door. They remain hidden in the smoke and sawdust of this retreat.

The arrest was a year ago, but the journey began before that, probably since before puberty. I'm only certain of my actions here in Dewers. They began two years ago on the inescapable night my wife, Mary, was attending a woman's circle dinner at the Methodist church on Main Street and the children, Billy and Sue, were sleeping the night at their grandparents' house, my parents, Mr. and Mrs. William Thompson, Sr.

My family name, Thompson, can be found on the documents incorporating this town. They started the First National Bank and obtained a considerable amount of farmland through war deeds. All of this enabled the family to accumulate money. You might say we are old money. At least that's what my wife thinks she married. When we announced our engagement, my father and Mary tried to get me to enter the banking business and take over after my father retired. I did not see this in my future. I went to law school as a compromise to keep them quiet but surprised both of them when I announced I'd be teaching at the state university and not going into private practice as I waited for my father to retire. Carrying on the prestigious family name as an attorney would secure Mary's social standing and ensure my father a continued legacy.

As her family were not original citizens but had located in the area because of her father's job, Mary took every advantage of being the daughter-in-law of the town's banker and elder family. There is an advantage to this: all of the time Mary spends with her various civic duties gives me free time away from her. Free time put me in the courthouse today and on this street seeking comfort in anonymity.

Mary insists we keep ourselves in top physical shape so we don't lose our high school physiques. Slim and blonde, she still turns heads. She says it makes her feel sexy when men, or women, comment on my body. She likes how my thick, black hair is naturally wavy. She encourages my fishing, saying it gives me an overall golden tan. She insists we work out on a regular basis at the local gym. It keeps me with a 32-inch waist, admirable pecs, and a firm abdomen. For my physique I am thankful, but it never has been anything but show for her. My looks garner few favors when we're alone in bed, but it has garnered favors from others, as has Mary's.

With all of Mary's antics and my father belittling my chosen teaching career, I welcome the nights when Mary is busy and the children are visiting grandparents. I also welcome the time it allows me to be alone with my college buddy, Gary, and the fishing trio: Danny, James, and me. When I can arrange free time, we meet up at our favorite bar on The Square, Squeaky's.

On the ill-fated night all the men except Thomas Turnbull were in the bar. As a farmer, he was still working in the fields. Gary Warren was seated at the bar, talking to James Calhoun and the bartender, Danny O'Conner. Gary had a martini in one hand, a cigarette in the other, and sat talking to James at the bar. Gary caught sight of my entrance and waved me over to the section of the bar where he was holding court. He motioned to the bartender to give me my usual, vodka with a twist of lemon. Since I was on my own for the night, Gary insisted it be a double.

Even when we first met in college, I felt as if he was a longtime friend. Rising from the bar stool, he hugged me, patted me on the shoulder, and started off with the obligatory questions concerning family. "How's Mary and the kids?"

"Mary is terrorizing the ladies circle tonight. She'll be in a good mood when she gets home, nothing like bossing around a group of women to make her happy. She'll be keeping them there until well past nine p.m."

Gary Laughed and then took a deep drag off his cigarette. "So you'll have to leave to get home before her?"

"It doesn't matter what time I get home," I said, thinking it didn't even matter if I slept in the same bed anymore. "My mom and dad are babysitting and the kids are sleeping over with them. Dad thinks he's great with the kids, but I get a slightly different version when they return home."

James strolled over to where I was talking with Gary and caught the cynicism in my words. "Your father is always bragging about his grandkids."

"Yeah, because Dad doesn't think he can brag about his professor son. He's never forgiven me for taking a full-time teaching position."

As usual, Gary defended my father. "Give the ol' man a break. He's only recently accepted the right of women to vote."

I can't believe he supports my dad. Gary attends demonstrations for equal rights, equal pay for women, anti-discrimination; he even talks about the rights of homosexuals. Basically Gary believes no one should be harassed by the law, evicted from their apartment, or prevented from earning a living because of their sex or private lives. Of course, this is not known publicly, at least here. He reserves his more liberal opinions for Chicago. Dad and he have a mutual agreement. Gary refers investors to the bank. Dad refers depositors to Gary for their insurance needs. Dad believes Gary is one of the good ol' boys because he's in a legitimate business: insurance sales.

"Maybe Dad should brag about you, Gary, since he's convinced I'm a failure. He certainly thinks you're a golden boy."

"What do you mean 'should'? How do you think I get all my business? And I *am* a golden boy. Why, just look at my clothes."

"Hey, remember this is me, Bob. I lived with you four years in college. I know your dirt, so yeah, in your dreams. Tight bell-bottom pants, a shirt with a weird pattern. All that's missing is the disco ball. What'd ya do, leave it in Chicago? Good thing Dad doesn't know what you do in the big city." James was attentively listening to our conversation. "So, have you got James stranded here, forcing him to listen to you?"

"No, we were describing next year's Chevy. He just got back from Detroit."

James's family owns a nearby Chevy/Buick dealership that James turned into a financial success and is all too eager to brag about it. His father had lost a lot of money due to alcohol and betting on the ponies. James worked hard to bring the business back to life. Mary and Judy -- his wife -- are members of the same bridge group and they often go shopping together.

James began shuffling from foot to foot as if he could not stand still. His face became flushed. Grinding his teeth, his jaw was taut. "Hey guys, there's more to my life than cars. Have you heard about the fishing cabins on Lake Warren? I was there last weekend with my brother and his family. The fishing is great. There's a dock at the back door, and the cabin sleeps six. There are woods all around. It's private. I think it's what this group needs, some R and R."

Lake Warren is a state park about a hundred miles south. A lake created to provide drinking water for the town of Warren. "Sounds like a good place. Except, I'd rather it be a husband-only weekend. No wives, no kids. Now that would be a *real* R and R weekend."

Gary sighed. "Hey, what about me? Am I excluded because I'm not a husband? I don't think I have kids."

"And I'm not sure you ever will, unless you've got someone hidden in Chicago," I say. Most weekends Gary would close down business and go to Chicago where he has a small studio apartment on the near north side. Though I have hinted at my desire to see it, Gary has never been forthcoming with an invitation. I ask him, "You spend so much time there. Are you sure you can find time for us lowly folk in this backwoods town?"

Gary's eyes caught the pool table light and sparkled with a look that seemed reserved for a sexual come on. Then the eyes began wandering. I could swear he' was searching both of our bodies. He leisurely sipped his martini then cocked his head to the side. "I may have a special person in Chicago, but the person is not marriage material."

I wasn't sure what Gary had in Chicago, but I was sure he was not celibate. "Just don't get anyone pregnant, or you'll have no choice but to have a family."

With downcast eyes, Gary stared at me. "I don't think there's any danger of that happening."

James could not resist his own jab at Gary. "Having some problems with sex are you?"

"I'll have you know everything is working. I can demonstrate for you if you would like."

All our hands flew to cover our eyes. James was first to speak. "Not here, not now."

"I couldn't agree more. Keep it zipped. I saw enough of you naked in college."

With hands on his hips, Gary puckered his lips and squinted his eyes, "Ah, come on, you don't know what you're missing."

Danny, the bartender, had little business and as a matter of fact, we were the only three in the bar. If he has time, Danny will listen to customers and commiserate with their sorrows, laugh at their foibles, or rejoice when someone is happy. He knows most of the town's secrets. His grandfather opened the bar and when Danny's father didn't want to work there, he told his grandfather he would manage it. It has gained a reputation for being a man's escape while wives shop. Not that women are not accepted in the bar. They are, but the men would rather have it to themselves. Danny learned from his grandfather all of the eccentricities: what a customer drinks, who doesn't like ice and who does, who wants extra lemon, who wants lime. Elbow on the bar with chin cupped in his palm, Danny was listening with interest to our conversation. "That sounds like a great idea. If I can get a weekend off, I'd like to go with you."

As this was spring planting time, Thomas was not with us. His farm requires constant attention at this time of the year. "If we want Thomas to go with us, we we'll have to wait until he's done in the fields. Probably early summer," I said.

James stopped shuffling and his jaw relaxed. I almost heard a sigh when he spoke. "Early summer it is. I'll check with the park on the availability."

That night keeps replaying in my head. Sometimes it's a horror movie. Sometimes it's a comedy. Sometimes it's a love story. It's always the beginning of a journey that takes me from my comfortable family life to a new land where I'm a stranger, unfamiliar with its morality, its rules. In my dreams I'm flying, circling in constant flight, chasing an elusive wind. Trapped in the flight, my wings ache to land. I see others soar, but I can't. I barely clear the treetops, and I go nowhere, while all the others fly everywhere at will. If I can't soar, I want it to land. Each flight brings me closer to the clouds. Each attempted landing nearer the ground. Today, I'm not sure if I'm soaring, or if I'm on the ground; but, during these past two years, I've come to realize my uncertain flight began long before this affair.

As a kid, my brother, William, Jr., and I would horse around. We'd do the usually stuff: jump on the beds, play practical jokes, talk about girls, and make fun of each other. What held my attention most was when we kidded each other about our growing sexuality. It was natural to see each other naked. Mom and Dad had wanted us to have separate bedrooms, but we wanted to sleep in the same room so we could talk late at night. We saw each other naked every day. We dressed and undressed in front of each other. My fascination began when Willy, his nickname, started growing pubic hair. Noticing a change in his voice, and the beginnings of a beard, Dad thought it time for the sex talk. He called us together and we both got the lecture. He said, "I don't want to repeat this, so I'll talk to both of you at the same time."

We'd already heard most of it from our friends, but we didn't tell Dad. We wanted to hear his version of the story. All Dad talked about were erections, male ejaculation, and the shame of getting a girl pregnant before you're married. He didn't even talk about intercourse, nor did he mention masturbation. We both had learned more from our friends.

After that talk, I began looking for my pubic hair, as well as my erections. Willy could not hide his morning "woody," as he called it. I was jealous and would kid him about it. "Well, look at Willy's willy this morning...looks awfully small to me."

Will would get out of bed, come over to my bed, and stick his dick in front of me. "Until you can match this, I suggest you shut up, or I'll make you play with it."

Play with it? What did he mean by that? None of my friends talked about playing with erections. They just said you had to have an erection to screw a girl, nothing about somebody playing with your erection. Over the next few days I asked around, until I found someone to tell me. It was my friend, John. "Hell, yes! It's better than masturbating by yourself. You sit back and let someone else stroke you; better yet, have someone put it in their mouth and give you a blow job. Who cares if it's a boy or girl when you get a chance to get your rocks off?"

This was news to me. "Where did you learn all this?"

"My older brother," John said. "He found a book in the library about sex. I haven't found any sissy boys to whack me off or give me a blow job yet, but I'm looking."

"What's a sissy boy?" I asked.

"That's a boy that's willing to play with your dick or give you a blow job."

I was embarrassed at how much more John knew than me, but I was also embarrassed that I wanted to try being that sissy boy.

Next time Willy bounced his dick in front of my face I hesitantly reached out and touched it. He let me keep my hand there while he spoke. "What's this? Does little Bobby want some? Take it and tell me if you think my willy is still so small."

I took my hand and put it completely around his stiff erection. He came almost immediately. "Now look what you've done. Mom will have a fit if she sees this," I said.

Will pulled his underwear up while speaking. "Well, wipe it up." Then he walked off to take a shower.

We had a few other similar encounters before Willy went off to the army. We never got to talk about it. He died within a year, a shooting accident.

I was afraid to go any further with my new found experimentation. I was a football star and being called a sissy in the locker room was not good for your reputation, but I couldn't keep my eyes off the other naked men. Besides, I was taught in church that sex before marriage was sin in the eyes of God. If I could lose my beloved status with God over sex with a girl, I imagined that sex with a man would bring eternal damnation. And I was sure that even thinking about it fell closer to the damnation side than the beloved.

In college, I learned much more from Gary. I asked him once why he never talked about girlfriends. "I'm one of the sissy boys you've talked about," he said.

I took this opportunity to learn more. He told me he was a homosexual and had known since he was young. When we were old enough to go to bars, I accompanied him on a couple of his trips home to Chicago. Despite my experiences there, I still considered myself a heterosexual. Experimenting was just part of learning to be a man. I had a girl waiting for me and we were going to get married after graduation. That's what was expected of me, and that's what I did. That night in the bar changed it all.

Chapter 3

Clara May on Thomas Turnbull

Ever since Thomas started crawling, he seemed confused. He'd crawl toward his mom, stop halfway, turn around, crawl toward his dad, sit, and then crawl out of the room. The confusion didn't improve with age. When he came to me in high school, his eighth grade teacher wrote a note. *Clara May, Thomas is a confused boy. He is shy in class, but when called on, he usually has the right answer. He started to play basketball and then dropped out. He did the same with track. He has potential, but he will need to be coaxed along. And, he has a healthy (too healthy) interest in girls.*

I thought Thomas had gotten his act together by the time I met with him. He was on the Varsity football team, President of the Future Farmers' Association, and the Senior Class Vice-President.

In our high school career counseling session he told me, "Miss Clara May, I know you're supposed to help me decide what I want to do, but I don't know where to start."

I asked, "Do you want to stay in town?"

Thomas took a while to respond. "I don't know."

I knew the answer already, but I had to ask. "What about college?"

Thomas laughed. "Miss Clara May, you've seen my grades. What do you think?"

His grades were not stellar, and college would be a stretch. However, he had good leadership skills. "If not college, what about working at the factory?"

"No. I can't be locked up inside doing the same thing over and over." This was the first time I had seen Thomas have a firm opinion.

His dad was a farmer, so I asked, "What about farming?"

I was surprised at his response. "My first thought is to say never, but I've been thinking. What if I first go into the military? I could see the world. Maybe meet some more girls, ones who aren't so … so uptight."

When I discussed this with Frieda, she thought I'd be shocked. "Isn't that what most kids think about in their teens?" Frieda's grin made her look like a hog in slop. She was so proud of her insight. "He's got it bad. I've had to break up Sue and him more times than I can remember. Making out at the locker, in the cafeteria, waiting for the bus. Oh yes, military is definitely for him. He needs to get laid."

As I remember, he was more worried about smoking his next cigarette than about studies. Frieda said, "I don't know when he finds time to study. He's always with Sue and he smokes like a chimney. Who pays for those cigarettes?"

Thomas only had a part time job. I said, "He must use money he gets from helping his dad on the farm, or his dad buys them for him."

I had a chance to talk to Thomas after church before this affair hit. I asked him how he was doing and he said, "Sue and I are doing okay. Dad can be a pain when it comes to farming. He's always done it his way, and by God I should, too. I can usually ignore him, or he forgets what he said."

I asked, "Are you happy you came back home?"

Thomas looked perplexed. "I miss the freedom. Wearing a uniform has its benefits. "

And that statement about freedom says it all. When I go to town for supper, he's usually at Squeaky's or the Washington Inn. His involvement in the affair confirms my suspicion that he's trying to drown his wanderlust in alcohol.

Chapter 4

Thomas Turnbull

The sky is the color of dishwater. Standing on the back porch in the dingy morning light, I light my first cigarette of the day and take a long deep drag. It's too early for a beer, but I could sure use one. Herman, the German Shepherd, realizes I'm on the porch and barks. He's impatient. When I open the door to let him out, he sniffs the cold air and hesitates before running off to take a pee. Indian summer is over. It's time to find my heavy coat and gloves. I would like to finish plowing the cornfield before winter sets in, but it looks as if this may be my last day in the field.

The crops are out and from the back porch I can see the vast prairie,. Except for an occasional rise, only the horizon limits my view. With the tall corn harvested, neighbors are exposed and subject to scrutiny -- and there's a lot of scrutinizing to do. There's been a summer hiding in the tall corn. You can see only what's on the road in front of your house. We now live on paved roads so company, or anyone passing by, catches you by surprise. If you live on a gravel road, no one can sneak up on you. With dust trails there are no unexpected arrivals.

Mom and Dad live across the road in the house I grew up in. It's Victorian, and it's the original house built for the farm. Mom can keep track of us from her front window that faces our driveway. There's no obstruction to her view. If only my parents could be hidden in dust clouds or behind corn. I appreciate what they do for Sue and me, but they're a little too close. It would be nice to have some distance or at least a cornfield to shield us in the summer.

I get on the tractor because it's where I'm supposed to be, and where I've learned to be. The usual warmth I feel when looking at the vastness of an open field is now a cold sweat. There are eyes peering through the ashen clouds, staring at me like I have put my shirt on backward or left my zipper open. There's no hiding behind stalks of corn. They're gone. Truthfully, I'd rather relax with my morning cup of coffee, read the newspaper, and when Squeaky's bar opens at noon, go to town, have a drink, and shoot the bull with whoever might be there. I'm especially fond of Danny, the bartender. Unfortunately, that's the last place I should be.

Today I'll have to concentrate on driving, lest I keep going and disk the neighbor's field, not that he would mind me doing his work. I'd rather not. I have enough land to keep me busy. I should be relieved not to be in court, but I'd almost rather be there, even though my attorney says it isn't necessary. There may be an out-of-court settlement. Bob said he'd take care of the details, and I should tend to the farming.

I want people to stop staring at me when they think I don't see. I want to hear laughter again when I go to the grain elevator, not an abrupt end of conversation. I want the grocery store clerk to look me in the eye when she hands me change and not at her shoes. I want to look at children without their mothers yanking them away. I want to look at my parents' house and not see Mom peeking out from behind the lace curtains checking me out. She thinks it will keep me on the straight and narrow. Mom's put me on the church prayer list, but it's a little late.

I answer only to the weather when working in the field, not my wife, not the sheriff, not my friends, not my father, not my mom. And since it's uncontrollable, I take it as it comes. Except for the tractor, it's quiet in the field. I have time – time to think, time to consider my past, and time to consider where I'm going from here.

Most people think farmers have it easy, that we have no need for an intellect. All we have to do is to keep the tractor and equipment in good working order, as well as keeping a good supply of gas. They're wrong. I'm a marketing analyst. I'm focused on the price of commodities and the grain futures market. This morning's report indicated the price of corn and soybeans is rising, so my initial thought is I should not sell now.

My livelihood, and that of my family, depends on important decisions I make: Will prices stabilize? Will they rise? Will they fall? Is it the right time to plant? What's the right kind of corn seed this year? Should I risk the year without buying expensive crop insurance? Then there's the selling of crops: getting a decent price is the only opportunity I've got to earn enough income to survive until next year's crops come in. If I were still raising livestock, I'd have to keep tabs on that market.

The barn fell down a few years ago due to erosion from the stream behind it, so there is no livestock, which is one less thing I have to worry about. Looking at the space where the red barn once stood, I feel as if an arm or a leg has been severed. I don't miss the chores like milking the cows or baling hay, but I do miss the simpler times that accompanied them. Fresh cream straight from the cow was used for hand-cranked ice cream in the summer. Now no one has the patience for making ice cream at home. Likewise, no one takes the time to enjoy a watermelon that's been chilling in the cattle water trough. I can see my cousins in a spitting contest to see who can spit the black seeds furthest. Grandma said not to swallow any because a watermelon would grow in your stomach. When Aunt Mary's stomach was getting big, I thought she had swallowed some watermelon seeds, but Grandma said she was pregnant. I still thought it was a watermelon, that is, until one day she had a baby in her arms. You didn't need as many things then. Money was tight, but it never seemed to control life. Perhaps it was just the innocence of childhood.

Innocence went the way of gravel roads, passenger trains, and ten-cent movies with cartoons. Mom and Dad would leave my friends and me to freely roam The Square. Aunts, uncles, and cousins were always parked nearby in their favorite spot. Everybody you knew was either in their cars or walking The Square. My sister and I could always count on the waitress at the Rexall counter to give us a free Coke if we shared our fries. If we ran out of our allowance, Grandpa was always good for a dollar and Grandma for a quarter. We would stretch our quarter allowance to include candy, popcorn, and a movie. Today there's no way out of this town except driving yourself or walking. There's no Greyhound bus. And the theater burnt down last year. I left this town for the Navy and where did it get me? Back to where I started.

This year, the decision on when to sell the crops is not entirely my own. There's an immediate need to pay attorney expenses. Even though it appears the market will be increasing, I can't wait. I could take out a farm loan against the crop sales, but that option is not the best. A loan entails more expenses for the interest, thus less income. My wife says she can help, maybe find a job in town at one of the local stores. She heard of a sales job on The Square. The grocery store needs cashiers and there's always the night shift at the factory. It increases production in the winter, utilizing the idle farmers or their wives. Neither decision is ideal. If she works during the day, I'll have to make sure I'm available to get the kids on the bus in the morning and greet them as they come home after school. If she works the evening shift, I'll be responsible for cooking dinner, making sure their homework is done, see to it they take their baths, brush their teeth, then read them a bedtime story before they fall asleep. My daughter is in third grade and my son first grade. They're too young to manage on their own. I could ask my mother to help, but that would mean admitting my wife and I can't handle a family on our own. Mom would love to lord that over my wife. There is also the fact that the more my wife is out in the public, the more she is open to scrutiny and whispered rumors. We're already the object of town gossip because of me. I don't want to make it any worse on her. She's going to apply for a couple of jobs. If she gets one, we'll decide. All the options keep me away from the boys and the bar. Maybe it's not a bad idea.

I'm nearing the end of the field and can see the house. The kids are waiting at the road for the school bus and Sue's watching from the drive. Our house is good for a tenant farmer. Mom and Dad gave us the land as a wedding present. We had the house built and moved in on our wedding day. A toaster would've been better. There are no free gifts from my parents. I may own the land where the house sits, but not the land I farm. That land is Dad's.

When I returned from the Navy, Dad was ready to cut back a bit on farming and offered some of the land to me. My plans had been to use my VA educational benefits and go to agricultural school. But I like farming and I was not interested in being stuck in a lab or behind a desk managing someone else's farming habits. And what did I get? I settled for someone managing me – Mom and Dad. They have good intentions, but are set in their ways and believe I should also be set in those same ways. At least I'm on the tractor and in the field. And I must admit Dad can be helpful.

The house is tan brick -- a one-story ranch style -- with three bedrooms and a full basement. It's easy to see. It sits on an acre of land carved out of the field I'm working on. The surrounding trees are still small. In the back yard, near the field, is the kid's swing set. They're so proud of it and show it off to their friends saying, "It was not bought at a store, my daddy made it."

As I begin to turn, I see the bus pull off with the kids. Sue waves to the parting bus and returns to the house. She will be gathering up the clothes. This is laundry day. Then when the wash is started, she'll clean up after the kids, dust, and vacuum. Or is this the day she has her job interview? I don't know how we'll manage if she has to work. Winter will be fine because I won't be in the field, but spring through fall will be difficult. I may be forced to rely on Mom's help. God forbid!

Having made the turn, I lose sight of the house. Plainly visible is the water tower and a block from it is the town Square. In the middle is the courthouse ... where the attorneys and the judge will be meeting, where my wife and I obtained our marriage license, and where the birth records of my kids are kept. If the proceedings are not successful, it will soon house my criminal record. In the Methodist church off The Square on Main Street, is where Sue and I were baptized, where we were married, and where Johnny and Mary were baptized.

If today doesn't go well, can any of us show our faces at church again? We have rarely gone since the affair hit the local papers and the gossip mill. Having repeated these words since my Sunday school days, they now haunt me:

Our Father, which art in heaven,
Hallowed be thy Name.
Thy Kingdom come.
Thy will be done on earth,
As it is in heaven.
Give us this day our daily bread.
And forgive us our trespasses,
As we forgive them that trespass against us.
And lead us not into temptation,
But deliver us from evil.

I can't get past evil. Me. Am I evil? I don't think of myself as evil. A criminal? I could go to jail. I could be put in a mental hospital. Where did I go wrong? I was tempted and I gave in. Did I do the trespassing on others or did they trespass against me? I definitely know it's been evil for my family and me. Was the sin already in me? I think that's what original sin means. But, then again, is it? What was that Sunday school lesson? Is this what goes through a criminal's mind? Do they plan ahead even though they say they don't? Can you really attack in a quick uncontrolled rage? It all makes me feel dirty, sleazy, like some bum walking the street exposing himself. It wasn't like that at all. It was tender caresses by someone who knew where to touch, a mechanic who knew how to fine tune a motor for maximum output, someone who knew how, where, when to plant seeds for optimal yield. I yearn for those feelings to put out the fires of my personal hell, my disgust.
For thine is the kingdom,
The power, and the glory,
For ever and ever.
Right now I see no power, no glory, no forever.

So caught up in my own self-pity, I don't see the row's end. I just miss the ditch, brake hard, and head back the other direction. My life is endless turns, back and forth, constantly changing direction and ending up in the same spot. Perhaps I should have made a career out of military service. Sue had not wanted me to enlist, saying, "Let's get married when we graduate from high school and take our chances with Selective Service."

There were rumors of the United States becoming more involved in Vietnam. Sue said I could join the National Guard if I felt serving my country was a duty, but I understood that if no one served, we all would lose, whether there was a war going on or not.

A month before graduation I went to the recruiting office and joined the Navy. I thought it a safe bet. Off shore, on a ship -- how dangerous could it be? Our marriage could wait a couple of years and if not, it wasn't meant to be. My father, a veteran of WWII, is the only one who supported my decision. Friends and family thought I was insane since I could have a deferment if I went on to college.

My problem began in the Navy, but I don't believe that staying home and getting married would have prevented it. I started drinking more and more when on shore leave, which led to prostitutes to relieve the anxiety of months without sex. They were easy to find in Southeast Asia. I wasn't sure what was sinful anymore.

My father's "birds and bees" education, as he called it, came reluctantly one summer as we walked the soybeans pulling weeds. Since we were alone, it was a time to talk man to man, or in this case man to boy. The previous school year I had noticed a change; I was not only growing more pubic hair, but also frequently getting erections. Girls became an attraction. One girl in particular caught my eye, and I wanted to know all about women and sex before going back to school. Growing up on a farm, I knew there was a difference between the make-up of females and males. My cousin and I had played *I'll show you mine if you show me yours* a number of times. It's one of the advantages of still having an outhouse. You could hide from your parents without notice. I knew a man had to have sex with a woman to have babies. I'd seen it in animals. I was confused about how humans did it.

I still remember the exact wording of my question, "Dad, if I have sex with a girl, do I have to take off my clothes, or can I just unzip my pants?" By this time I had discovered masturbation, so I knew how my plumbing worked. I also knew that I could rub myself without taking off my pants and cum. But would it work with a girl?

I think my dad nearly cut his finger with the hoe laughing, "I suppose you could just unzip your pants, but most couples like to get naked." Now, as a young man with raging hormones, sex in any form excited me, but getting naked was another story. That was the extent of the birds and the bees from my father. I learned much more in the school locker room and the Navy.

When not working on the farm, my retreat was the library. I claimed to have a lot of homework requiring time away from the noisy house, TV, talk, and my sister. I had a part-time job stacking books that came with privileges. I could go places others were not allowed. One day I discovered the adult reference section with its books on sexuality. A particular book caught my eye. It was about aberrant sexual behavior. I believe it was Kinsey's book. I was amazed. The initial sexual arousal and final climax of sex is very visual in a man, but, according to them, not so in a woman. I learned that intercourse was not a one-sided event. Once hard, the man needs only friction, then cums. What's the difference if it's your hand or a vagina that provides the friction? I had no idea there were alternative means to climax, or that anything was happening to the woman. There are all means of reaching a climax: oral sex, anal sex, sex with more than one, sex with another male, and two females having sex. Who knew women got aroused and climaxed? Who knew you could have sex with another man? I committed the pictures and words to memory. One day I would try these for myself.

I looked at girls with a new vision. I looked at men with curiosity, wondering just how it would feel. I had kissed a number of girls, but a man? I began to look at men differently, mentally commenting on the size of their cocks, the look of their naked bodies in the shower. Could seeing them naked arouse me? I wanted a woman. Though I heard talk of sex in high school, that's what all I thought it was -- talk -- except for those girls who disappeared in the middle of the year only to reappear the next.

When I went to Chicago for my induction physical I was a virgin. I was horny, and I was anxious to leave this country town and have a taste of what I had only read in books. There was no chance for modesty or privacy while in the line for physicals. It was all hanging out for the world to see. I saw and was not comfortable with what I saw. I had to concentrate on not looking and comparing. Why was I so interested in another man's size? Basic training didn't help and being on board ship meant I was close to men dressed and naked for an extended time. While in the Navy, for all intents and purposes, there were no women, except for the pinups and magazines. Strangely, there were a group of men who had none, myself included.

In retrospect, I think I was trying to prove my masculinity while in the service. I enjoyed losing my virginity to prostitutes, yet I still questioned my sexual identity because I was curious of the rumored sexual affairs between men on the ship. Heterosexual sex was readily available when on leave, but long stretches at sea were frustrating. Others on the ship were whispered to be eager and readily available, and the urge became more important than the gender of the person satisfying that urge. The armed forces steadfastly maintained the facade of sexual purity. What a joke.

My stomach growls, and with a glance at my watch, I notice it is lunchtime. I stop the tractor, pull a cigarette out of my pocket, light it, take a drag. Then I pull out the lunch Sue packed – baloney sandwiches with crunchy peanut butter on squishy white bread. I grab the thermos and pour myself a cup of coffee to go with lunch, wishing it was a Budweiser. Glancing back at the house, Sue is driving off in our '66 pink Plymouth to take cookies to school. Today there's a Halloween party. The kids are right about that car. It looks like Pepto Bismol. What can I say? It was the end of the year and a good deal.

Having finished lunch, I start disking the field again; my thoughts return to my service time. In addition to sex, it taught me release through alcohol and smoking. Often it was easier to pick up a guy in the bars surrounding base. Trouble was, you often didn't know it was a guy. More likely than not I was drunk, and lady-boys were very good at disguise. As it turned out, having sex with men required fewer social skills. It was obvious what you were there for and it was often carried off without discussion. Everyone did it. I had left my righteous morality back home, but at times I heard the preacher's words on the sinfulness of unmarried sex. Regardless of my sexual exploits in the service, I still wanted Sue and planned to marry her upon discharge.

Sue had the wedding planned when I arrived home. Other than my parents providing the invitation list, I had no part in it. My only requirement was to show up on time. Mom had even chosen the best man and groomsman. Tom, my brother, was the best man, and my cousin, David, the groomsman. It was a cake and punch wedding. Since the reception was in the church hall, champagne was allowed only for the toast. Later I found out it was sparkling grape juice, not even real champagne. We were escorted on the obligatory trip around The Square in our car with tin cans dragging behind and soaped windows reading *Just Married*, all typical of marriage in this town. Farmers have little expendable money, so celebrations are simple except for the food.

Everyone is proud of their cooking and likes to show it off. Anytime there is a pot-luck dinner at church, county fair, or funeral, food is involved. Mom won many prizes for her apple pie. Aunt May's potato salad makes my mouth water just thinking about it. My cousin, Sue, makes deviled eggs that often disappear before they even make it to the table. My Aunt Ellen's red velvet cake would make me sell my soul to the devil, except I think I might have already.

Sex with Sue is just about as plain as our marriage ceremony. The missionary position is the limit of her repertoire. I've suggested doggy style, but she says it feels unnatural for her. I would enjoy some oral sex, giving and/or receiving. She's not interested. I have a desire to experiment with what I learned in the service, go a little on the wild side, even if it is something most consider kinky or taboo. After the two kids, any sex would be fine. Sue is always too busy, too tired, or the kids need too much attention. I wonder, is there some inner psychological conflict over my sexual desires? I don't know what bothers Sue.

I continue with working the field, back and forth. The repeated turns and the unending flatness of the fields lull me into complacency where time is lost. It's like when you are on a road trip and suddenly realize you've gone over 100 miles without a recollection of towns or scenery Looking up to the house, I see my kids waving for me to stop. I have lost track of time again. I didn't see the bus drop them off. When I get to the end, I stop. "Hey, kids, what's up? Your costumes look great."

Clamoring for attention, each wants to tell me something. They end up in a cross talk, but I get the message. "Are you going to Grandma's tonight to trick-or-treat?"

As usual my daughter gets the upper hand and speaks. "We're going into town after that."

"I may not be able to go with you. I want to finish this field. I'll miss you, though."

"Okay, but you'll miss out on the fun."

"I'll be here when you get home. And I get first dibs at the candy, especially the chocolate. "

"That's not fair."

"I could be bribed."

Off they go, trying to out-race the other to tell their mom. I could never tell them that I would rather go to the bar for a drink, not the one on The Square but the one by the railroad track, the Washington Street Inn. No one cares about your business there.

The wind has shifted out of the north, grey clouds are darkening, and I think I feel some light snowflakes hitting my face. I should stay in the field. The cold is better than drinking in a bar with probing eyes staring at me, even if they don't talk.

Suddenly I remember the radio was playing *Let It Be* as I left this morning. It's a sign. Let it be. So for now, let the land be. I need a drink. If I go now I can make it home for the trick-or-treating.

Chapter 5

Clara May on Danny O' Conner

Right after this whole affair hit, we were talking about Danny in my bridge club. Millie had just downed her second vodka martini. She laid her cards on the table so she could point her crooked index finger at me. It was shaking so much from her Parkinson disease I was getting dizzy. I said, "Go ahead and ask your question Millie. You're making me crazy with that shaking."

Millie was irritated with me for pointing out her tremor, as if no one could see. She continued to point her finger in my general direction as she asked, "You've known Danny his whole life, being a next door neighbor and all. What's wrong with him? Why hasn't he married?"

Her questions irritate me. She usually has some ulterior motive. She doesn't always quite tell what's on her mind. I'm going to call her bluff today. "Is it really any of your business Millie? Why do you ask, or are you just nosey?"

She huffed like a horse that had just run a mile and squinted her eyes in a direct stare. Then she lit into me. "You, of all people think I'm nosey, Clara May, the town gossip. I want to know because my granddaughter's been seeing Danny and the relationship doesn't seem to be going anywhere, especially now. With all this publicity of the affair, I told her to drop him. Sounds like he doesn't know what he wants."

"Yes, I know Danny very well. Since he lives just down the road from me, I see him most every day, but you know that. He doesn't tell me about his dating. His dad is an SOB who rules the house with an iron fist. The boy hasn't exactly got a good family foundation to build on. His granddad was the most positive thing in his life and he's gone now. Did you ever think it could be your granddaughter who's at fault?"

Oh, this caused Millie to fume. She was ready to spit fire. I could see the smoke rising as she spat the words at me, "I'll have you know my granddaughter is a fine outstanding woman. She's church going, virtuous, and a good housekeeper."

Hazel had had it with us and broke in. "You two hens stop pecking at each other."

With those words, I could not hold in my laughter. When I stopped laughing, I leaned over to pat Millie on the arm and said, "Honey, I don't know any more about what's going on than what we've all read in the papers. I know he's lonely and upset. I don't know if he's guilty or not and I don't know what he thinks of your granddaughter."

And that was the truth. Danny hadn't talked to me about the affair. I know his dad visited him the other day. Danny and I were having a morning cup of coffee when he came in. We heard a car on the gravel driveway and recognized it as his dad. The car door slammed with more force than necessary to close it and then we heard his heavy steps on the porch stairs. He came in without knocking, holding his frayed black Bible. The color had faded to gray but his name, stamped in gold letters, could still be seen. After thumping it on the kitchen table, he looked at me with eyes closed into slits. Then, with flared nostrils, he addressed me. The words rushed from his mouth like water through a burst levy. "Clara May, you need to leave. I want to talk to my son. Alone." He then swiveled his outstretched arm and pointed to the door.

Danny's eyes were pleading for me stay. I gave a near smile, as if to say sorry. Rising to place my cup in the sink, I said, "I'll be going now, Danny. If you need me call." His dad watched my every move and his eyes followed me to the door.

Tiger, Danny's cat, was on the back steps. I stopped to pet her. She gave me a reason to linger. I could hear his dad's enraged words. "I knew if you went to your granddad's house you would turn out to be no good. First you have to go and own that bar. Now, this. What next, murder? Don't you know God's word? You're a sinner."

I didn't want to hear anymore, so I left. Since then, Danny and I haven't had much time together. I stop by every now and then and he's been over to fix a few things. I've told him what's done is done. Move on. Hold your head erect.

Chapter 6

Danny O' Connor

Damn, what's that noise? I part the curtains just in time to see James' red Camaro go by honking. Holding a coffee cup to my head to get its warmth, I think *Crazy man and his cars. Loves that red Camaro.* You'd think he's a smart-ass high school kid. I part the curtain again to look at the overcast sky and see Clara May on her way into town. I wonder what the old girl's up to today. Yesterday she told me where she would be, but I forgot. Clara May thinks neighbors should know what neighbors are doing. Never can be too careful. She said she heard tell some Gypsies were through here the other day. Could be, but then again, she could be remembering when she was younger. Ah yes, she was going in town for groceries because Frieda is coming for tea and then this afternoon she's getting her hair done up. It's blue hair day at the beauty parlor. Well I'm sure there will be a lot of gossip because today is the preliminary hearing. Wonder if she'll stop and tell me what she's heard, probably will. She always does. We talk over a gin and tonic. Doesn't seem to bother her any that I'm a part of that affair.

I'm not ashamed of what I did, but I am sorry for the scandal it's caused the community. At least it's been good for bar business. Town folk are curious about where they think it all started. Wives would like to keep their husbands away but secretly want them to go have a drink to see if they can catch any gossip. They think maybe I'll spill the beans.

Let them say I'm a deviant. I only wanted anonymity. What does that mean anyway? Who knows? It's just what they label me. I don't have children to protect. My dad already thinks I'm in the hands of the devil. My sister doesn't live here anymore. And Mom? Mom does as Dad wants. It's hard to tell what Mom is feeling. My major worry is that prison time is a possibility. If I'm in prison, what do I do with the bar? I get a headache thinking of it, so I try not to. I have no control over what happens in the court.

This morning my headache is not from the affair but from a hard night of bartending. I was going to have a relief bartender work last night, but he wasn't available. As it turns out, it was good to work. It kept my mind off what was to come today. And if people talk, they're going to talk. I might as well be there to hear it. I figured there would be a lot of people. Another reason to work, I get the tips.

My busy night was thanks to the bowling alley. The leagues have a week off in order to resurface the lanes. Bowlers don't have their usual hang out so they came into Squeaky's. Other than the bowling alley, it's the only other place in town they deem "respectable." Thank God the affair hasn't changed that. They could go to the Elks, but they don't like the neighborhood and it doesn't stay open late. They ran me ragged last night. Nothing special in their drinks -- the usual beer or "and" drinks: vodka and soda, gin and tonic, scotch and water. Women were the only ones ordering fancy drinks. They'd come to the bar, order their drink, and then sit on a stool while I made it. When I turned to place the drinks in front of them, they'd look at me with these big eyes. I wasn't sure if they were trying to see through me and discover why I was involved in this affair, or if they felt sorry for me. Hell if I know. Maybe they were saying *Stay away from my man.*

Men normally leave the women at the bar and go off downstairs for a game of pool, but nobody played pool last night. Men didn't stray far from their wives: No separate man-talk over cigars and beer. No going in the corner to talk fishing. No group discussing the merits of the various new cars. Not that these topics were not discussed -- they were, but in mixed company. Men are afraid of being talked about if they're seen in a group, and they're right. People will talk, especially in this town.

I wanted to tell them to go huddle in your groups. I certainly wasn't going to gossip. I longed to say *Hey, this is not how things happened. Go have fun. Don't worry about the gossip. Play pool. Play cards. Tell your fishing tales.* We are not guilty of any lewd conduct in the bar, unless you consider talking. I couldn't chance having my license suspended or worse yet, having it revoked.

I would never jeopardize the bar; it, and this piece of land where my house sits, is all I've got. There's not enough farmland to feed a cow, let alone me. Besides, I don't know how to farm. I can't even grow a decent vegetable garden. I rely on the generosity of Clara May for my vegetables. In exchange, I do odd jobs for her. I pick apples for her in the fall. Last week I reattached a downspout and changed the oil in her car.

Clara May asked me once if I knew she and my granddad had dated. I told her I did, but if she had some juicy stories, I'd like to hear them. "Oh there were some good times all right. You young kids don't have a market on that. My dad was pretty well off. He had this Model T Ford that he let me drive and if it wasn't available we took the horse and buggy. Went to Chicago on the train to pick up that Ford. Oh, Lord -- it could tell some tales! You know your granddad proposed to me and I turned him down. We grew up together. He was more of a brother to me than a potential husband. Nearly broke his heart, or at least that's what he told me. Should have taken the offer, 'cause nobody better came along."

It's beginning to get chilly standing in the kitchen, time to turn the heat on. As I adjust the thermostat in the hallway, the grandfather clock chimes, reminding me I need to call my relief bartender and make sure he can work today.

I don't want to face my customers today. They talk around the affair. It's like they're riding the merry-go-round trying to catch the gold ring. They're afraid to lean out far enough to get the prize. No. I'm afraid I'd tell them off tonight. I'll see if George wants to work.

"Hello, George ... yeah, a little tired today from last night ... it was a good ring. People were drinking a lot ... no I'm not going to the trial. Bob is the only one today ... I'm doing fine, thanks for asking. Say, could you work the place today ... great, that's great. I'm too tired to face the customers right now, especially today ... no, no, I don't mind you asking. It's nice to know someone cares about me and not just the decline of morality in this town ... change is in the safe and ready to go ... 'bye. I'll see you tomorrow."

George is not a gossip, but customers feel free to ask him questions. He can talk as much as he pleases. The other day when we were cleaning the bar he said, "Danny, I don't care about the rumors, and you shouldn't either. What you do in your private life is your business. I'm not talking about the affair when I work. If anyone asks, I tell them to talk to you."

Work's taken care of. Now what do I do with my day off to keep my mind off the hearing? First, another cup of coffee. I leave the hallway and go for coffee, and I notice the kitchen is beginning to look dingy. There's some peeling paint on the outside wall where the porch roof leaked. I can't repair that in this weather, especially when it looks as if it will snow. The kitchen hot water faucet is leaking. I could repair that as long as I don't need to go to town for parts. A loud meow interrupts my repair thoughts.

"Who's that I hear meowing outside? So you think it's time to come in do you Tiger? Get too cold, did you? Looks like we're going to have to fix this door girl, it's sticking again." Taking my cup to the kitchen table, I sit so Tiger can have some lap time. With her purring, I grab a note pad, a pen from the end of the table, and begin to make a list of chores that need doing around the house. There's a lot. I've not had the energy to do much since this whole affair started.

In a way I'm glad a trial is finally happening. At least I'll know what the state's attorney plans to do. Up until now, he's been tight lipped about it. Bob knows him and even he can't get a thing. We know the charges, but they could be reduced. We could get a plea bargain. The attorneys thought it best if each trial were separate. We'd know the game plan. Bob is first. Nothing left to do but wait. I should have put Clara May onto it. She can weasel information out of anybody.

"Okay, Tiger, down you go. It's time to make a list and get started." I haven't cleaned the house out since Granddad died last year. This will be a start. I'm not sure he did any cleaning after Grandma died. Granddad lived alone here until I moved in. I welcomed the chance. Life with Mom and Dad had not exactly been grand. A few years back, Dad found religion and let everyone know it. If it hadn't been for his new evangelical conservatism, I might have been able to talk to him about the sexual feelings I had. All he wanted to talk about was how Jesus saved him. After his revival experience, no matter what subject we wanted to discuss with him, it always came around to religion, his religion.

It was one of those tent revivals that often came to town. Dad, Mom, my sister, and I all had to go. My sister and I whined to stay home, but Dad would have none of it. This was a part of learning to be a good Christian. With sulking faces, my sister and I piled into the back seat of our new Chrysler.

A massive white tent was set up in an empty lot on the edge of town with a central pole piercing the center. On top of the pole was a large cross. A young man with a yardstick guided the cars to parking spaces on the grass. We took one of the last spaces. Cars behind us were parking on the roadside. My sister and I quietly commented because we couldn't let our dad hear: "The tent is ugly."

My sister took another look then scrunched her face. "The circus tent last year was much nicer. It was candy striped."

She gave me an idea. "Maybe we can pretend it's the circus."

That was our plan until Dad intervened. "There will be no pretending this is a circus. When we get in you will sit still and behave."

I guess we had not talked softly enough. The August night was hot and humid. There was not a whisper of wind, but we had to wear church clothes. I was in long pants, a white shirt, tie, and a sport coat. Even before entering the tent, I was sweating and started to take off my coat. Dad saw me and said, "Leave it on. I don't want you looking like some ragamuffin."

It was crowded as we entered. There were a number of people from our church sitting in the folding chairs that said *Harvard Funeral Parlor*. All of the seats in back were taken because it was the only location to get what coolness might come from the evening air. Besides, who wanted to sit under the watchful eye of a revival preacher? We had no choice but to take four open chairs in the front row.

Posters on either side of the stage advertised the revival. *Five Days of Heaven on Earth. Largest Tent Revival in the State. The Reverend Jack Hamilton.* Five days! I could not stand that many nights.

A large woman entered and sat down at the electronic Hammond organ. She played a number of hymns that excited the people. Some were clapping and others were dancing in the aisle. Then, over low music, a man walked to the microphone and said, "Tonight, this first night of our revival, you will enjoy heaven on earth as Reverend Jack Hamilton brings you the love of God in Jesus. Do I hear an amen? Yes. I say, amen."

With the *amens* the music grew and grew to a pitch. Finally, the man at the microphone said, "Now I give you the Reverend Jack Hamilton!"

The people rose from their seats, including Dad, who frantically waved for us to stand. The Reverend raised both of his hands to the rooftop, "Thank you. Thank you. Praise the Lord. Praise Jesus." He then lowered his hands in a patting motion indicating the people should be seated.

I remember little of what the Reverend had to say except that he wanted us all to take Jesus into our hearts. Accepting Jesus into our hearts was the only way to be saved. I thought if I can be saved from coming here again I'd take a chance on Jesus.

What I do remember is the altar call. The preaching over, Reverend Jack Hamilton invited people to come forward and accept Jesus as their savior. "Let your heart soften to the spirit and the word of God. Let Jesus lodge himself in your heart. Come dedicate your life to Jesus."

Much to my horror, Dad rose and stared open eyed at the stage. My sister and I looked at Mom, who motioned for us to remain seated. My father started clapping and raising his hands toward the tent roof. "Yes, Lord, yes, Lord, I'm here. I open my heart to you. I seek you. I have craved a pure, perfect heart. I will be born again."

Dad kept waving his hands and earnestly trying to get me to stand up. Finally, he grabbed me by the arm and pulled me up with him. My eyes pleaded with Mom, but she could do nothing. Holding my arm, Dad dragged me to the altar. I kept looking at Mom. Her eyes were squinted and her lips were tightly shut. She looked like she was trying to suppress her laughter. She turned her head to look at my sister and with her hand, waved me on. I followed Dad, turning my head and pleading with my eyes as he dragged me to the front of the tent.

As Dad knelt, I had no choice but to kneel with him. The Reverend Jack Hamilton quoted scripture, "The Lord whom ye seek, shall suddenly come to his temple." And Jesus saved Dad and me that night.

Dad insisted we go all the nights, but Mom intervened after the second night. "We are not going tonight. The weather is hot and the kids and I are staying home. You can go if you want." I guess you can say I was "saved" – saved by Mom's determination not to return.

Dad attended each revival meeting. Our attendance at church became regular. Dad made himself well known to Pastor Wallace and Pastor Wallace became well known to us. Dad thought Pastor Wallace was the authority on all things moral and he was right up there with the Pastor in his condemnation of the evils of alcohol and sex. The result being that he turned his back on the bar business, his relationship with Granddad became strained, and any talk of sex was forbidden.

After Dad was saved, home life became hell. I had to account for every minute of the day. There was no staying after school for anything. Movies and dancing were looked at with an evil eye. The kicker came when he found "smut" material hidden in my dresser. It was a men's muscle magazine. Dad hit the roof. We had a major fight. Mom stood by sheepishly, hovering in the hallway and biting her knuckles. "Dad, you have no right to go through my things," I said.

Dad's face was red and his fists were clinched tightly, "As long as you live in my house, I have every right to do what I please. And remember, you are not 18 yet. Until you are, you do what I say."

My face was becoming as red as his and my stomach was doing summersaults. Shouting would have made me feel good, but I knew a calm steady voice angered my dad, so that's what I aimed for. He wanted a fight, somebody to get as angry as he was. I would not give him that satisfaction. Autumn leaves fell with more force than my words. "Well, you're right. I'm not 18 yet, but I don't have to live with you. Granddad needs help. I'm going over there to live with him."

I knew this would set him off even more and it did. By this time, my sister was standing next to Mom. She was still chewing on her knuckles. My sister, twisting her hair and putting the ends in her mouth, had a smirk on her face as if to say *I'm glad it's you and not me*. Dad looked over at the two of them, "What are you two doing? And you, missy," wagging his index finger at her, "don't be so smug. You could be next. Now, both of you, go. Find something else to do."

Mom and my sister disappeared from the door, but I didn't hear any footsteps on the stairs. I figured they were holed up in my sister's room next door. The walls were thin and Dad talked loud enough, so they could hear. "Fine. Live with your grandfather. Enter into the devil's den. Next thing I know you'll have gotten some girl pregnant."

Laughing was not going to help me any, but I couldn't resist. When I calmed down enough to talk again, it was through chuckles. "Oh, that's laughable. Me ... get a girl pregnant. First, you've told me nothing about sex. You don't know if I like girls. Second, going out is like asking for a release from prison. You have eyes and ears everywhere I go. You know everything I do. When would I have a chance?"

He brought his fist up as if to hit me. I flinched and backed away, sitting on the bed. "You know you're not too old to get a good whooping." Dad had rarely spanked me, but when he did, I remembered it. "Get a suitcase. Pack your things. Go stay with your grandfather. But don't expect any visits from us and don't go asking for money. You want to be on your own. Be on your own. And here. Here is the smut material. I don't want it in my house. I don't want it in my garbage. I don't want it in my burn pile."

Dad then turned his attention to the hallway and gave instructions to my mother saying, "Anne, get on the phone and call. Tell my dad his grandson is coming to stay with him. Tell him I have no interest in discussing it. Tell him he better keep Danny out of the bar. There is no telling what he'll learn there." At this point Dad paused, intently looked me over then said, "No, he can do whatever he damn well pleases. I wash my hands of it."

I wanted to tell Dad that those words were not too Christian, but I knew he wouldn't get it. A loving, kind, and forgiving Christian was not his brand of Christianity. He believes in hell fire, brimstone, and the evil of sinful ways.

Until Granddad died, those were the last words I heard my father speak. I packed my belongings and Granddad came to pick me up. Dad would not let Mom go with me and he wouldn't let her kiss me or say goodbye. I left quietly without slamming drawers or doors. Clouds moving across the sky made more noise than me that day.

The ride to Granddad's was short and silent. When we got there, Granddad helped me with the bags and I went to my usual room. As I was climbing the stairs, Granddad spoke. "Come back down when you're settled, and let's talk."

I welcomed a chance to talk to someone sane. Just existing at home had been rough. I hoped this would be easier. "Coming right down, I'll unpack later."

Granddad had a glass of sweet tea for me, and we took seats in the living room. An upright piano still held family pictures, including Grandma and his wedding portrait, Mom and Dad's picture, and pictures of us grandkids. Grandma's lace doilies still covered the end tables and the lace curtains she cared for hung in the windows. Each spring before Easter, and each fall after Labor Day I would help her take them down. She'd hand wash them and then we'd put them on the stretchers with the small sharp points. No matter how hard we tried, we'd always prick ourselves. My reward for helping was a cherry pie. I could use a cherry pie about now.

Granddad noticed me looking around. "Yep, seems as if your grandma is only out visiting someone. I sometimes sit here and ask myself, *Now where is it she's gone again?* Then I remember she's not coming back."

I fingered the doily. "I really miss her."

Granddad's blue eyes glowed and as he looked at me, there was tenderness. He leaned over and patted me on the knee. "Okay, Danny, I knew this would happen sooner or later. Your dad's been working up to it for a time. What happened to set him off?"

I explained to Granddad the happenings of the day that started with Dad finding the magazine. He never stopped smiling and never took his eyes off me. "Well, now nothing wrong with a few pictures." I think he knew then that I was different. He never asked me why I had the magazine and he never asked to look at it. I was embarrassed to tell him I liked to look at the men's bodies. I didn't think he'd understand and I needed him on my side. He accepted me as I was and that's all I needed.

Granddad continued. "Let's talk about a plan for you. You got one more year of high school, right?"

"Yes, I graduate next year."

Granddad shook his head in agreement. "Then what? Have you got any plans?"

I hadn't thought about any until he asked, so I hesitated. "I don't think college is for me. Maybe the Army?"

For the first time he looked troubled. "Son, you know you would probably go to Vietnam. Are you ready for that?"

War scared me. Earlier this year one of our neighbor's sons was killed in the service. "I don't know. It seems as if no one is happy about going to war. But I'm not a chicken. I just don't know if I willing to put myself in a position to be killed."

Granddad held up his right hand. "Hold on. No one's talking about you dying. If you decide to go to the service, we'll talk about it then. I have an idea."

Thank God someone was willing to talk to me like I was an adult. I could make choices on my own. "What idea is that?"

Granddad fiddled with his pipe, loaded it with tobacco, lit it, and then leaned forward. "How about taking over the bar when you're 21? It should come as no surprise to you that your Dad has no interest in it. I don't want to let it go. You're friendly with people, a good talker."

I couldn't believe this. Someone with a plan for me. I said, "Are you kidding? That would be great!"

Granddad took a puff on his pipe, letting the smoke settle. "Well then, here's the plan. You finish high school first. I've talked to the foreman out at the factory and he says if you want a job, he can get you on. You work some with me on the weekends and in the evening. You'll learn the business. When you turn 21 you'll be ready to take over and I'll be more than ready to let you. In the meantime, settle in and let me worry about your dad."

I graduated from high school and went to work at the factory. Vietnam grew worse, but I never was in the armed forces. I turned 21 in 1964 with a big celebration at the bar. Nurturing a hangover, I was tending bar the next day and Granddad was rocking on his porch.

I never acted on my sexual interest. I dated girls, as was obligatory in high school: Homecoming, Prom, and sock hops. I never enjoyed the dates. I was never sure why. My friends were constantly talking about their make-out sessions. I listened because they were friends but was never interested.

Granddad died last year. He left me the bar, this house, and plot of land. Mom and my sister occasionally visit, but I never saw Dad again until Granddad's funeral. My sister left town after high school graduation. We talk on the phone, but she's never come back. Granddad and I talked about dating and getting married but there was never pressure. He said as long as I was happy, he was happy.

I've made friends at the bar. The Square affair five -- Thomas, Gary, James, and Bob -- are among the closest. We play cards, pool, and fish. It's not that I was ever lonely, but after Granddad died, they, and Clara May, were the only ones I could confide in. I could talk about feelings. I could be honest about missing my granddad. They became my family. The fishing trip to Lake Warren changed everything, and here I am today waiting for word of the court hearing.

Now I've gone and let my coffee get cold. No matter. I've got to get going on these chores. Just then the phone rings, "Hello. Oh, hey, Gary ... no I'm staying home today and doing some fixing up around the house ... I'm not going to tend bar tonight either ... yeah, I'd consider going down to Washington Street later this afternoon. Should be safe enough there   see you later today."

Chapter 7

Clara May on James Calhoun

The mid-day news tells me Peggy Sue has been hospitalized, what the market price of corn is, how much I can get per pound for pigs or beef cattle, and that John Meyer died but says nothing about the trial.

Frieda thinks we ought to give them a piece of our mind. "I'm going to call that station and tell them what news we really want to hear. Imagine, not reporting on the trial."

I'm frustrated, too, but not enough to call. Besides, they'll think we're just a couple of old biddies with nothing better to do. "Did you ever think they might not have anything to report?"

"Well, if they don't have anything to report, they should say so."

Frieda can be a pain in the butt; however, she's a good friend. "Did I tell you that on my way into town this morning for a gallon of milk, James almost ran into me? He was driving his fancy new red car." James is one of The Square Affair five.

Frieda starts chuckling, and it makes her fat rolls jiggle. "I remember when his daddy got him his first car. Most kids get rusty used ones or had to drive the farm truck, but not James -- his dad owned the Chevy dealership. His son was going to drive a new car. Ran off the road and totaled it in less than a week. Old man didn't blink an eye."

The accident was just down the road from me. "I remember James came to my house to call his dad. Found him in the bar, and he drove out here drunk. Nearly took out my mailbox coming into the driveway. Thank God James doesn't take after his dad."

"He may not be a drunk, but he's involved in this affair. Could be worse than drinking."

Frieda remembers, "He was trouble in school. Doesn't surprise me that he'd be promiscuous in his sex life."

"Frieda, what would you know about promiscuity? You're a good church lady."

"I'm not a prude," says Frieda.

"Selling is the right profession for him. James is a born talker."

Frieda responds, "I remember. You sent him many times to the Principal's office for disturbing the class with his talking."

I say, "It's a good thing he had a built-in career from his dad. James would not have done well in college, but he was determined not to make the same mistakes as his dad. Remember how he almost lost the business? He was always on trips to Las Vegas for some car show or another. If you ask me, he went there to gamble and drink."

"Do I remember?" Frieda says, "I had just bought a new car and it wasn't running right. I went back in to give James' dad a piece of my mind. I was told he wouldn't be back for another week. That's when I changed from Chevy to Ford."

"But you drive a Chevy now?" I asked.

"When James took over I wanted to give him a chance and despite his antics in high school, he's done very well by himself." Frieda changes the subject. "Why do you think it is that James and Judy are doing so well? This affair doesn't seem to have affected them much."

"Well, let me see. Where did I put my crystal ball?"

Chapter 8

James Calhoun

Judy should have left by now to teach her second grade class, but I haven't heard the garage door or the car. She must want to talk to me. I'm sure she wants to know what I'm going to do today and hear again why I'm not going to the courthouse to be with Bob. Exiting the bathroom I hear her call, "James, are you coming down?"

I don't want to talk this morning. Nightmares kept waking me up last night. I was in jail with my friends, Bob, Gary, Thomas, and Danny. The jailors made us strip, searched us, and then refused to give us prison clothes, saying they had run out of uniforms. We were forced to make a go of it in our birthday suits.

The jailor rattled his keys to get the attention of the other inmates and paraded all of us through the halls to the accompaniment of catcalls and whistles:

"Hey, sailor, bend over and pick up that paper for me."

"Hey, brown eyes. Would you wear lipstick for me tonight?"

"Leave your purses at home, did you?"

"Blondie, I got a quarter. Come see me later tonight."

Our cell was located in the middle of a large round room completely surrounded by the other inmates so that our every move could be seen. And all eyes were on us.

Judy pleads, "James, please come down. I need to talk to you before I leave for school."

"All right, all right, I'm coming. I didn't sleep well last night. I've got a headache. Your yelling is not helping."

Judy takes a deep breath, holds it in, and then slowly exhales. She knows it will not help anything to become riled or excited, but she cannot avoid repeatedly turning her wrist to look at the Bulova Watch. It was my present to her for our anniversary.

Can't put it off, or go back to bed. "Okay, okay, what is it that's so important?" I ask and see Judy as I'm rounding the curve in the stairs. "Good God, what the hell are you wearing?"

"It's Halloween, or have you forgotten? I'm dressed as a witch for the school party."

I give her a long look and unsuccessfully hide my laughter. "Very convincing. I imagine some of your students think you're a witch without that outfit. Black is your color -- it is very slimming."

I'm sure Judy would like to laugh at my comments, but she apparently has more serious things on her mind. "Thanks, I think. I waited for you because I want to make sure you'll be all right today."

I can't be angry with Judy in that outfit. She has been surprised at this mess but never angry. Her concern has always been my welfare, our marriage. The gossip doesn't seem to bother her. "I'm going over to the dealership in Lincolnville, to see the new showroom. It'll take my mind off the trial. It's far enough away that I don't think they'll know what's going on. Besides, there'll be big wigs there from Detroit. Even if people know, they won't bring it up in front of them."

Judy follows me into the kitchen as I get my first morning cup of coffee. "Why again is it you don't have to go to court with Bob?"

I wrap my hands around the cup and take a sip of coffee before answering. It gives me time to look at her eyes. It's amazing, still no anger. "I don't understand all the legal wrestling but to the best of my knowledge, I'm not required for the preliminary hearing. Since Bob is an attorney, he said he would work with the attorney representing us. It's clear as mud to me. I'm trying to not create waves."

Judy leans over to give me a kiss on the forehead and her hat tumbles onto the counter. "Sure you don't want me to stay home? I can call in sick. Everyone will know I'm not sick, but they'll understand."

I pick up the black witch's hat from the counter and place it on my head. "Perhaps I should be the wicked witch this Halloween. Everyone seems to think that's what I am these days."

Judy takes the hat from my head and replaces it on hers. "I'll be the wicked witch for the day." She looks at the broom sitting in the corner where she left it after sweeping the kitchen last night, and then continues. "I'll be needing this broom to fly to school unless I hurry, and I'm afraid my butt may be a bit too big for it to stay in flight. Despite all that has happened, I love you and we'll get through this."

I know Judy is speaking the truth; she never could lie. She blames it on being a minister's daughter. "Thanks. I know you care, and I love you." We walk to the front door together and open it. We both shiver in the cold wind. "I hope you've got some warm clothes on under that outfit because it looks as if you are going to need them."

"I don't, but I'll be running after the kids all day trying to keep them from eating too much candy. Besides what would a witch wear under her outfit?"

"Maybe a black lace bra and black lace stockings studded with rhinestones."

"There is no chance of that. Believe me. 'Bye. Take it easy today." Judy gives me a last kiss and goes to the car.

I stand shivering at the door until Judy backs out of the driveway. I wave and then close the door. I look out the window beside the door and see an overcast sky. It could snow today.

How can people like fall? The red, yellow, gold, orange of early fall have all gone and what color's left on the trees is brown: brown leaves, brown bark, and brown earth. Come to think of it, everything's brown. The grass is brown after the first frost. Harvested corn stalks are brown. Soybean stalks are brown. The sky is gray-brown with impending snow. Pumpkins rotting on the steps and porches are brown. Burning leaves are brown. It's time to put on brown leather gloves. Hell, it's a depressing time of year. Thank God new car models arrive in the fall. New cars, new sales, new colors -- something I can look forward to each year.

I can't resist a look at my new red Camaro. Driving it today to Lincolnville will be a needed diversion from the sordid affair I've gotten myself into. I walk into the kitchen for another cup of coffee and then open the door to the attached garage to have a look. It's power and virility in red. Who cares if it is my mid-life crisis? That's what Judy calls the car. It would have been better than the affair. Can't get into too much trouble over a car, but it is a thrill behind the wheel. Look at that white racing stripe. It's almost as good as sex. I pat the car hood then return to the kitchen feeling like a high school kid again. I remember getting my first car from Dad and driving around The Square to show off. Is this what a mid-life crisis at 40 feels like?

I grab more coffee, head upstairs to shower, and get ready to go to the meeting. Undressing, I catch sight of myself in the in the reflection on my varsity football picture. I'm definitely not the high school football player any more. There's not even a trace of rippled abdominal muscles. I've let myself go. Too much time sitting at my desk. Too much time sitting on the bank fishing. The only physical activity I get is walking the golf course and I only do that to please potential customers.

As I go to the dresser to get my underwear, I notice other pictures: our wedding photo family portraits, baby and graduation pictures of the kids. Picking up the wedding photo, I stare at us. What went wrong, Judy? We were perfect for each other. The All-American couple, we have two kids, one girl and one boy. Thank God they're both in college. Judy and I told them about the arrest and court case. They were quiet and only asked if their mom and I would be getting a divorce. Honestly, at that time we hadn't thought about divorce. We told the kids we wanted to work out our problems and stay together. But the final decision hasn't been made.

We told them that we'd like to take a family vacation over Christmas. We'll know more then and could talk. Judy suggested visiting her parents in Arizona. I don't know if I can tolerate her father's sermons. As a retired minister he can be very judgmental and is not shy in letting you know his feelings. He uses us as his congregation.

After showering, I wrap myself in a towel as best I can. It used to go all the way around with plenty to tuck in. Now it barely covers me. As I'm shaving I notice more grey whiskers in the sink than black. Is this what middle age is all about? I get a sports car to show I'm not impotent? I let myself go? I get pudgy? Dad turned to booze and gambling and I turn to deviant sex.

Having shaved and dressed, I telephone the office. "Marge, hi. Wanted to make sure you remembered I'm going to Lincolnville today ... no I won't be in at all ... any problems I need to take care of? ...I'll call in to make sure everything is okay ... 'bye, talk to you later." I know she knows I'm not coming in because of the court date. Marge is great. She didn't say a word. Never has mentioned it, even in passing conversation.

I grab my trench coat from the hall closet, go to the garage, and get into the Camaro. Keys in hand, I settle into the seat and inhale deeply. Oh yes, the smell of a new car: almost as good as sex. I rub the rich velvety leather thinking of a voluptuous thigh. Let's go for a ride, baby.

Judy and I recently moved to a new house. It's located about a mile outside of town nestled in an old forest along a creek bed. On the way to work I would normally go for coffee with friends at The Square Cafe, but I've not done this since the arrest. I have no intention of stopping today or going anywhere near The Square. I'll take country roads and pick up the highway outside of town.

All this emptiness depresses me. I want to see the green of newly planted corn standing in parallel rows like soldiers at attention. I want to see the wheat flowing with the wind, golden and ready for harvest. I want to smell new mown clover drying. I want to see cattle grazing in a newly harvested oat field. I want to see green trees. This time of year everything is dying.

Good -- the long stretch of straight road where I can floor the car is clear. Forty, fifty, sixty, eighty, ninety and nothing is distinct. Red shapes could be barns, white shapes could be houses, and there could be people. That could be a tractor. Oblivious to the world outside, all that matters is me in this red Camaro, me and no one else. At this speed, there is no affair. The road turns ahead and I have to slow down, come back to reality at a reasonable speed.

Ahead is Tom's farm. I see him in the field headed away from me. Good, that means I won't have to ignore him. Not that I don't want to talk to him, I do. I would love to talk to him, to see how he's doing, how he and Sue are managing. The attorney told us to avoid contact as much as possible. What were his words? He said that if we were seen together it would look as if we were not repentant. Perhaps he said remorseful. It doesn't matter. Our being seen together would create more rumors. There's enough gossip already, so why add fuel to the fire? I want to say, "Piss on you, these are my friends. Am I supposed to lock myself up in the house, read old issues of Reader's Digest, watch Lawrence Welk, or reruns of 'Gun Smoke'?" I miss fishing with my buddies. I miss drinking beers at Squeaky's.

I roll down my window and wave at Tom. I know he won't see. I know no one will see. I give a finger to the wind. Judy and I are okay. So to the rest of you, fuck off. Not that that helped anything, but it felt good to be defiant.

Finally, it's the state highway to Lincolnville. Damn, a slow moving car and I won't be able to pass it because of hills in the Cedar Creek bottom. Just my luck, on only part of the highway with a stretch of no passing zones, I'll be behind the little old lady from Pasadena. Wait, I recognize that car. It's the blue Chevy Impala I sold to Pastor Jenkins. It's not exactly a little old lady, but it might as well be. He's just as persnickety and a lot less pleasant. Jenkins has a strong sense of Christian self-righteousness and has no problem inflicting it on others. I would not be surprised if he stopped to give me a sermon. That would ruin my happy defiant attitude. Well I'm not going to give him the chance. Growing up in this town has its advantages. I'll take the back roads and avoid the state highway.

Once free of Pastor Jenkins, I drive on a deserted road through cornfields and on to the forest around south creek. My thoughts return to the affair. Judy thinks part of the blame should be hers because she encouraged me to get out on my own more. She told me: "Go ahead have a poker night. Play pool with the boys. Take the boat fishing for a weekend." She knew I was not interested in shopping, which was her favorite pastime, so I took her up on the offer.

Meeting the other guys was innocent. Gary's agency handles insurance for the car dealership. Of course Bob and his family are common names in this community. Bob and I became friends because both of us would often end up at Squeaky's for a beer when our wives were playing bridge and we're both members of the country club. Fishing is a passion for both of us. I knew Danny's granddad. He and my dad were good friends. Danny likes to talk to me about his grandfather. He thinks I have good stories through my Dad. I remind him I'm only a few years older than he is so there's not much to tell, but he likes to hear the stories I have. Thomas and his dad, Joe, are both customers of mine and of course, Thomas is a frequent customer in the bar. He's more frequent in the winter when he's not in the field. And that's The Square Affair five. We became good friends over beer, pool, and fishing.

There's the slight rise in the road ahead. This baby can really make your stomach do a flip over the bump. Here goes. That was great.

I'm acting like a kid who just got his driver's license. I'm a 40-year-old man for heaven's sake. What am I doing playing dumb high school tricks? I'm acting worse than some sex-craved teenager with too much testosterone. I don't remember craving this kind of sex as a kid. I've got to pull myself together. Judy wants to go to counseling. Whatever it takes, she wants to stay together, and I think I agree. I'm not willing to start a new life at this age. What would I do? I've got a lot of time and money invested in the dealership and I'm not about to walk away from that. I wouldn't feel right selling it. Judy says the town will soon forget the whole thing after the court hearing. She has more confidence in the goodness of the town people than I do. I've a lifetime of their antics.

That's Danny's truck in the driveway ahead. I forgot he lives out here in the woods. He must not be going to work at the bar today. Seems as if none of us want to be seen. I'll lay on the horn, wake him up. If I can't sleep, he shouldn't. I wonder if he remembers the incident his grandfather had with Pastor Wallace, Judy's dad. Pastor Wallace has not preached or lived here since his retirement, but still holds a grudge against Squeaky, the original owner of Squeaky's Bar.

Squeaky was running for mayor and the good pastor thought it was not right for a bar owner to be mayor. Pastor Wallace believes liquor to be the root most evil. When Squeaky discovered the Pastor was preaching on the evils of alcohol, and particularly the evil of Squeaky's bar, he went to the church to confront him. Pastor Wallace saw Squeaky in the church congregation and he thought the man had come to see the error of his ways. From the pulpit, Pastor Wallace was brimming with joy. He was happy as a kid on Christmas morning. He sang hymns with a fervor few had seen. He read the scripture with a renewed spirit. You would have thought he could fly like the angels right up to the rafters and through the roof.

Just as the pastor was reaching a fevered pitch on the evils of drink, Squeaky stood up to speak. In his odd high-pitched voice -- thus his name -- Squeaky began. "Pastor Wallace, isn't Joe Turnbull here an elder in your church? And what about John Smyth? I believe he's also an elder. Oh yes, and I see Billy Jenson over there. I believe he's head of the Pancake Festival. Well Pastor, they were all in this week for a pool game and a few beers. Matter-of-fact, they're in most weeks for a few drinks. Oh, and let's not forget the ladies. Dorothy Turnbull comes in most Friday afternoons with her bridge club for a little toddy. I believe she's head of the Ladies Auxiliary. Clara May likes to talk to Frieda over a gin and tonic. Frieda has a beer. You better get the shepherd's staff and start searching. You may have lost some of your flock."

Pastor Wallace's wings were clipped. He fell from his invented piety with a thud all the way to the next county. He quickly called for the organist to play a hymn, *How Great Thou Art*, to cut off Squeaky's rant. Squeaky had won the round, but the battle was far from over. For as long as Pastor Wallace remained in town there were no more sermons on the evil of Squeaky's, just on the evil of alcohol. Squeaky won the election by a landslide. Judy tells me her dad, the good Pastor, drinks a bit now and then himself now that he's living in Arizona. Maybe he thinks it's okay in retirement without a flock to herd, or he's just hypocritical. First Pastor Jenkins on the highway and now remembering Pastor Wallace, I don't need this today.

Good God, it's Clara May coming toward me. What's she doing out at this time of day? Her driver's license should be taken away, but since she lives in the country there would be no way for her to get around. She needs to move in town. Living in a small town everyone knows you and your business, so she would get all the help she needed.

When Mom died, everyone was there to help. There was enough food to feed the entire town. Customers would stop by just to see how I was doing. This is their good side. It can also be a curse when everyone knows your business. Secrets are hard to keep. It will be common knowledge that I was driving around in the country before lunch. I am sure Clara May will come up with some juicy story to go with it. Might as well roll down my window and wave.

"Hey, Clara May. Don't look too long. Keep your eyes on the road. Yes, it's me James in the red Camaro. Please don't bother to wave. Hands on the wheel, that's a good girl."

Her car remains in perfect condition because everyone avoids her. As soon as she gets home, she will be on the phone to pass along the gossip. Where would this town be without the Clara Mays of the world? Maybe I should get a bumper sticker that says *James is up to no good*. I could interchange it with *James is being a bad boy*. Today it would say, *James is a very good boy, he has to be*.

Chapter 9

Clara May on Gary Warren

What can I tell you about Gary? People feel he's aloof, better than the rest of us. My friend Freda says it best. "Gary looks down his nose at us. He thinks Dewers is a two-bit hick town and not good enough for him."

I told Frieda, "I don't think he's aloof. I think he's lonely and doesn't know how to find friends here. He's got his insurance clients, but they're not friends. Without a family he doesn't fit in."

Frieda wasn't buying any excuses. "Most of the town's blaming him for the affair. We're not good enough, and he doesn't even spend weekends with us. He goes to Chicago, and he's not a member of any church."

I said, "So what difference does that make?"

"What difference does it make?" Frieda was on the warpath. "Why, Clara May, this is a God-fearing town, and if I can do anything about it, it will stay that way. I find it hard to trust anyone who is not a regular church-goer."

I wasn't letting her off without an argument. "John Dunhill goes to church every Sunday and I wouldn't call him a good person."

Frieda wasn't backing down. "Yeah, but we all know John. Known him for a long time, and know to stay away from him. There's other places we can get groceries in this town than his store, but there's not much choice of where to buy insurance. Gary's it in this town."

Should I admit I see Gary often? Why not? I'm sure Frieda knows anyway. "Gary's okay when you get to know him. We meet regularly for a gin and tonic at Squeaky's. He fills me in on what's happening on The Square. You know he can spy on The Square's going-ons from his apartment?"

Frieda's mouth dropped forming a wide O. You could drive a semi truck through it. It took her a minute to recover and close it before she could speak. "Why, Clara May, I never. I hope you don't have plans on continuing after this whole affair."

"I have all the more reason to see him now. He'll tell me what's going on and be truthful about it. I have no intention of dropping my friendship."

Again Frieda's mouth drops, her head jerks up, and she puffs up her chest like a proud peacock. "I hope you know what you're doing, Clara May, consorting with the likes of him."

Truth is I didn't know what I was doing, I often don't. Doesn't bother me. I dive in feet first. I have a hunch Gary's not too sure of himself, either. He's basically a good kid. I didn't know him or his parents in school, but I've never let that stop me from forming an opinion. We meet once a week at Squeaky's. It began as a thank you drink. I had upgraded my insurance policy for the farm and he suggested we go out for a drink. I discovered he loves to tell tales as much as I do. Okay, we both like to gossip. I have gin and tonics, and he has vodka martinis. We both have a good time talking about the town.

In our last conversation before the affair broke, Gary was as bubbly as a bottle of fresh seltzer water. "Clara May, I'm getting used to this town, never thought I'd say that. You think I might be catching something, getting a fever?"

This was a surprise to me. I responded, "I don't know. You want me to get a thermometer and take your temperature?"

Gary held up both his hands as if to push me away. "No, I don't think so. You probably still use a rectal thermometer."

Gary had just taken a sip of his martini, and we both were laughing so hard it was coming out of his nose. He started coughing, and I was afraid he couldn't breathe. I asked him, "Are you all right?"

Through coughs he got out, "I'm okay, but don't make me laugh when I'm drinking a martini. Just because I'm an insurance agent doesn't mean I have good insurance."

He seemed okay, so I thought I'd give him a nudge. I wanted to see if I could get more from him. "What's changed your mind about Dewers? I thought you were a die-hard big city man. Is there some secret life here you've not told me?"

As Gary looked down at his drink, he lost his smile. "There are a lot of secrets in this town. You, of all people, should know that."

Huh, I'm hitting some pay dirt. "That's true, but do you have a secret that's changed your mind?"

Gary took another sip of his martini. I tried to read his face but wasn't sure if it was surprise or anger. His eyebrows were slightly arched. His lips were firm, but with the jaw slightly dropped. His eyes were wide. I could see white at the tops. "It's that I've gotten to know people better. I'm enjoying myself at the Rotary Club. I've even given some thought about attending church, but I think I'll stay away from Pastor Jenkins. Maybe I'll try the Universalist Church next door."

It's my turn to be surprised. "Church, you? My goodness, I better make sure I've got lightening rods installed before God strikes with a bolt."

Gary and I laughed again and when we stopped our laughing, he had a quizzical expression: eyes open and fixed on me, relaxed lips with the hint of a frown. My students would do this when they were truly listening. It said he was interested in what I was saying and paying close attention. "Clara May there is something, but I think you know."

Do I keep the cat out of the bag or shove it back in? He's brought it out. I carefully chose my words. "You mean your homosexuality? You're trying to tell me you prefer men?"

Looking me straight in the eyes, Gary sighed deeply. "Yes, I am. And I'm happy because I've found others in this town."

It's my turn for a drink and a sigh. "Doesn't surprise me, you or the others. We've always had men content to be life-long bachelors. No one paid them much mind. We called them eccentric. My uncle Jake never married, kept to himself. I think he was a homosexual. He liked to take trips to Chicago on the train. It was the only time he left town. I'm sure he found what he was looking for there. Just like you probably have.

"If you were one of my students, I'd say you'd be a smart ass to cover up your feelings. All male eyes, except yours, are checking out girls. In the locker room you're silent as others brag and fantasize about female dates and how many bases they reached. You'd make snide remarks and have a tough boy attitude. There would be deep, forbidden longings you don't understand. You'd be a kid more comfortable in home economics than shop. Your type usually runs from Dewers at the first chance they can. What I'm trying to say is I've known from the beginning."

Gary's face relaxed and he had a broad smile as he rose from his seat to give me a hug. This was the last conversation I had with him before the affair hit the papers.

Chapter 10

Gary Warren

I hate mornings. How did I ever get through college with morning classes? If it hadn't been for Bob waking me, I don't think I would've made it. I would've flunked every morning class. But I did make it, and look where it's gotten me: Dewers Town Square.

Clearly visible from my window is the entrance to the men's restroom at the courthouse, and watching it is what got me into trouble. Well watching it didn't get me into trouble; it was being nosey. I checked it out one day and discovered it was being used for more than a quick piss. There will be no one today. The restrooms are closed for good, but let's have a look this Halloween morning to see what else is going on. Clara May might call to quiz me and I don't want to disappoint her.

Henry, the jeweler, has arrived. Mr. Banks, the high school principle, is going in for his morning coffee at The Square Cafe, and Officer Bob is parking his patrol car. He's following Banks into the coffee shop. Mr. Majors is coming to open up his clothing store. Looks like he's got a new cashmere coat. I'll note that for Clara May. I see Doc Marvin with his black bag. Come rain, shine, snow, or sleet, he walks to work. It's a little early for Marge's hat shop. She usually doesn't make it until just before opening at 10 a.m., but it looks as if Mary Key is waiting anyway. I hope she's planning of returning that dreadful hat. It looks as if some bird has built a nest on her head. I wonder if Clara May has seen it. I'll have to ask her. Maggi, the florist, is walking in. She's got a funeral this morning and probably has last minute arrangements. It's Gertie Henderson. My predecessor sold her a policy. It will be a goodly amount for her kids. Husband died a few years earlier. Along with the Thompsons, their families are the oldest settlers of Dewers.

Speaking of the Thompsons, it doesn't look as if William, Bob's dad, is at work today.

Maybe he's decided to come in late. I'm not sure if he lets the gossip bother him. We've not talked since the affair hit. I hope it blows over before golf season comes around again. I'm hoping for another round before winter, but I don't think that's going to happen. I miss William saying, "Hey, there's Gary, my boy -- how's my insurance salesman?" Drives Bob crazy when he calls me his boy, but I like it.

I am not Dewers born or Dewers raised. I'm from the big city, Chicago. No one knows my family here. There are no remembered good old' days. I have buddies at the bar and of course there is Bob, who was my college roommate. I have no kids in school. There is no wife to go to PTA meetings.

You get the picture. I'm not known. I'm not fond of small town life and I go to Chicago every chance I get, which raises a few eyebrows. I overheard Frieda on The Square the other day. She was talking to Clara May. "If he's going to do business in Dewers, he could at least enjoy what we have to offer." What Dewers has to offer is gossip on The Square, unending talk of the weather, church, and bake sales.

Most people see me as the man they owe money to for their insurance. Insurance they won't see because they'll be dead, or insurance they don't want to collect because it means a loved one has died or some catastrophe his hit. When a tornado hit near town last year, I did win a few friends. With their belongings strewn over cornfields, people were in shock. They needed help and they needed it fast. Faster than a speeding bullet, super insurance man came to the rescue, but they view that as my job, which means it's nothing special. I have ulterior motives -- selling them more insurance.

William Thompson and I used to be good friends. He and I hit it off from the first time I met him. He said, "Gary, you've got a good head. Your father should be proud of you." This was odd, because Bob had me believing he was a horse's ass.

Dad wanted me to start an agency in Dewers and William was willing to help. "That is a great plan, Gary. The guy who owned the insurance agency next to the bank just died, and his wife is looking for someone to buy the business." William was more than happy to have me come into town. We struck a deal.

William financed the purchase of the business and then he took me to the country club for drinks. He also had something else on his mind. "You know Gary, that building is also for sale. The wife is going back to Iowa and doesn't want anything to do with it. I bet we can get you a good deal. It's great for you, a two-bedroom apartment above, and no problem getting to work. Laughing, he said, "Hell, you could put in a fire pole. People will look favorably on you for staying on The Square where you're easy to visit. Good visibility. Folks will see you as they walk The Square shopping. Make sure you're open Saturday afternoons. People will stop in just to talk. Have some coffee to offer them."

How would this work? I had just graduated and was already in debt for the business.
"William, I'm not sure I can get a loan for the building also."

He smiled, laid a hand on my shoulder, and said, "Gary, let me handle that. I'm the banker."

The deal was closed. I was grateful, but I also knew it was not a one-sided deal. He would refer customers to me for their insurance deals. He finances a home purchase and arranges insurance through me. We had a good thing going.

In the beginning, William was only someone I could use to achieve my goals, but he asked me to play golf with his buddies. I've grown fond of him. I got to know the elite of Dewers. I had access to their inner circle but never became a part of that circle. William got me into the Rotary and the Elks. I'm too old to be a good catch for their daughters and without a wife, I'm an odd man out at parties. Most damning of all are my Chicago weekends. But despite these shortcomings, ones my father constantly reminded me of, I was fitting in.

When you're a big city native, small town life can be, well, small. Life in Dewers is centered on family, weather, crop and livestock prices. My only interest in any of these was to insure them. New babies need to be covered. There's always a threat of bad weather, and bad crops. I need to keep tabs on the feelings of the farmers.

William and Bob were making progress in softening me up to the unseen benefits of small town life. People really care about how your day is going when they ask. Realizing how good fresh biscuits in the morning smell. Knowing that personal misfortune brings help out of the woodwork. Everyone celebrates and benefits from a good harvest. Everyone is an aunt, or uncle, or grandparent, or cousin, or knows you through a family member. Religion is a way of life, not words spoken in church. I was considering spending more weekends in Dewers.

Most townsfolk -- if they're interested, and most are -- think I go to Chicago to see my family. They're partly right. Occasionally, I visit Mom and Dad for Sunday dinner or if there's a birthday, but it's not much different than being in Dewers. My sister comes with her dentist doctor husband and the kids. It's grandkids this, grandkids that. What cute clothes. Don't get me wrong, I like my nieces and nephews, but enough is enough. Send them outdoors to play and lock the doors. Tell them they can't come in until their ready to sleep or their parents are ready to go home. Dewers has taught me to be a bit more tolerant. The kids can come in an hour before bedtime.

My sister says I am too particular about dress. You can call me a dandy or a peacock. I like it, but wearing my latest fashion in Dewers is putting a spotlight on me. Last thing I need is to be any different than I already am. Imagine me, a peacock strolling around The Square. I'd like to let my hair grow long, but no man in town has long hair. It's all crew cut, flattop, or wavy short. I save the designer clothes for Chicago.

Jealousy is most likely a major cause of the belligerent behavior toward my sister and her family. Mom and Dad understand her and her dentist husband; they are involved in their lives. Even though my parents are sophisticated big city people, they haven't a clue about my lifestyle. All they know is that there'll be no children coming from their son, no male heir to pass on the Warren legacy. I never understood this until I lived in Dewers. I now know that unless you live in my world, you cannot know my world. Heterosexuality is all my parents know. It's like they're in Paris and don't know French. How do they get around? How can they befriend a person when they don't speak the language?

It's not that my parents have a problem with my lifestyle because they don't. When I told them I was a homosexual, they were upset but I never doubted their love. Dad's only comment was, "You know son, getting ahead in the business world is tough when you're single. Businessmen expect their colleagues to be married with a family. Who's going to accompany you to the parties if you don't have a wife? You can't take your boyfriend, and you can't be swishy."

Swishy? Boyfriend? I barely had sex in Dewers until I observed unusual activity in the courthouse restrooms. I discovered anonymous sex there. Problem is, it's become an addiction. It bothers me, the restroom sex, but I can't stop. Even when I'm in Chicago, I seek out the restrooms when there's no need. For Christ's sake, I can take men home to my apartment. Maybe I need to get a long-term partner.

This affair has made me wonder if it's worth the trouble of living a double life in Dewers. My agency is successful. I could hire an office manager to run the day-to-day business and I could handle what I need to from Chicago. Right now, as an outsider, I'm receiving most of the blame for the affair. It takes the heat off the locals, Thomas, Bob, James, and Danny. Problem is, if I leave, one of them will be the new target. People always feel a need to blame someone.

Blame it on original sin. Blame it on the devil. Blame it on the weather. Blame it on our fathers. Blame it on our mothers. The fact is, no one is to blame, unless you consider God or the devil. That's it. Let's blame it on one of them. Pastor Jenkins already blames the devil. Maybe I'll join in.

The Square Affair five, as we have been named, haven't talked since the arrest. It's our attorney's advice. I haven't a clue how they're coping. We used to talk about sexual desires, who else in the town has similar desires. We'd discuss our fears of discovery, and alibis. We never talked about quitting. I need to talk to my friends. I miss them. I miss our laughter, our secrets, the danger, and the intrigue.

How do friendships happen? How does a trip to the movies turn into a marriage? How does a thought, a vision, an urge, a longing become reality? Who knows? If I did, I'd be a marriage broker, not an insurance salesman. And even if I knew how I became a homosexual, I wouldn't change. I like who I am. I dislike the secrets I have to keep. I long to have an honest discussion. I want to share my passion for men. I want to talk about married men I meet, how they bitch about their wives. I want to talk about my real life the way heterosexuals do. Even in Chicago I'm forced to live a secret life, except in the company of my homosexual friends and even then, we have to be careful. There are still police raids and people who would love to do us harm.

Until I met the other men, Bob was the only one in Dewers that knew my double life. We met in college and pledged the same fraternity. Though the university town is larger than Dewers, it's not a metropolis. Bob was happy to be away, to be free of scrutinizing eyes and cupped ears ready to report his every word. I was in culture shock outside of Chicago. We were unlikely roommates, one skeptical, one elated. We found common ground in being free of family and their expectations. Bob's dad was expecting him to be bank president. My dad was expecting me to be his protégé. I came to agree with my dad and Bob pushed further away from his.

I made no attempt to keep my Chicago life secret. It intrigued Bob. He would often go with me when I returned on weekends. My flamboyant friends treated him like royalty. He was the innocent farm boy and they were waiting to convert that innocence into some sophisticated sin. Bob gave in a few times, but he would never totally let go. Apron strings were tied too tightly. Being seen with homosexuals was not in the moral code of Dewers.

I'd like to feel guilty about introducing Bob to my world, but I don't. I'm sorry that I couldn't offer him advice on how to deal with his marriage. I regret that I wasn't able to snag him before he became engaged. I know married men who play around, but they're tight lipped about their double lives. They play a game of denial, but it's really Russian roulette.

When I moved to Dewers, Bob and I had a routine. We'd meet every Wednesday evening at Squeaky's for drinks. Drinks led to weekends of fishing and sex at Lake Warren and eventually to the courthouse bathrooms for sex. He discovered them on his own and often went without me. The danger of being discovered aroused us, pulled us into its web, and onto the cold concrete floor. The longer you go without being caught, the more you want to go. This must be like cocaine or heroin. We had an occasional romp in my apartment, but we preferred the sleaziness of the restrooms.

We met at the bar on Wednesday nights because nothing gets done on that night in small towns. It's reserved as church night. I'm always at Squeaky's, never at church. Bob is usually with me unless there's a men's group or a planning meeting for the pancake breakfast. Bob's wife always goes to church night. She's got her fingers into everything. Danny owns the bar and is always there. Thomas is another fixture when he's not in the fields. James is off and on. I guess you could say Wednesday is our church night. We have our own unique fellowship.

One night after a few too many martinis, I was showing off. As usual, conversation got around to sex. They wanted to know if everything was working okay. After all, I don't have a wife or girlfriend. I offered to show them, but they refused. Almost slipped up that night. Turns out it wouldn't have mattered. I had missed some obvious signs from my friends.

The married men were tired of their lives. It was just before the July 4th festivities when the discussion got heated. Thomas started. "I'm tired of going to my parents for wiener roasts and fireworks. I realized they are just across the road, but I'd like to relax in my own yard with my family. They always have their friends over." He took a sip of his beer then continued. "Maybe I'll do it this year."

Bob held up both hands, as if this would eliminate any more burdens. "Oh God, I know what you mean. My son graduated from kindergarten this year, and Mary insisted on having a big graduation party. Can you believe it? Kindergarten! She said it was so we could meet all the other kids and their parents. I told her I'd lived here my whole life. I know the parents."

James thought he had us all beat. "I not only have to be nice and reward the employees with Christmas presents and bonuses, I've got to do something for the customers. And we have a summer thank you picnic. I've got little time to be alone to shop or to simply sit down with my family. There are the General Motor's functions, new model roll out parties, dealership award parties, and Christmas parties. Only good thing, my wife doesn't like going out of town. I can be alone, explore, be adventurous, and play around. But you know what I'd like to do. I want all of us buddies to go fishing at Lake Warren."

I had the feeling something more intimate than friendship was brewing. Availability was determined, and a remote cabin secured. Our fate was sealed.

Thomas kept asking, "Are you sure the cabins are remote? What will be the sleeping arrangements?"

James said the cabin sleeps six in two bedrooms. He also wanted to know what we should wear. He kept checking the weather to determine if it was going to rain or be hot. He wanted to know if there were storms forecast. He especially wanted to know, "Is it okay to sleep without clothes? I usually sleep in the nude. Will that bother anyone?"

Thomas was the first to respond. "Hey, I haven't compared sizes since high school and the military. We can see how you measure up."

James didn't miss a beat in his response. "You've got to remember some people are showers, and some are growers." We all knew what he was saying, but why was he saying it? What does it matter?

Danny had been listening behind the bar. At this point in the conversation he broke in. "Save it for the lake. No one's taking any clothes off here."

I took a sip from my martini and with a little swish responded, "Are you afraid somebody will show you up?" Actually I wanted to know if their erections were any of the anonymous ones I'd seen in the courthouse restrooms. I should have stopped it at this point. That voice in my head, that tickle in my gut said, *Gary, you know where this is headed.* Trouble was, I didn't want to hear that voice. I didn't want it to stop. I needed others to share my secret life and suspected they did, too.

Danny's eyes squinted, and his lips slowly grew into a smug smile, which threatened to become a broad grin, "You'll just have to wait and see."

Bob was quiet, but taking in the conversation. He placed his chin on his right hand surveying all of us before speaking. "What are all of you, some sex craved maniacs? Do all of you sleep naked? You'd think you've never seen a man's dick before."

In college I learned a lot about Bob. I said, "Have you changed your sleeping habits? Every night for four years, I saw you strip before going to bed. And I believe you were constantly checking out men in the shower." I almost added, *before you actually had sex with them.*

I pulled out my pack of cigarettes, and, as I was tapping out a new one, glanced at the new health warning. "And they say these are hazardous to your health. This group is hazardous to my health."

The weekend finally arrived. With James' boat in tow, we set out Friday evening to Lake Warren, stopping at the liquor store on the way for a couple cases of beer and ice. I already had my vodka in the cooler. We'd buy some groceries at the local store, but this insured we had the most important stuff: alcohol.

We pulled in as the sun was sinking below the lake's surface. Away from other cabins, on a hidden cove in the lake, and surrounded by tall trees with thick underbrush, our cabin was perfect. We were ready.

I was first to hop out of the car. I took a deep breath, "So, this is what nature smells like."

James unfolded himself from the back seat along with the cooler of beer and vodka and asks me, "Miss the traffic noise and exhaust fumes yet?"

As a matter of fact I did, but I wasn't going to admit it. "I'm not homesick yet, if that's what you're asking."

Making note of the fading light, Bob began unpacking the car. "If you don't want to do this in the dark, you nature lovers might want to help me."

I found my vodka and cigarettes and ignored Bob. "This much nature and clean air is going to ruin my lungs. I need a drink and a smoke before I can go on." With that, I took a swig of vodka and lit a cigarette. I would have preferred a martini glass, but I hadn't packed one.

Bob dropped what he was carrying. With intently focused eyes, he tried to intimidate Thomas and me. Thomas had also stopped to light up a cigarette. "Okay, whose got the keys?"

I blew a plume of smoke at Bob, while holding out my hand with the keys.

Once inside, it was time to choose bedrooms. Danny, I, and Bob took one. Thomas and James took the other room. Each room had a double and a single bed. Danny took the single. "You two have slept together before, so you get the double. I'll take the single."

Bob corrected him, "We didn't sleep together. We slept in the same room."

Danny responded, "Same thing. You've seen each other naked."

I hardly could keep from laughing. "Yeah, Bob, whatever you say." I couldn't resist a tilt of my head and a downward glace at Bob. He smiled and quickly looked away.

After settling in, we pulled out sandwiches and had dinner in front of the fireplace. When it was time for bed, we were all pretty tired. None of us took much notice that evening of each other as we stripped off our clothes. Morning brought a chill in the air and a change in us. Danny was the first to wake up, "God, it's cold in here. Who let the fire go out? Move over guys. I'm coming in bed for some warmth."

Danny climbed into bed on my side and snuggled. His back was to my front. We were spooning each other. Bob woke up shivering and cuddled up to me on the other side. Suddenly I got an erection. Next Danny got an erection, and then Bob got an erection. Bob spoke first, "You know you've got your dick between my legs."

Danny commented, "And you've got your dick between my legs."

We lay still for a few minutes with no one's erections showing any signs of going away. I was the first to stroke Danny. There was no mistaking the sound of Danny's moaning so Bob reached and stroked my erection. We became entwined and then the inevitable ejaculations.

It was Bob who first leaned over to kiss me. Then the three of us were hugging and kissing. We fell asleep again cuddling.

I woke first and ran into Thomas and James kissing in the kitchen. "Excuse me. Did you two have a good night?"

As they turned around, I could see that if they didn't have a good night, they were going to have a good morning. Both were erect and red faced. Thomas spoke first. "We were just ..."

Finishing the sentence, I said, "Just kissing, I think."

Thomas tried to change the subject, "But we're not ... we didn't. And how did you sleep last night? We heard a lot of commotion in your room."

There was no need to lie. "After we had sex this morning, we all slept very well."
It was James' turn to look surprised. "You, all three, sex?"

I responded, "Yes, James, don't get bug eyed. Stop drooling. You knew it was going to happen, and you've done it before, both of you."

I turned around and noticed that Danny and Bob had walked in. Danny spoke. "Well, well what have we here, a little hanky panky?"

I was in a mood to be smug and responded for them. "There's no need to deny it. I've seen both of you many times going into the courthouse restrooms, far too many times for just a pee. I see the coffee is done. Let's all put on some pants and go on the porch for a cup. I still need my morning pick me up."

It was so quiet on the porch. I think you could hear fish swimming. Everyone was staring into their coffee cups and no one was drinking, except me. "I don't know about you guys, but I like my coffee hot. If you don't want it cold, you better start drinking."

Almost in unison they all raised cups to lips and drank. Danny put his cup on the porch floor then spoke. "Gary and I are single, and the rest of you are married. I had some idea from the bar discussions that something might be going on. But you guys are married. Have we all been in the courthouse bathrooms?"

I said, "Yes, they have. I've seen you all coming and going and I'm no stranger to those concrete floors. Once I knew it was good for anonymous sex, I kept watch on it from my office and apartment. You were all good about your timing. Nobody went on Saturday when The Square was full, but all of you must have known Sunday late morning and afternoon was a good time because everyone's in church or having Sunday dinner with family. Late morning, early afternoon is also a good time. Kids are still in school and there aren't many people shopping. You'd park on the outside of The Square and pretend you were using the courthouse grounds as a shortcut to the other side."

Bob was watching with an open mouth. "Why didn't you tell me you knew all of this? You knew I was having sex there and I knew you were, and occasionally we did together, but the others?"

I said, "I didn't want to ruin a good thing. Obviously you all are into anonymous sex. I understand. We're in a small town: small town attitude, small town gossip, small town life. You've urges you don't understand, and one day, when you innocently go for a pee you find the source of those urges. I've known I liked men since high school, but no one told me either. Bob discovered he liked men while in college with me but fought it and got married anyway."

The married men still weren't willing to talk. I wondered if they just needed to have some time to come to grips with the fact that their secret life was not so secret anymore, at least among us.

Finally James spoke. "Let's grab some breakfast and get out early on the lake. We'll see if anything is biting."

Bob started laughing, "Danny will bite if you want him to. He did this morning."

Danny gave Bob the finger and went inside to get some breakfast.

The rest of the morning we concentrated on fishing, talking about what line to use, what bait, best places to buy equipment, but nothing about sex. We caught enough fish for a good dinner and headed back to shore for lunch, beers, clean the fish, and a nap.

After our naps we gathered on the porch for a drink and a smoke. We commented on the lush tree growth that gave us privacy. Thomas said he walked by the closest cabin and found out they couldn't see us. I observed the others and was sure after supper they'd start talking. They'd have enough time to digest last night, the morning, and they'd be forming questions for which there would be no good answers. Danny volunteered to cook the fish, and I said I'd do the potatoes and vegetables.

When Danny and I were in the kitchen alone, he asked, "How long have you known?"

"A while," I responded.

Danny's forehead wrinkled and he skewed his mouth like he was trying to form a thought but couldn't quite get it out. Finally he spoke. "How do you think they can do it, the married guys? They're married with children. It's hard enough for me and I'm single. As it is, I think Clara May suspects, or possibly even knows."

"I'll let her speak for herself," I said, "but I think she knows."

Danny stopped talking as the others came in to see how dinner was doing.

Thomas slipped in an aside like a school kid looking to get into trouble. "Is it ready yet, or have you two been doing something other than cooking."

"No and no, and if you don't get out of here, I'm going to flick cigarette ashes in your potatoes." I would have, too. "I suggest you guys get the table ready to eat."

Thomas was trying to be a wise guy. "How fancy do we have to be?"

"We're not eating it out of the pan, or with our fingers, if that's what you're asking." As Thomas left to set up the table, I couldn't resist. "Make it pretty."

I hoped the guys were doing okay and that they would talk tonight. I thought they would because they wouldn't miss an opportunity for sex that's not so anonymous. I almost said "without guilt," but I was not even there yet.

After dinner and a few drinks, we finally got down to some serious talk. "All of you have been in the bathrooms?" Thomas asked. All heads nodded yes. Thomas continued. "Then that means we've probably had sex with each other."

I could easily answer that question. "I am sure of that. At least you've been in the bathrooms at the same time."

Annoyed, James asked, "Okay, now that we've established that. What the hell does it matter? Should we play pin the name on the dick? What I want to know is where do we go from here? We know we're all looking for the same thing."

"We can plan more fishing trips, but too many will raise suspicion. And what do we do in the winter?" Bob offered. "What about your place, Gary?"

I wasn't sure how to answer that question, but I tried. "I would like nothing better than to know I could have regular sex with the men of Dewers, but there are only so many card games or insurance chats we can have. Occasionally is fine, but not on a regular basis."

Danny asked the hard question. "I know I go to the bathroom because it's the only sex I can get without going out of town, and I'm guessing that's the same for Gary. Why do you three married guys go? Are you closeted homosexuals, or just not getting it at home?"

James answered first. "I'm not sure why. I can't complain about sex at home, but once I discovered anonymous male sex, it kind of took hold of me. It's a craving. I don't neglect my wife, but this excites me in different ways, ways I don't think my wife could."

"Where did you first find out about it?" Bob asked.

James responded, seemingly without a thought. "I was at a new model roll out in Detroit. I was staying at a Holiday Inn. One night I went to the lobby restroom. We'd been out drinking, and I couldn't make it to the room. I went into a stall, and this guy in the next stall put his hand under the divider. I didn't know what it was about, so I ignored it. Then he passed a note saying he'd give me a blowjob. I don't know if I was drunk or what, but I did it. I liked it, and did it every night I was there. It wasn't always the same guy. Late at night there was always someone in the restroom. When I got home, I went to the courthouse bathrooms on the off chance there may be someone there and there was."

Thomas was listening with great interest. When James was done he spoke. "I was horny as hell going into the service. I'd heard there were always girls near the bases that were easy. I found them, gave them a try, and it was okay. Then one night, I'm with a few guys in a bar off base. I was feeling horny but I wasn't driving, so getting laid by one of the girls was going to be difficult. Just like James, I was approached in the bathroom. Later I found out where I could get regular blowjobs, even on base. I wasn't looking for sex in the courthouse, but one day I was in town and had to pee and there it was. There's no negotiation, no waiting for the kids to go to bed. It's pretty much there when you want it."

"You still haven't answered my question." Danny looked concerned. "Why do you do it? What if your wives found out?"

There was an alarming silence, as if none of them had thought about that before. Bob was the first to speak. "I have often wanted that very thing to happen. I can't speak for the others, but I knew I liked to be with men before I got married. I went ahead with the marriage because it was the right thing to do. The only thing to do if you live in Dewers is get married or move away. "

I commented. "I'll say he knew he liked men. Should have seen him in Chicago."

Bob turned red and gave me the finger.

Thomas was not looking at us and I thought the conversation was bothering him. I asked, "Thomas, are you okay?"

He replied, "Yes. I'm thinking about Danny's questions. Alone in the field, I've had a great amount of time to think about what I'd tell Sue. It frightened me to think she would find out, but like you, Bob, I wanted her to find out. I imagined the embarrassment, hers and mine. I thought if it came out, I'd never be able to see the kids again. When I thought about it, I'd stop going to the courthouse for a few weeks but always went back."

Bob was twisting in his chair and wringing his hands. "Do you know, I would dream that Mary was killed in an auto accident, or was diagnosed with terminal cancer? It was an easy way out. I wouldn't marry again, maybe move to Chicago with the kids. I despise myself for those dreams, but can't stop them."

James was getting visibly excited. "I for one don't want to talk about what my wife wants or what she thinks. There are four men with like minds here, and I want to talk about what I want."

We all laughed a bit too hard but that had broken the ice. There was a lot of bed switching that night. The next day we fished some, drank a little more, and after dinner had another conversation. This time we talked about Squeaky's.

Danny wasn't shy to talk about the impression he had formed of us all. "Gary was the very picture of a homosexual. I saw through his Dewers face, especially after he'd had a couple of martinis. Bob and Gary seemed a little too chummy to have been just college roommates. It seems as if every night you guys were there, in some way there was a discussion of the courthouse restrooms. One night, Thomas was complaining that they were locked on a day he had to pee badly. James would always complain that they were in poor repair and dirty. He wanted the city to make more of an effort to keep them clean, for the sake of the tourists. But Bob, you were the strangest. You would agree with the others about how the restrooms looked and why were they locked sometimes, but your dad's bank is on The Square. Why would you need to use the courthouse restroom? And, of course, since I knew what was going on, I put it all together."

Thomas was concerned about what would happen after this weekend. "We have to be careful now that we know."

"In what way?" Bob asked.

Thomas responded, "We'll want to talk about the restrooms. We'll want to talk about our weekend. We can't have our conversations wander into that direction. We already know a few drinks can loosen our tongues. It could ruin a good thing."

James was concerned. "I know there are dangers in us continuing with this behavior, but I'm not willing to stop. What about the rest of you?"

Thomas looked worried. "I've always been concerned, but I can't stop either."

"As you well know, I can watch out for the sheriff or other odd people hanging around. If I see anything suspicious, I'll let you know on our nights at Squeaky's."

Danny had a suggestion. "Since I'll most likely be tending bar on nights that you all will be in, I'll try to keep you on track." He paused a moment then spoke again. "I have an idea. When I think the talk is getting out of hand, I'll ask a question. *Has anyone seen Clara May today?"*

Everyone agreed this was a good tactic and we had another night of sex.

Despite the bedroom romps and the conversations, we did get in some good fishing. We talked about some of the other men who came in to the restrooms. Some of the names surprised me, but the life-long residents of Dewers were not surprised. It was agreed they would not be brought into our fold. For the first time since moving to Dewers, I thought I could make it a home.

Plans were made for another weekend, and then a third weekend, but no one gave up the restrooms. There've been occasional meetings between Bob and me in my apartment. We thought the courthouse basement restroom ideal because it has the mystique of danger, a clandestine affair under the noses of everyone in Dewers. No excuses would be needed. We were simply going to The Square on an errand. However, someone noticed and tipped off the sheriff. Our mistake, thinking that nothing goes unnoticed in this town. And that's why I'm looking out the window today wondering what's going on in the courthouse

Chapter 11

Clara May on William Thompson

Frieda and I are in the car on the way to The Square for dinner when Frieda drops a bombshell. "Oh, I forgot to tell you what I saw in the cemetery this morning."

"What a brave person you are, going to the cemetery on Halloween. What were you doing there? Were you lying down next to George to see if your grave will still fit your body?"

"So, I've gained some weight. No, you'll never guess what I saw?"

"A ghost."

"No. I saw William Thompson and he looked like he was talking to ghosts."

"I'm beginning to worry about you Frieda. Did you see these ghosts he was talking to?"

"Clara May let me tell this story, and you keep your mind on the road. You almost ran that stop sign."

"Don't be a backseat driver. Talk."

"William was at the family plot staring at his parent's grave marker and he was waving his hands in the air. He raised a clenched fist like he was cursing God. He got down on his knees and touched his boy's grave, as if he was giving him a good night kiss."

"He is big on his family and the reputation they built here, but this sounds a little crazy, even for him."

"I know. Sometimes I go visit George's grave and talk to him while I'm arranging flowers. William looked like he was really talking and someone was listening."

"Did you wave or stop to say hello?"

"No. He didn't look in a mood to talk."

"You're letting me down here, Frieda. I count on you to gather information when you see or hear it."

"Hold your horses. I'm not done yet."

"Hurry up. We're almost at the café."

"While I was at George's grave, Harry the groundskeeper stopped by."

"And ..."

"And he had talked to William just a few minutes earlier. William was worried about Bob and talking it over with the family."

"You mean the dead family. Sounds a little nuts to me, but family always comes first to William."

Frieda is one of the greeters at church so she notices who comes and goes. "He and Rose have been very distant at church. They come in at the last minute, sit in back, and leave early. I don't think they want to talk to anyone."

"Would that anyone be Pastor Jenkins?"

"Could be."

"Looks like the girls are at the café. This will be an interesting supper."

Chapter 12

William Thompson

I never thought I'd welcome the chance to be with banking regulators, but today they'll keep me in my office and away from the people of this town. A town my family forged from prairie grass. A town my bank mortgaged. A town my friends live and work in. A town in which I married Rose. A town my children call home. A town in which my son is buried. A town whose history defines my life.

I don't know what time Rose, my wife, got to sleep, but it was late. I awoke early, quietly robed, and walked downstairs to make coffee. I'm absent-mindedly looking out the kitchen window now and notice the sky has a dark cloud cover. It looks like snow. I could have used a sunny day to brighten my mood. No luck with that today. My dog, Pete, begins nudging me with his nose. "Okay boy, I'll let you out, but it's cold." As I open the door, Pete looks at me with his brown eyes wondering what happened to the warmth. "I know, Pete. I wish it were warm, too. Better get used to it. It's going to be cold for a while. Out the door. No barking."

The drip of percolating coffee is soothing. The aroma brings me back to childhood: Mom's coffee bubbling on the iron cook stove, biscuits in the oven, sizzling bacon. Good thing she's not here. Bob's affair and legal problems would not sit well with her Baptist mind. She'd have the Bible out making him swear he'd never again stray. I don't know if it would help.

This affair has me tied in knots. Rose is refusing to talk to Bob. I've got my family's name, heritage, and hard work to protect, so I try not to talk about the affair at work. I've been entrusted with the bank, the land holdings, and stock. It's a burden I gladly accept, but managing it gives the appearance of autocratic rule, being a hard ass. The bottom line, the buck stops with me. It's hard to turn it off when I'm out of the bank. Town gossip is unsettling. I feel like I have a stomach ulcer that can't be treated, or there's a fallen tree in my path that I can't get around or move. The agony I see in my son and wife increases the pain. Rose used to be my remedy for a bad day. She'd rub my shoulders, talk to me about the happenings in her life, church social planning, the historical society, and it soothed me. Now her conversations are all about the affair. Just last night over supper she said, "Sue gave me a cold shoulder today. I was at lunch in the café were a group of my friends were eating. None of them would even look at me." There are no more back rubs, nor more scotch and water waiting for me when I get home.

The bank probably won't be affected by this scandal. I can't be as positive about my family. My wife is livid with Bob and his wife.

I wish I could shield my grandkids.

I wish this affair would go away.

I wish Rose could find some love for her son.

I wish I could have a conversation with my son without Rose stepping in or someone getting angry.

I wish I could understand what's going on with Bob.

Rose spent most of the night staring: first looking at William, Jr.'s photo, then his coffin flag, then Bob's photo, then the photo of the grandkids, then the family Christmas photo, all the time crying. Rose blames herself for Bill, Jr.'s death, and insists I'm the cause of Bob's sexual behavior. She kept quoting *Time* magazine that says homosexuality is a pernicious sickness and Bob is a deviant. Is he a deviant? He's different, but I can't believe he's sick. I can't believe he's evil, malicious, or willfully intends to cause harm. He's my son. He's my flesh and blood. I am capable of love. I love my son.

Rose forced me to read the Time article. *The mother — either domineering and contemptuous of the father, or feeling rejected by him — makes her son a substitute for her husband, with a close-binding, overprotective relationship. Thus, she unconsciously demasculinizes him.*

So Rose blames me for making Bob less of a man, says he was doomed because of our actions. Hogwash. I don't feel I've ever rejected Rose. Is she contemptuous of me? She'd never admit to being domineering.

I don't know what to think, and today I won't have to. I'll be with the bank auditors all day and then later, dinner. There won't be time to worry. I enjoy greeting people on my way to work but not today. Pouring another cup of coffee, I return to the bedroom to shower and dress. As is usually her habit, Rose laid out my clothes last night. I hope I don't wake her. I can't put up with my wife's babble this morning.

Showered and dressed, I find the winter lining for my coat and head out the door to the garage. Once in the black Buick, I feel safer, protected from the world. Outside the windows there's still no sign of the sun, just dark, long hanging clouds. My neighbor, Dr. West, waves to me as I back out of the garage. No doubt he'd love to gossip. He'd never mention Bob's affair, but talk around it, hoping I'd bring up the subject. I have no intention of letting that happen. I don't want to talk today.

I head in the opposite direction of work to check on a piece of land. My brother, Michael, manages the bank's farm department and this piece of property is part of it. I'm worried about the renter, Charlie. He had a heart attack last month. Michael says we should take the farm away from him, but the farm income is all Charlie has. His wife died of cancer a year ago and his son is in the army. I'm told the son will come home and help as soon as his tour of duty ends. I can't let the farm be taken away from Charlie without investigating myself. As I pass by, I notice the crop is nearly out and that multiple combines are working the field. His neighbors are finishing the job. I'm satisfied. There's no need to intervene.

Pulling into Charlie's driveway, I begin to back up so I can turn around when I see Charlie in his overalls and denim jacket waving at me. It'd be rude not to stop. I roll down my window and speak to him. "Charlie, how the hell are you?"

"Pretty damn good for an old fart like me."

"You can't be old, Charlie. You're the same age I am, and I'm not old."

"When's the last time you looked in the mirror, Bill?"

"When I shaved this morning, but I saw a young man."

"You need to go visit the doc for new glasses."

"Perhaps you're right. Charlie, how are you feeling?"

"I'm feeling great. Itching to get back on the tractor seat and into the field, but Doc West says I need to take it easy."

"I see you've got plenty of help with the crops."

Charlie sighs heavily and glances at the cornfield before answering. "I don't know where I'd be without Jim, Bob, Joe, and Earl. I'm glad to have good neighbors. I didn't ask. They appeared one day and started in on the soybeans. When they finished them, they headed to the corn. Looks like they'll finish it today."

"And in good time. Winter's around the corner."

"You're telling me. I can feel it in these bones."

"When's your son headed home?"

Square Affair

95

"He says sometime around Christmas unless they make him stay longer, but he doesn't think so. I worry about him over there in Vietnam."

"Charlie, we all worry about the boys over there. They're always in my prayers. Say, Charlie, don't you worry about losing this land. The crops are out in good time and your son will soon be home to help next spring."

"Thank you, Bill. That's a load off my mind."

"How's it going without June?"

"I miss her, but the other widows and the church take care of me. It seems I'm never without something to eat. You think they're after my money or my body?"

"Well, Charlie, I'd say unless you've got a stash under your mattress, they're after your body."

"Imagine that, I've still got the charm at 50."

"You still do. Got to run. See you later."

Charlie waves as I drive off. For the first time in awhile he has a big grin on his face. I need to protect the bank's interests, but sometimes leniency is in the best interest of the bank.

The cemetery is on the way back into town. I glance at my watch, realize there's time to stop and turn right, through the iron gates. A tall granite obelisk at the entrance is dedicated to the civil war soldiers. Some Thompson family members are mentioned. Crumbling gravestones, markers of the early settlers, surround it. Their names are as unreadable as their lives are forgotten. But look around the town and you can see them: Stewart's Opera House, Jones Men's Wear, Castle Building, James Watson Public Library, John Watson Memorial Hospital, Clayton and Bald Bank Building, and Thompson National Bank. Beyond the old graves, a gentle hill overlooks Bottom Creek where a number of lamb head stones can be seen. They are the children who died in one plague or another. The rusted iron bridge with wood runners carried devastated families in black carriages home to mourn as it did Rose, Bob, and myself the day we buried Bill, Jr. Our family plot is just beyond the bridge on top of the facing hill overlooking the creek and the children's graves.

A large mausoleum marks our plot and is readily identifiable because it's meant to be noticed and impress. Inside are the remains of the family patriarch and matriarch, James Madison Thompson, and his wife, Mable Anne Baker Thompson. Large steel double doors guard the mausoleum, while an image of Gabriel in stained glass provides reassurance of God's love. It does little to reassure me or brighten my day. Simple round top stones engraved with the individual's date of birth and death mark the graves of other family members. William, Jr. is among them.

I pull the car over, careful not to park on the graves. I exit the car, salute, and bow to our patriarch and his wife. He was a general in the Cavalry. It's my way of thanking him for the legacy. Mom, Dad, Grandma, and Grandpa are buried to the right. Before talking I look to make sure no one is around to hear. "Thanks for taking good care of the money and land, guys. Grandpa, we still live in your farmhouse, though I'm not sure you'd recognize it. We have indoor plumbing and electricity. The outhouse is still standing. We left it to remind us of how far we've come. I've been known to use it when I want to get away. No one, especially Rose, will come looking for me there. Mom, I'm still married to Rose. I know you thought it would never last, but it has. Did you really dislike her that much? Did you know she's organized an exhibit of your quilts at the museum? She has. And Dad, she was instrumental in getting your old farm equipment displayed. They're both complete with a gold plaque. I hope you all are taking care of William, Jr.

"Mom, I'm sure you've already put in a request for an audience with the big guy about Bob, that is if you know anything about what's going on down here. In case you don't know, he's in trouble, and there's a court date today. He had a homosexual affair in the courthouse restroom. I love him, but is his affair an affront to God? Should I care what he does in his bedroom? Was his marriage a mistake? I'm so confused. I want to ignore the gossip and listen to him. I say business will be fine, but I wonder if it will. And what about Gary? He's a part of the affair. Gary's my friend and business associate. Did he get this thing going with Bob?"

A noise disturbs my talk. A tractor is coming to dig a new grave. The driver is Harry, one of the grounds men for the cemetery. "Hey, Bill. Stop by for a little visit to talk to the family did ya?"

How do I respond? I can't tell him I'm talking to my dead relatives. "Just checking out the plot. I was told one of the headstones was beginning to lean." It's not really a lie. Rose told me a few months ago one of the older headstones looked as if it were ready to topple.

"I saw that the other day. Want me to have a look at it later?"

"That would be good of you. Thanks, Harry. Who's being buried today?"

"It's old Miss Hardy, such a shame. Taught many of us in first grade, but not a single person to pay their respects. Pastor Jenkins will say a prayer at the graveside. Outlived all her family and friends. Maybe Clara May will show up. I'll say a special prayer as I dig the grave. Well, gotta go before this storm takes hold. Nice seeing ya, Bill. Don't stay out here too long. You may grow to like it and want to move in."

"'Bye Harry. Keep warm. I'll also say a prayer for Miss Hardy, too, and don't be so sure about nobody being there. Funerals are sacred in Dewers. People here feel they've got a duty to honor a fellow citizen passing on. "

Right now I wouldn't mind moving in. I return to the graves and address them all. "What do you think guys? Junior, where did I go so wrong? Rose and I've read about homosexuals. Well, it's more Rose than me. Most experts blame us for Bob's behavior. I'm certainly not submissive to Rose. Granted, she runs the house, but we try to make joint decisions concerning big things. I control the money. She's never complained.

"I taught both of them how to fish. We went hunting together. It seemed masculine to me. I shared my secrets of good whisky. We smoked cigars together. Junior, everyone knows you were to take over the bank. Did I slight Bob? He never wanted to be part of the bank, or at least that's what he said. It upset me, but eventually I let go. However, I don't think I've moved on. Bob's kids are smart. I can wait until they're old enough to maybe run the bank. Mom, Dad, I'm sorry, but my brother's kids are too, ah … too attached to money to do a good job. I love my nephew, David. He's a good attorney, but too keen on himself. I've avoided talking to him about Bob. I don't know what to say. I don't understand my feelings. He has to know. Everyone in town knows. He's said nothing to me. Perhaps he doesn't know what to say, or he's embarrassed. Hell, we'd all like it to go away."

How pathetic, I'm here talking to dead people and neglecting the living. I've avoided the subject with Rose, except when she wants to pontificate. When I try to talk, she withdraws into her shell, closes up, changes the subject, or says she has sewing to do, and disappears into her room.

Our only conversation with Bob was a disaster. We asked Bob if we could talk to him, at his house, alone. He said the kids and Sue were out, and he'd wait for us. It was a cool July evening, so Rose worn a light coat. Bob greeted us at the door. Rose handed him her coat, but she didn't wait for Bob to hang it up. With arched eyebrows and narrowed eyes, she looked at Bob head on. Her pursed lips exploded with righteous anger. "Is it true you are a homosexual?"

Bob was not surprised nor did he look away. He met Rose's eyes. "I'm not sure what I am at the moment, but yes, I engaged in homosexual activities."

Red blotches appeared on Rose's neck. Her ears were turning red, and with staring set eyes, she attempted to demoralize Bob. I could see the spatters of her spit. "I find that filthy, dirty, and disgusting."

Bob stood his ground, never taking his eyes off his mom. His voice was even, calm, no hint of anger, almost cold like a breeze after a summer rain. "I'm sorry you feel that way, Mom."

Rose was on a roll. Bob couldn't get off that easy. "Sorry! Sorry doesn't get it. What about the kids? What about Mary, the marriage? What about us, our reputation? Didn't you care? What about God?"

"I care a lot, Mom. But how can I deny what I feel inside? I don't know anymore what feels right."

"What you feel? What's right? What's right is to be an outstanding citizen, a good father, and a faithful husband. What's right is to live by God's law and to be moral."

"Don't you mean your morality Mom? Don't you mean I wasn't faithful to your ideal of a son? Don't you mean I'm not William Junior, your perfect son? Don't you wish it was me who died and not Junior?"

"How dare you?"

"No. How dare you? Do I ask you and Dad what you do in your bedroom? No, I don't. That's between you two. I'm no different than the Bob you knew a month ago. You just know more about me now and I can't help if it you don't like what you know."

Bob's icy responses to his mom only succeeded in fueling her anger. I thought I could see flames coming from Rose's hat. "Your Dad and I don't have sex in public." Rose doesn't like talking about anything intimate, even with me. I can't believe she even said the word sex.

At this point Bob got our coats. Unflinching, he looked his mom in the eyes. His eyes were ice. They spoke of distant concern as if Rose were a stranger and her dilemma to be pitied. There was no love in them. But if he was angry, I didn't hear it in his voice. "Mom, here's your coat. You should leave now, while I can still call you Mom. Don't talk. Leave. If you say anything else I may not be able to say I have a Mom."

With those words, Rose turned on her heels, stomping out of the house and down the stairs like a child who hasn't gotten their way. I turned and with tears in my eyes, hugged Bob. "I will always love you." And I do. I may seem like a mean sob, but I'm not. I didn't know what to do then. And now I do the only thing I know I can do -- keep the family business alive.

A voice calls to me. "Hey, Bill. You're still here."

Harry was back from digging the grave. "I lost track of time. Thanks, Harry. I've got to get to the bank. Auditors are coming today."

Chapter 13

Clara May on Judy Calhoun

James' wife, Judy, is in the Monday night bridge group so we try to stay away from any comments concerning The Square Affair, but the other night Judy brought it up herself. "Okay ladies, you've been holding your tongues tighter than the cards in your hands. It's time we break the ice on this affair business."

I was the first to speak up. "I can't speak for all the girls, but I for one am tired of talking around the issue. And it must be working on your nerves."

No one else was willing to talk, so I suggested we go to the kitchen for a snack.

"Not as much as you would think, Clara May. Dad does enough worrying over my sinful life for the both of us."

"And Pastor Jenkins isn't any better."

"The worst thing is, I don't have anyone to talk to. The lawyers don't want the wives to communicate. Teachers at school are afraid to bring it up, and my friends are keeping their distance."

"I'm always available if you want to talk. We can have some coffee and pound cake or a drink, whatever pleases you."

Judy sighed, "Thanks, I'd like that."

The next day I was talking to Frieda when she asked, "What did Judy have to say about the affair?"

"Now you talk. Where was your tongue on bridge night? I'm sure it was wagging while Judy and I were in the kitchen."

"No, none of us talked. We were all too shocked that Judy brought up the topic. Oh, we had plenty to say and ask, but we didn't want to offend her."

"I think she'd welcome being offended. She'd welcome any talk." I said

"So ... what did she say?" asked Frieda.

"Frieda, were you this annoying to the principal?"

Frieda smiled, "Probably."

"She didn't say much. Just that she was lonely."

"It's such a shame because she fought so hard to get out from under her father's control." Frieda said. "Remember when she started using makeup. She'd hide it in her locker and put it on after she came to school. Her father came to school one day to meet with the principal on another matter and Judy was in the outer office talking to me."

"I remember. He told you off."

"He said, 'Miss Frieda, how could you possibly let young girls walk the halls looking like hussies?' I told him I didn't think they were hussies. They're just teenagers."

I remembered. "He gave us a sermon about it the next Sunday. I could see Judy in the pew in front of me as she sank down. Her neck was red. I greeted her after church and she wouldn't look at me. She mumbled, 'Morning Miss Clara May' and then ran off with tears in her eyes."

"James and she seem to be handling the affair best of the three married couples," Frieda comments.

"They've been married the longest, and I expected that has something to do with it."

"Not that you'd know Clara May, you've never been married. I was married 50 years before George died. If you make it to 25 without any argument causing trouble, you're probably home free. Nothing much bothers you after that."

"Is that so?" I asked. "Would it have bothered you if George had an affair with a man?"

Frieda could hardly talk through her laughter. "If it kept him happy, I probably wouldn't mind, but I'd still give him a hard time. I say if you've got a good man, don't give him up, but I'd reserve the right for an affair myself."

"Such modern thinking for an old lady."

Chapter 14

Judy Calhoun

As a minister's daughter, some fancy me as an embodiment of Polly Anna, the cute small town child who wants to see the best in everyone. I should always be optimistic and God forbid I should ever have a negative comment. I did not learn any such trait from my father, Pastor Wallace. Father was a stern man with a firm belief in hell. He thought most of his parishioners were sinful and wondered if any of them were worthy of salvation. Adam's fall from grace was as real to him as butter and jam on his morning toast. Being his daughter did not get me any slack. No one escapes his wrath. I'm not sure he could see the good in any person. So if anyone expects me to rescue Dewers from moral decay, they're barking up the wrong tree. They should try Pastor Jenkins, but Dewers is pretty entrenched in their ways. And the jury is still out on whether it will come to the rescue of James and me.

Others in Dewers say I'm a rebel child defying my father's moral code. Anna Jones, the first grade teacher, told me the other day, "Judy, you're nothing like your father. You enjoy a drink or two. You're a member of the bridge club. You like to shop and buy things. Your dad must have been strict growing up."

I wasn't sure how to respond. I'm certainly not an image of my father, or some naïve ingénue. I'm not a whisky-guzzling prima donna either. I like to think I exist somewhere in the space between. "You're right, I'm not my father, and he was a strict man. I think I'm a good Christian, just not a hell-fire and damnation person. I don't judge on first impressions."

Anna's downcast eyes made me believe she was disappointed or unbelieving. I couldn't tell which. The afternoon bell rang, so I didn't have time to ask. It did make me think of my father like others saw him. I was Father's precious little girl, but Father is far from my ideal man. Unlike the way he behaved with parishioners and friends, I received kind words, kisses, and hugs, most of the time. I quickly learned that if I wanted his affections, I existed by his rules, no exceptions: Church was a time to sit still and be quiet. I ate what was given to me on my plate. I could argue with my mother, but never in front of him. I could disagree with him, but never argue. When he was in the study with the door closed, the house was to be silent. It was best to go play outside.

Our major disagreements came when I entered puberty. Father sat me down for "the talk." You would think he would be embarrassed to discuss the changes in his daughter. The girl stuff he left to my mother. Mom told me that I'd just have to endure sex with men if I wanted a happy marriage. I'd say I more than endure it. I like sex. Father took me into his study and closed the door. In previous occasions this meant I was in trouble, so I was apprehensive and doing a checklist in my mind of things I might have done to upset him. I couldn't come up with any, at least in the last few days. He directed me to sit in the green wing back chair. It's the one he'd have his parishioners sit in when they came to the house for a talk. If I had done something wrong he made us stand, so I knew the talk was not about something I did, yet.

Father took his Bible from the desk, handed it to me, and then sat down across the desk from me. The Bible was black and originally had his name engraved in gold on the front, but all that could be seen now was some gold specks where the name had been. The black was worn and grey in spots. The once smooth leather cover was cracked and held together with tape and its binding was broken. Pages were frayed and dog-eared. I saw bits of church bulletins sticking out. I knew without opening it there would be countless notes scribbled in the margins. One year, Mom suggested we buy him a new Bible for Christmas. It has a permanent place in his book case gathering dust. I asked him once why he never used it. "It's special because you kids bought it, but all my useful notes are in this old one." The Bible was proof of Father's devotion to God's word. I knew I was holding an object sacred to him, his ark of the covenant carried with him wherever he went.

"Judy, that book you are holding has everything you need to know about how to live a good and proper life. It's God's word, His moral code for us. Soon you will have urges to be with boys, and they will want to take advantage of you. I know I can't keep you away from boys. They're at school. They're at church. They're on the streets. I expect you to conduct yourself at all times like a lady, a Christian lady."

I wasn't sure what he meant. Be like a lady? Did he mean like my mom?

I knew he'd let me know. He continued. "A proper lady wears her skirt an appropriate length below her knees. She does not wear excessive make up. She never wears garish red lipstick. You need to tame the lust in men and maintain an attitude of chastity. Christ cannot be found on the painted smile of a seductively dressed woman. You must not let your inner pride show by wearing too much cosmetics, fancy jewelry, or expensive clothing."

I wanted to say that it didn't matter because he would never let me buy expensive clothing, but I knew better. This was a time to keep my mouth shut.

Father was on a roll. I sat and held on to the Bible, knowing he had more to say about it. "As a Christian, how you dress is important. Your look reflects on the Lord."

Yeah, and on you, I thought.

"That Bible you're holding tells you all you need to know about being an outstanding Christian woman. Christians must dress in a *well-ordered, decorous, decent manner,* without causing shame or embarrassment to God, themselves, or others. Now open my Bible. First look at Proverbs 4:23: 'Guard your heart above all else, for it determines the course of your life.' Now as for your sexual purity look at 1 Corinthians 6:18: 'Run from sexual sin! No other sin so clearly affects the body as this one does. For sexual immorality is a sin against your own body.' And lastly take a look at Matthew 5:28: 'But, I say, anyone who even looks at a woman with lust has already committed adultery with her in his heart.' Substitute the word man for the word woman here – the moral issue is the same."

Dad sat back in his chair with a resolute smirk that said, *I've done the best I can. It is now up to you.* Of course he would not say that because he felt he always did his best when it came to God's work. Father never expected anyone to question his authority, especially a woman. He was the true head of his wife. She never spoke back, why should I?

Father came around from behind the desk and stood before me. I rose, placed the Bible in his outstretched hands, and gave him a kiss on the cheek. I turned and left the room without looking at him but I could feel the penetrating eyes examining me as if I were naked before him. Running would have shown disrespect. I walked slowly and erect until the door was closed then hurriedly climbed the stairs to my room.

When I heard the car in the gravel driveway, I knew Father was off to the church. I grabbed the phone and pulled it into my room. Julie was my best friend at the time. "Julie, you will not believe the lecture I just got from my father. He thinks if I wear make-up, or too much jewelry I will be a harlot, some jezebel ... what does it mean? I don't know, but it can't be good if Father doesn't like it. He says if I even think about boys it is sinning...no, I will not do exactly as he says. I'll find a way to date and I'll find a way to wear make-up ... thanks. That's a great idea to come by your house on the way to school. He'll never suspect. Your dad's an elder in the church."

I got away with the deception for a while, but Father eventually found out. I was grounded for at least a month. I was forced to go to a religious college where woman have hours. Dorm doors were locked at 10:00 p.m. We still managed to sneak out and see the boys.

Father had not wanted me to marry James. He hoped I would find some suitable man at college. By suitable he meant a man going on to seminary. That was not in my plans. I'd remain single first. I was not going to marry a minister. Father knew James' dad was an alcoholic and a gambler, and he felt James would follow the same path. When I graduated from college I accepted a teaching job in the Dewers school system as a second grade teacher and announced my engagement to James.

Father said, "I'm not marrying you to that man. He does not come from a God-fearing family. If you go behind my back and marry him, you'll no longer be my daughter. I will never speak to you again."

I was 21 with a paying job. This time I stood up to him. "I don't need your approval or support. As I remember you telling me many times, your father was not a God-fearing man. You pride yourself in overcoming the odds and becoming a spokesman for God. Ask anyone in this town. You're living proof that the lowly can become the chosen of God. I am marrying James."

Father was waving his Bible at me with one hand and shaking his fist with the other. I thought I could see fire coming out his mouth like Moses before the burning bush. "How dare you disrespect your father? I have earned the position of authority I hold. I did find God despite my family."

"And I might find God despite my family. What happened to sin of pride, of self-adoration, or is that just a sin for women? I have friends from college whose dads are ministers. Any one of them would be more than happy to marry James and me. You won't be missed."

Mom must have had a talk with Father because he eventually conducted the service. He would never admit it, but his pride would not allow another minister to marry me. Father could not stand before his congregation if they knew his daughter had called his bluff. What kind of Christian would he have raised? Children should obey their parents.

Whatever the town thinks of me, I know I'm a loving wife. Like any married couple, James and I have had our troubles. James overextended himself when he remodeled the car showroom. We had to negotiate loans, and though the kids were young, I went back to teaching. A young 6th grade teacher caught my fancy. I fell for him. It never became an affair, but James thought it had. I still had to regain the trust of my husband. This affair is the worst crisis we've faced. I will stand by him as long as he wants me. James finds it hard to believe that I still love him, so I take every opportunity to let him know.

Halloween day is not a good day to be absent from your second grade class, however I was prepared to stay home with James if he needed me. When I left home this morning I made sure to ask him again. He took my witch's hat, placed it on his head, and said no. He did wonder if he shouldn't be the wicked one for the day. No costume would be needed.

Halloween is always a busy day. The kids make decorations in the morning and in the afternoon we have a school parade followed by a party. It'll keep my mind off the trial. All the other teachers will be busy today so they won't be able to ask me questions.

Since there is a student teacher assigned to me this semester, I am able to leave the room and go to the school kitchen to work on party refreshments. Walking the hall to the kitchen, I run into Sue Turnbull, Thomas's wife. She is carrying two trays of cookies for the afternoon party. "Morning, Sue. Let me help you with those."

Sue has dark circles under her eyes and looks as if she has lost weight. "Thanks, they were getting heavy." Suddenly she realizes who I am. "Mrs. Calhoun, is that you under the witch hat?"

"Please, Sue, call me Judy."

A slight smile comes across Sue's otherwise solemn face. "I haven't been too observant recently. Pretty much been wrapped up in the kids and myself. I'm dropping these cookies off for the party before I go for a job interview. Need every bit of money we can get now days."

I'm not sure how they are making it financially. James and I have kids in college. We both work and it is still tight sometimes. The attorney fees are causing us to watch our budget more closely. Looking around I see there's no one near or coming in the door. "How are you and Thomas doing? Since the attorneys want to keep us apart, we don't have a chance to support each other, even the wives."

Sue looks around herself to make sure there are no ears listening. "It seems strange talking to you because my kids are in your school, but I've got to talk to someone. Pastor Jenkins is out of the question. I think we all know his stance. He probably thinks it's our fault. Thomas has been too moody to talk. He's not going to Squeaky's anymore, but I can't say the same for Washington Street. When he's not there in the evening, he's drinking at home. Now that it looks as if he will be done in the field, there's nothing to keep him occupied."

"You've got to get Thomas to talk. It's the only chance you have of working it out. Would he be interested in a job at the factory? I hear they're hiring this winter."

Sue starts looking at her watch and I know the conversation is over. "I've got to get to my interview. Thanks for the encouragement."

I felt like I had done nothing but open her wound more. "Call me if you want to talk. To hell with the attorneys."

And to hell with Father. He called yesterday, not to see how I was doing, but to make sure I was not visiting with the other women. "You know, Judy, it makes you look guilty if you're talking with the other women. I didn't bring you up to disobey your husband, but in this case I think it would be acceptable. I warned you about James. Pastor Jenkins says things look pretty bad. He's going to preach on it next Sunday."

I thought, *Just great, Father*. I'll stay with James even if he doesn't love me. I will never give you the satisfaction of leaving. I wanted to tell him these things, but I didn't. Guilt was creeping in. Damn you, Father.

Chapter 15

Clara May on Sue Turnbull

After ladies' circle at church, Frieda and I head back to her house. She asks, "How do you reckon Sue Turnbull is doing? I hear tell she's applying for a sales position at Montgomery Ward."

"I'm sure it's hard on her," I said. She was Thomas' high school sweetheart. Her family's been farmers almost as long as my family has been here. Dirt runs in her veins. Her mom and grandma never would have thought of leaving the farm for a job in the city. A farmer's wife should be by his side. I continued, "Sue loves being in the fields, gardening, canning, and helping on the farm in any way she can. She'd be devastated to leave the farm for another job."

"But women are getting jobs off the farm all the time."

"Not Sue, she likes farming. Home economics was her favorite class in high school. She said she had no need of learning any other skills. She was going to be a farmer's wife."

"I bet she's wishing now she had at least taken typing, shorthand, or bookkeeping."

"Farmers have lots of records to keep so I was able to talk her into bookkeeping, but that was it."

"If she doesn't get the job at Montgomery Ward maybe she could get one at the factory."

"Work like that would drive her crazy. She's too much a free spirit. Montgomery Ward would be best. She can talk to people there."

"What's her mom and dad think of her getting work outside the house?"

"They're not too happy. Of course, it's hard to tell if they're upset over Sue having to work or the affair." I stop in front of Frieda's house. "Here you are ... home again."

"Why don't you come in and have some coffee or a drink. I'm sure you've got more to tell me."

Chapter 16

Sue Turnbull

"Jimmy, Jane: hurry up. You're going to be late for the school bus."

Her curls bouncing, Jane stomps down the stairs landing on the kitchen floor. Still in her pajamas, she stands staring at me with pursed lips and hands on her waist.

"I'm not going today."

"You're going," I tell her. "Now get upstairs and put on your costume."

Jane squints her eyes and works hard at producing tears. "I don't like the costume. I want to be a princess not a clown."

I would like to throw the bowl of oatmeal at the wall, but I have a job interview today. I don't have the patience to clean it up. Clinching my fists, I take a deep breath, and resist the urge to shake Jane into submission and try my best to be calm. "Jane, I made the costume because you said you wanted to be a clown. It took a lot of time to get it just right. Remember, you helped pick the fabric. You will always be my princess." I thought, *Yeah, you're a princess that's for sure. God help me. What are you going to be like when you get older?* "Go put on your costume. Do you want to be the only one at school without a costume?"

With a snivel to match her fake tears and crossing her arms, Jane stomps her foot, turns to go back up the stairs whining. "I'm not going to like it."

"You don't have to like it, but you have to wear it." God help me. Why did I ever have children? She is going to grow up just like her grandpa, set in her ways and determined the world will revolve around her.

Just as I'm wondering if it's too late to give Jane up for adoption, Johnny comes down the stairs, all smiles with his six-shooter drawn. "Hands up, Mom. Hand over that toast."

"Oh my, oh my! Don't hurt me, cowboy! You can have whatever you want." Does he know his mom really is a damsel in distress and not acting?

"No, Mom, I'm here to save you."

"Thank you, Johnny. I need to be saved today. Do you think you've got time for a bit of breakfast before you go off to capture the villains?"

Johnny puts his gun back in the holster strapped around his waist and swaggers to the kitchen table. "Can I have peanut butter and grape jelly?"

"Of course, sheriff." Though I love my kids, right now I want to get them on the school bus so I can go for my interview. I yell upstairs, "Jane, hurry up."

Jane appears at the end of the stairs in her clown costume. I want to chuckle but can't. If Jane knew how funny the costume is, it would start a new round of stomping feet and fake tears. Large red floppy slippers fit over Jane's regular shoes and make her look as if she could fall at anytime. There's a wig of curly red hair coming out from under a coned hat with a tassel on top. Multi-colored dots on the white fabric remind me of the dot candy I loved as a kid.

Jane holds up the red nose for me to see. "I'm only putting this on for pictures."

Still struggling to keep my laughter at bay, I can barely get out the words. "The costume looks great without it. Wearing it for the pictures will be okay."

Johnny is not as kind as I am. "You look funny. How are you gonna walk in those shoes? Mom, mine is so much better. Do I have to be seen with her?"

The honesty of kids always amazes me, no matter how often I hear it. If only grown-ups could speak simple truths. "Johnny you've got to ride the bus with your sister. You'll get off at your school. She'll get off at hers. Nobody but the kids on the bus will see you with her."

Jane knows how to get the upper hand on Johnny. She practices a lot. "Who wants to be a lame cowboy? You're not funny or cute. At least I'm funny."

I roll my eyes. At least Jane knows she's funny. "Funny thing is, neither one of you will get breakfast if you don't eat. The bus will be here any minute now."

I no longer want to laugh. Events of the past weeks flash through my mind. I'm playing the part of a sad clown without painting a frown or tears. I need the bus to be on time. Holding back the tears and putting on a fake smile is getting more difficult as the minutes pass.

Impatiently, I rub the kitchen window to clear its fog as if it was a magic lamp and a genie would grant me a wish. "The bus is just down the road. Get your coats on." I put my coat on and walk with them to the road. As the bus doors close and it pulls away, tears begin to form, and they feel like icicles on my cheeks in the autumn chill. I wave to the bus until it's a distant yellow smear on the country road and when I finally take my eyes off it, I see my husband, Tom, in the field.

I'm flooded with emptiness where there used to be warmth. My stomach is performing somersaults as if it were hungry. Despite the cold, my face is flushed and I feel hot. A knot forms in my throat the way it did on our first date. I feel the touch of his lips on mine and want to shove him away, and I want to draw him close. I want to beat him on the chest with my fists and tell him to leave. I never want to set eyes on him again. I want to wrap my hands around his broad chest and cry into his flannel shirt. I want to stay on the side of the road and watch him work the field. I want to turn and never see him again. My only certainty today, I've got to find employment before we go broke.

Suddenly I feel cold and quickly turn to go back inside. Out of the corner of my eye I see Tom's wave from the field and ignore it.

The closet is full of flannel shirts, overalls, pants, and work shoes. There's a high neck long sleeve black dress I use for funerals, but it's not appropriate for a job interview. At the back of the closet I find the low cut red dress I wore to Chicago last summer when Tom took me out for our anniversary. We stayed downtown at the Palmer House and had dinner in the Empire Room, complete with champagne. We toasted 10 years of a happy marriage. Perhaps it was the alcohol, maybe being away from the kids, the excitement of the city, or the cheek-to-cheek dancing, but we had passionate sex that night and again the next morning. I knew we should not be spending money when we were barely getting by, but my parents had given us money for our anniversary and offered to keep the kids for a weekend. I slip into the red heels hoping to recapture some of that weekend, but my image is a blur because of tears. Was he faking it that weekend? I would like to believe not, but reality at the moment is illusive, an oasis I'm seeking to find.

I throw the shoes to the back of the closet. I can't wear them or the red dress today, not for a job interview, and definitely not in this cold weather. All of my clothes are for a farmer's wife who works alongside her husband: driving a tractor or truck, scooping grain, mowing grass, or gardening. What other dresses I have are old and faded, ones I wear in the heat of summer. Good thing today is cold. I pick a pair of pants and a sweater that Tom bought me for Christmas last year. It will have to do. Besides, I prefer pants.

Placing my wedding ring on the dresser, I sit at the mirror to apply make-up. I routinely remove the ring so as not to damage it when working on the farm. Never before has my hand felt empty without it, but today it's as if a part of me is missing. Is this what an amputee feels when describing a phantom limb? I can see the impression left by the ring, and there's a white band as if it's still there. I slowly lift my hand, aware that it's lighter. With a closed fist I bring my fingers to my eyes to closely examine the ring finger, its indention, its white band. To me the absence is obvious. Will it be as obvious to others if I have to remove it? From my jewelry box I pull out a gold ring with a sapphire stone. It was my grandmother's ring. I place the ring on my finger and think it's beautiful but not a substitute for a wedding ring.

As I powder my face in the mirror, I'm acutely aware of bagginess around my eyes. The red lipstick doesn't cover fine lines at the edges of my mouth. I have a great body. My breasts remain firm. I wear a size seven. Even in my 30s I'd be a good catch, but there are the two kids. Would a man want me and children?

The phone rings bringing me back to the present. "Hello. Oh, hi, Mom ... Tom's in the field ... I can't keep him home if he wants to go ... yes, I'm just getting dressed now ... I'm wearing pants with the sweater John got me for Christmas. Don't have a dress that's appropriate ... they are all too summery ... yes, Mom, I put on make-up. And lipstick ... no, it's not too much ... I'll be able to see the kids off on the school bus and they can stay with me at the store after work ... Mom, I've got to go or I'll be late ... I'll remember to drop cookies off at school ... Yes, I'll be careful driving. 'Bye."

I would like to cancel the interview, go to bed, and pull up the covers, but we need the money. I take one last look in the mirror before pulling on my winter coat. As I open the door, I realize it has begun to snow. Great, I was hoping it would be a good day. It's not snowing hard. Maybe Tom will stay in the field and finish. Dear God keep him away from The Square today and, above all else, away from the bars. He doesn't need an excuse to drink. While you're at it God, give me the strength to face The Square and get through this interview.

Every time I open the garage door, I'm taken aback by the color of our car. Tom's family has always done business with the Plymouth dealer, so naturally he had to have a Plymouth. His friend, James, owns the Chevy dealership, but even he could not talk Tom out of the Plymouth. As I look at the car, I want to vomit. As a matter of fact, the Pepto Bismol pink color looks like I've already thrown up on a perfectly good white car. If only I had an inconspicuous car. People can see me coming. It's easy to spot in a big parking lot. No danger of losing it, and no danger of someone wanting to steal it. It sticks out like a sore thumb. Thieves would have to repaint it immediately.

It's all I've got, so here goes. Tom and I have lived in Dewers since birth, so it's not like either one of us can hide. I back out of the garage, turn around, and exit the driveway toward town. Tom is at the end of the field and I tap my horn so he knows I'm on my way. He waves back, but not too lively.

The court hearing is not until this afternoon, so I don't think I should run into Bob on The Square. The bank is not close to the store, which means I can avoid Mr. Thompson. However, this is a small town and you never know. If I can find a place to park in front of Montgomery Ward, it should not be a problem. God is with me today, or perhaps the devil. There's an empty spot in front of the store, and the meter has money on it. Let's hope the remainder of the day goes as well.

I adjust the review mirror to check my hair and face. If I get this job, part of my first paycheck is going to be spent on the hairdresser. Grey is creeping in on the sides. I would like to get rid of it. Okay it's the best I can do. Here goes. As I get out of the car, I notice a woman is cleaning the windows in preparation for the window-painting contest later today. She turns to grab the bucket of water, and I realize it's my cousin, Georgina. She has noticed me. It's too late to dodge her. Our eyes meet, and I want to escape back to the car. Georgina tilts her head to the left, and her downcast eyes seem to say, poor you, but, instead, Georgina asks me about Halloween. "Hey, Sue. Are you going to bring the kids to the window decoration party later this afternoon?"

The last thing I want to do is be in a crowd of parents but I promised the kids. "I'm headed in for a job interview, and I guess it depends on the outcome. I may get my mom to bring them up."

Georgina is cheerful and encouraging. Too much Polly Anna for me. "I hope you can make it. It's such fun. The kids plan the window design in the school art classes. They're so proud of their work. You've been keeping to yourself. Everyone would love to see you."

Yeah, I bet they want to see me. All the parents want to see the poor wife. How is she holding up? What will she look like? Has she lost weight or has it made her eat more? Are you still living with Tom? Are you planning a divorce? "If I don't see it today, it's up all weekend and I'll catch it Saturday or Sunday."

Georgina returns to the windows, but watches me walk to the door. "Oh Sue, are you doing okay?"

I knew it was too good to be true. There it is, the dreaded question. Someone has attached a concrete block to my body and I'm sinking. I'm going to drown in the questions. How do I respond? Do I respond? I've got to say something. Ignoring her is worse. "I'm okay. It will be better after today." With that, I hustle inside before Georgina can ask any more questions.

The manager's office is on the second floor and the staircase is at the back of the store. I try to keep my eyes focused on the stairs and away from the shoppers, but this fixated walking runs me into the minister's wife, Peggy. "Oh, I'm terribly sorry. I didn't see you. You must think I'm so rude."

Peggy takes being the wife of a minister seriously. She is the eyes and ears of the community for her husband. Nothing happens without her taking note. "Sue, where are you headed in such a hurry?"

I don't want her to know I'm applying for a job. Everyone will know by tonight. But, then again, I can talk about the job and maybe she will not quiz me about the court hearing. "I'm interviewing for a sales position."

Peggy smiles, but her eyes remain fixed on me. A false smile, since she's smiling only with her lips. I brace for the question I know she's going to ask. "Who's going to take care of the kids if you're working? You don't expect Tom to handle it, do you?"

Peggy's is so much a man's woman. She wouldn't think of working. Her place is in the home entertaining parishioners, being the perfect mother, barefoot and pregnant. She's at every PTA meeting. She was a religious music major in college, and she doesn't sing or play an instrument. What are you going to do with that degree? I clear my throat in an effort to talk. I cannot make eye contact. "We will do what we have to do to get by. Pull ourselves up by our bootstraps." How lame -- why did I say that?

Peggy ignores my comments and starts in on her latest project, saving the passenger train service and the Illinois Central Train Station. "I've been so busy with the Save the Station Campaign, I've not had time to keep up with other happenings in the town. We could use some help with passing out brochures. There's a potluck fundraiser at the church next week. Why don't you come and bring your wonderful meat loaf? We could use your support."

I glance at my watch, run my fingers through my hair, and, this time, look Peggy in the eyes. "Peggy, I can't talk now. I really have to go, or I will be late for my interview. It was nice seeing you." I climb the stairs with determination that I hope Peggy takes note of. Train station, my aching ass. She's no more interested in that train station than becoming a Presbyterian. She's trying to pump me for information so she can pass it on. Gossiping must be a sin of some sort. Or maybe being the minister's wife means you're free of sin. At last here is the manager's office.

I open the door and the receptionist greets me. "Good morning. May I help you?"

The encounter with Peggy at least helped to relieve my anxiety. My heart rate has slowed, and, to my surprise, I find it easy to speak. "Hi, I'm Sue Turnbull, and I'm here for the sales clerk position."

The receptionist hands me an application form and a pen. "Will you please fill out this application while you're waiting? You can have a seat over there."

The application is simple. They want: my name, address, schooling, any work experience. Can I put housewife as work experience?

After finishing the application, I return it to the receptionist. With her head down, she looks it over and then looking over the top of her glass with squinting eyes and a tight jaw, she addresses me. "Mrs. Thompson everything looks in order here. Have a seat and Mr. Holland will be with you a few minutes."

I turn from the desk and take a chair facing Mr. Holland's door. I want to see his reaction when he first looks at me. It will probably be the same as the receptionist. The penetrating eyes, tight-lipped frown that says, *Yes, I know who you are. You're one of the scorned wives.* It's not really pity, but more like disgust. How could a fine dutiful wife be in this position? They think I'm just as much at fault as my husband.

The office door opens, and Mr. Holland appears. He looks to be in his late 50s, early 60s and is wearing a dark grey suit with a vest. "Mrs. Thompson, would you come with me please?"

I feel like I'm going to the principal's office to be reprimanded for something I didn't do, but was somehow implicated. At the door he greets me with a handshake and ushers me into his office. He motions for me to sit at a chair in front of his desk, while he sits in the desk chair. "Mrs. Thompson, let me take a minute to look over this application."

The room has a tension that becomes apparent as he reads my application. A grandfather clock stands to the right and it's ticking a forced march to the chimes each quarter hour. There's non-descript music playing softly in the background daring someone to increase the volume. Mr. Holland leans back in his chair and its squeak is a groan of old age.

Finally he looks at me. I don't see any judgment in his gaze. His mouth is a fixed straight line, no smile, no frown. His eyebrows are not furrowed. I hope this is a good sign. "Mrs. Johnson, I see you have no work experience beyond being a housewife. Is that correct?"

I was afraid of this. "No, Mr. Holland, I do not, but being a house wife and mother to small children is a balancing act. It gives me great organizational skills and patience."

"Will taking care of the kids interfere with work, if you were to be hired?" he asks.

I reply, "No, my mom, and my husband's mom have volunteered to help."

We talk a bit more about time commitment and juggling being a mom with work and then he dismisses me. "Mrs. Thompson, I think that will be all for now. I've got a few other women applying for the position. When I'm finished interviewing them, I'll get back to you. It will be by the end of next week."

With those words, he ushers me to the door.

I think the interview went well, but you never know. At least he didn't ask about the affair. I saw no emotion in his face, so I'm not sure what he thinks. I've done all I can, and now, I've got to go. I don't have time to tarry. The bus will be dropping off the kids soon.

As I pull into the driveway, the kids are getting off the bus.

"Mom, it's snowing! How come Dad is still in the field?"

"He wants to get as much of the corn field ready for spring planting before winter sets in for good. Did you finish your homework, Mary?"

"I did the math, but I hate the spelling. It's too hard."

"Why don't you ask your brother to help you with it?"

"Johnny's too busy playing with this tractor set Dad gave him, and besides, he's only in first grade. What can he do?"

What a thought that is, Johnny just like his dad. I hope not, for it will get him in a load of trouble. Of course, I know that he's far too young to know what's in his mind, especially when it comes to sex. He still thinks girls are to be avoided at all cost. Just acting like a typical first grade kid. I want to protect both of them from the rumors I know will be flying around town. The other kids will not understand what it is the parents are talking about, but they'll hear, and, at the very least, ask questions. *Why is your dad in trouble? Will he have to go to jail? What was he doing in the courthouse?* I know John and I should sit the kids down and talk to them about what happened, but the question is how? They won't know what pervert means, as far as that goes, they won't know what any of the stuff means. All they know is that people look at them differently and avoid their father. They look at me with pity. I don't need pity and John does not need to be judged.

I'm at the sink beginning to fix supper, when I grab a knife to peel the potatoes and wonder how it would feel to cut my wrist, slit my throat. The blade's sharp. I've slipped, and accidentally cut myself. It didn't hurt. It would be such an embarrassment to my family. My mother would be furious, but, then again, I wouldn't be here. I wouldn't have to hear it. I wouldn't have to hear criticism from friends and strangers saying how they thought I was stronger. Didn't I think of my children being raised by John, a person of questionable moral character? And the church -- oh, my God, the church -- the ladies' prayer circle would be furious with me. I'm on duty next month to chair their fundraising event. The women prepare their best dishes to be sold the week before Thanksgiving, ready-made dishes for dinner, easing the work of those less able to cook. It also raises most of the budget for the altar flowers. Who would take over if I weren't there? I put the knife away and pull out the potato peeler instead. With it I'm less likely to slip up, do something I'd regret, couldn't undo.

As I glance up from the sink to the window, I catch a glimpse of myself in the glass. Unexpected, the figure looking back at me looks nothing like me. This person has the beginnings of crow's feet on the edge of her eyes. It confirms what I saw this morning putting on my makeup. They're not the sparking eyes that gave Tom a "come hither" look, but sad eyes that say if you're not nice to me I will cry -- in fact I may cry if you just look at me. Eyes that chase you away in fear you might be caught up in their sadness, eyes that are waterlogged with worry and see no release even if they could tear. The skin is drawn, dried out, almost like the old apple sitting in a bowl on the counter. The hair isn't black, but has spots of dirty grey; it's wild, sticking out at all angles, obviously hasn't been styled in awhile. I wonder how this woman's hair got that way, but, then again, I can't remember when I last washed it. Is this what I looked liked for the job interview?

I see a woman I don't like, one I would not be friends with, one whose husband deserves pity. What happened to the youthful girl who captured a prize in high school? She got one of the good boys, the dream of all high school girls, a boy on the Varsity football team, president of the Future Farmers Association, and Senior Class Vice-President. Yes, that girl caught her man. She even held on to her man when he went off to war, letting him have his time knowing that he might get killed, and even worse knowing that if he would only marry her now he'd get a deferment. He could stay home safe in her arms. No, she waited, dating no one else. That girl worked at the local IGA, lived at home, and saved money to pay for her own wedding. Her man came back to that girl. I cannot figure out where that girl has gone. Has she changed that much? Is this new woman driving her husband away? Is he now ashamed of being with her?

I learned about sex in the way most young women do. When I started growing breasts, Mom sat me down, and we talked about getting the monthly curse. She showed me various ways of protecting myself from getting blood on my panties. My mom took me shopping, and together we bought a training bra and Tampax. I remember how odd it was to call it a training bra. Was I training it or was the bra training my breasts? What exactly was it training them to do? I knew how you train a dog to do tricks, to urinate where you tell them to, but breasts? I knew boys paid more attention to girls with large breasts and cleavage, though I did not know why. Maybe it was to train the breasts in attracting men.

My mom briefly talked about boys getting girls pregnant, she also said God didn't like women to have sex with anyone but their husbands, and then only to get pregnant. It was made clear I would bring shame to the family if I were to have sex before marriage or get knocked up. As far as Mom was concerned, Eve should have never eaten the apple, for now all women have to suffer sex, monthly periods, and babies. I was sure my mother's fervent prayers were not for the welfare of anyone except herself. She prayed to God to reverse Eve's wrong.

My knowledge of sex and ways of pleasing a husband in bed came from magazines, and friends, sources of even more questionable authority than my mother. Mary is having an affair right under her husband's nose -- Bill thinks she spends all that time away from home at the gym, the beauty parlor, or at one of her committees trying to look like a rich man's wife. In effect, all she's doing is making her husband a cuckold fool. No wonder he was a part of The Square Affair, any excuse to get away from her.

No one really talks about sex, his or her sex, just about others, so I am not sure how I compare to the ordinary. I know how I compare according to the magazines, but I really don't believe them. I'm happy enough having sex with Thomas, but I wish he were more pleased with me. He's always anxious to have intercourse, but the act is finished quickly and I'm left feeling vacant, wanting more. I didn't even know women could climax until I read about it in a magazine a few years back on one of the rare occasions I visited the beauty parlor. I guess I did learn something useful from magazines. I've tried talking to Thomas about satisfying both of our sexual desires, but he shies away from the subject.

"Mom, it's still snowing, can I go outside and play?"

"Finish your homework?"

"Why don't you ever ask Johnny that before he plays?"

"He doesn't have any homework yet."

"Well, can I go out?"

"Yes, but make sure you put on your winter jacket and gloves. Make sure your brother has his on."

"Why is it always me?"

"Because you're older and wiser."

"Oh yea, I am older and smarter than he will ever be."

"When your dad comes around next time, flag him down and tell him supper is almost ready."

"Okay. 'Bye, Mom."

"Don't-- " *bang* " --slam the door on your way out."

I return to the potatoes and look up to see Thomas round the corner of the cornfield. I watch him driving away from the house, becoming smaller, finally disappearing over a slight rise in the field, and leaving me behind with the kids. I sit the potatoes aside, begin to clean the carrots and when I glance up again Thomas is reappearing over the rise headed toward the house. First a speck on the horizon, he could be a crow. It's only when he's closer that I can tell it's him. Strange, I knew it would be John on the tractor coming back this way, but for a moment I felt alone and wondered if it would be him or if he had somehow disappeared forever into the horizon.

God, I promised myself I wasn't going to think about what was happening today, what had happened to us, and now just this trick of distance has left me wondering if our present situation is no different. Eventually you reach the end of the ground you're working in the field. There is an end point, a place where you're finished. I'm not sure this mess Tom has gotten us into will have an end. I fear it will. I worry that my life as I know it will end in divorce. For now my life is back and forth, back and forth, just like working the field.

The door slams open again with an even louder bang. This time it's Johnny. "Mom, Jane says I will never be as smart as she is. She's mean."

"She's just older and smarter than you are now."

"When will I be older and smarter?"

"Soon, very soon."

"She made me come in to tell you dad says he's not done yet. And, oh yeah, he says he may not make it to trick-or-treat."

"Thanks."

"Can I go back out and play? It's snowing."

"Yes, just put your gloves on, and don't slam the door. It's giving me a headache."

"Mom, when can I get into my cowboy costume to go trick-or-treating at Grandma's?"

"Oh, shit, I forgot."

"Mom, you said a bad word."

"Pretend you didn't hear it. We will go after dinner. We need to be at your Grandma's house by 7 p.m."

"Thanks, Mom, 'bye."

"Gloves. Hey, come in when it gets dark."

"Okay."

How can he go to The Square today? I thought he wanted to stay away from the trial. He is going to go up there and have a drink at the bar. I bet he plans on meeting Bob or one of the others. No, it'll be Bob. He was the one going to the hearing. Tom will want to know what happened. I want to know what happened. I guess I can understand his eagerness tonight. It's just that you would think they would pick another spot than the very bar where it started. Maybe they have enough smarts to go to one of the bars near the train tracks, the part of town I was warned to stay away from as a kid. They will be safe there. People who go there do not talk, their business is their business, it's one of those don't ask bars and if you do you may find yourself with a fat lip, a concussion or worse.

No, I don't think Thomas will be home in time for dinner or for trick-or-treating. He needs time with his buddies to sort out this affair and see where he wants his life to go from here. As for me, I am willing to take all of him back, but we have to talk.

Chapter 17

Clara May On Mary Thompson

The night of the trial, Frieda and I go to have supper at the café on The Square. As we enter the café, Millie and some of the other girls from our bridge club wave us over to join them. Millie is fidgeting, impatiently waiting for us to get settled in. We have barely placed our order when she starts. "I heard you got quite an earful at the beauty parlor today."

"I did, and I see from your interest it has already made it around The Square, and I dare say to the far reaches of the county, maybe even to the next."

Millie doesn't want me to get an upper hand in the conversation. She launches into her opinions like Mr. Baker's bull when he escapes from his pen. "Can you believe it, men having sex with men under our very eyes? It's not natural. These deviants need to be cured or locked up."

Frieda is nervously shredding her napkin. "I don't agree with what the newspaper says. I know these men. They're not deviants. I'm not even sure what that means."

Millie answers, "I know what it means. A deviant is someone who doesn't follow the laws of God. Deviants pollute the minds of our children. Sex in the courthouse restrooms - these men are possessed with demons."

I tell her, "You've been taking Pastor Jenkins' sermons to heart. I, for one, think he complains a bit too much. Sounds like he's a little frustrated."

Mille rises. "He is a man of the cloth. How dare you talk about him like that? What's his sex life got to do with homosexuality?" She stomps away.

"Well, I guess she told us," says Frieda.

"But she's missed the good part." I say, and then add, "You haven't heard about Mary."

Frieda sweeps away her shredded napkin as she speaks. "Oh, I almost forgot. You said you got an ear full at the beauty shop today."

Millie stops mid-stomp, turns on her heel, and walks back to the table. "I still say you should not talk about Pastor Jenkins. Someone should keep this town on a moral path."

"And I take it that person is you," I reply.

All eyes and ears are directed toward me, but Frieda speaks first. "Well, out with it Clara May. Any one of us could drop dead with our next breath. I don't want that to happen before I hear about Mary."

"I was under the dryer in the shop when Mary came in. I didn't hear what Mary and Peggy were first talking about, but when Mary told us all to gather around, I was all ears."

Mary's family is originally from New York but she's been here since high school. Bob's dad, William, is right about her. She is a gold digger. Mary is good looking. She still has perky breasts. All her blouses have a plunging neckline. She still has a small waist. I bet she doesn't wear more than a size five. Lost all the weight she gained with her pregnancies. Costs Bob a lot of money keeping her in designer clothes, paying for tennis lessons, keeping up the country club membership, and making sure her house has the best of everything. Our stores are not good enough for her. She goes to Chicago to shop, even for her furniture and household goods. She is the self-appointed queen of charity and special causes. She rose to that throne on the back her husband's family tradition. She wouldn't have gotten there without it.

My grandmother's lemonade is bitter compared to Mary's forced nature. Truth is, I'd rather eat grandma's raw lemons than listen to her false banalities. It's always, "I've done this, I'm on this board, Bob and I give this much to the church."

I say, "Mary is showy about everything. If you've got to brag about it, it can't be too sincere. I believe even the Bible has something to say about it. We should ask Pastor Jenkins."

Millie stiffens and crosses her arms, but she is not going to walk away. I say, "There is also something in the good book about women being quiet."

Frieda balls up what is left of her napkin and throws it at me. "Sit down, Millie, and shut up. And you, Clara May, stop stirring the shit and tell us the story."

Chapter 18

Mary Thompson

As I drive up to Judy's beauty parlor, I notice a lot of cars. Today looks as if it is going to be the day I face the firing squad of Dewers' blue haired ladies. I'm not sure what I'll say to their questions, if they have any.

Judy greets me as I walk in the door. "Hey Mary, you're early, grab a cup of coffee and sit down."

"Looks like you're not too busy today," I reply.

Judy looks up from the customer she's combing out. "Yeah, it's kind of slow, Halloween and all. Most of my customers are finishing last minute details on their kids' costumes, or at school watching them parade around the hall."

"Well, I don't sew, but John's mom insists on making costumes each year, and that's fine with me. She seems to get a kick out of doing it."

As she talks, Judy returns to the comb out. "It's nice you have someone to do it and treat the kids."

"I guess so," I say.

Judy looks at me again. "You don't sound too excited."

"I'm not. For me, Halloween isn't much fun. Candy just adds pounds I have to shed, and it's a lot of fuss. Besides, the help of Bob's mom doesn't come cheap," I reply.

Judy stops, and with a look of surprise in her wide eyes asks, "What, she charges you?"

I reply, "Oh heavens no, that would be an admission that my mother-in-law is doing common work. I have a cleaning lady once a week, but she doesn't clean her own house at all. She has a maid and a cook daily. She sews the kid's costumes so she can have me beholden to her. She already thinks I'm a gold digger, married her son just because Bob's dad is a bank president. My dad is a lowly foreman in a factory. He's not fit for her society."

"What society? This town only has a few thousand people, most work in the factory, and the rest are farmers," says Judy.

I say, "Yes, but there are attorneys, doctors, judges, business owners, and my family isn't a part of that. Then there's the problem that I am not from here. I'm not old money, old landed gentry."

Clara May has turned off her dryer and is now intently listening. She says, "Don't listen to her, Mary -- you've done well for yourself. You're chair of the Woman's Welfare League, head up the 4th of July Festival committee, and you're a star tennis player at the country club."

I quickly respond, "She says it's all because of her and William. According to her, I would be a nobody if it were not for them. It's not easy living only blocks from your in-laws. She stops by without asking, usually when I'm getting ready to go out. Clucks at the house, runs her fingers in the dust on the tables. You know she still wears hats and white gloves. I tell her the cleaners are coming tomorrow, but I don't think she believes it. She blames me for Bob not going into his dad's banking business. She says he never would have left behind a lucrative attorney practice for teaching if it hadn't been for me. Bob just wanted to get away from them."

Judy motions in the general direction of east as she speaks. "The new houses they're building out near the lake are nice, maybe you and Bob should look into moving. It would put some distance between you and your in-laws"

I reply, "I would love it, a house on the lake, our own boat dock, perhaps a tennis court, but it will never happen as long they are alive, and William is President of the bank. First National Bank holds the mortgage on our existing house, and we'd use them for a new one. The apron strings are so tight, even a few blocks stretches the limits."

Judy takes the cape off Mrs. Janson, who has been sitting in the chair and then addresses me. "Come on, Mary, let's get you washed. I'll touch up your hair, give it a style, and send you out of here in a better mood."

I allow myself to be ushered to the washbasin where I'm concealed beneath a wrap with my head hanging over the bowl. So I wonder, *Is this what it feels like to have your head on the chopping block?* Everyone in the shop knows me, and of course knows Bob's family. I close my eyes as the warm water sooths my scalp. Now I feel even more like the accused on the scaffolding. Even with my eyes closed, I feel other eyes looking at me with pity. There are voices, soft whispers talking about Bob and me. I strain to hear, but the water is running and drowns it all out, but for a buzzing.

Before I came to the beauty parlor, I drove around The Square. I wanted to know if Bob was still in court. I didn't see his car, so I thought it might be over. However, as I drove off The Square, I saw his car in the bank parking lot. That was not a good place for him to park. His dad would have been looking out the window of his office, waiting. Bob, of course, would have had no intention of talking to his father so soon after the hearing but William, I am sure, had other plans. When the gossip started, after they arrested Bob and the other men, his father was furious. He came by the house, told me to get the hell out, take the kids with me and not come back until I saw that his car was gone. Bob and I barely had a chance to talk, but of course, big daddy had to be satisfied first. No one could stand in his way.

There had been reports that a group of men were having sex in the basement bathrooms of the courthouse. The county sheriff initially laughed it off, believing behavior like that may happen in the big city but not here in God-fearing farm country. Everyone here is normal, they graduate from high school, find a job, or go to college, then get married. Those who want a more exciting life than what this town offers leave and come back only for funerals and weddings. It was after unnamed sources complained that the sheriff sent a deputy to investigate. Initially the deputy found nothing, but he kept coming back at different times of the day and eventually walked in on the group engaged in oral and anal sex in the bathrooms.

Judy interrupts my thoughts. "Mary, are you with me, Mary?"

"Sorry, I didn't hear you," I reply.

Judy, through laughter, says, "You were off in lala land there."

"I know, I haven't been sleeping well." It's out of my mouth before I know what I'm saying. Of course they know I haven't been sleeping well. I can't look at her or anyone else in the shop. They all want to talk about me. I divert my eyes to the mirror. Thank God my beautician notices I'm flustered and asks me how I want my hair, giving me a reason to look in the mirror. I decide to go for it. I've broken the ice. I could only slip in and drown, but who knows, someone might throw me a lifeline.

I say, "Let's do an updo, something sexy. This is the day Bob's in court."

Judy is surprised that I've brought up the subject. She draws in her breath, afraid to let it out. I think she's going to choke. Her eyes widen, she drops the shears and comb on the floor. Picking up the two she knocks over bottles from the shelf behind her. This gets the attention of everyone in the shop. When I was at the washbasin, people were trying to disguise the fact that they were looking at me. Now, they openly stare. Their eyes pierce through me. I see them. Those under the dryers are turning them off, even though their hair is not dry. No one in the shop is even attempting to ignore the situation. They won't have to eavesdrop because I plan to tell my piece loud enough for all to hear.

Judy is finally able to speak. "Well, Mary, no, I didn't know it was today."

Who is she fooling? Of course she knows it's today, but I play dumb, saying, "Come on Judy, where have you been, off to the moon with astronauts? Everybody in town knows today is the big day."

Judy is taken aback and stammers. "I ... I knew it was soon, but I didn't know it was today."

Though the conversation is now underway about the affair, I'm hesitant to let them know I've been stewing over the trial.

I decide it's time to tell my story. To hell with Bob's family. I'll stand proud as a scorned woman. "It's okay all of you, I am going to talk about it. You all are gossiping, so you might as well get the story from the mouth of the offended. It'll have my in-laws headed for the gin, and nothing would please me more."

Bob's parents have been trying to push it under the carpet. You can push a little dirt under the carpet, but there is not much you can do to hide a mountain of it.

"Do you want me to tell you, or are all of you going to sit there with your mouths open? It's October, the flies are dead or gone, and we don't need any honey sweet mouths to catch them right now. Okay, you all got your hearing aids on? Can you hear me Clara May, 'cause you're screeching a little?"

"I can hear you fine, honey. You just start talking. If I need to, I'll sit on your lap to hear this," says Clara May. She pulls up a chair in front of me. Her hair is blue with a whitening agent.

June has already turned off her dryer. Multiple bobby pins hold in place her wet pin curls as she gets up and pulls a stool next to me. Charlotte, who has been sitting at the washbasin with a towel wrapped around her head, walks over and stands behind June. Judy's assistant, Bessie, who's has been putting large rollers in Maggie's hair stops. She turns the chair around so they both can look on as I talk. Maggie looks like some space alien. One side of her hair is as flat as a recently harvested wheat field, and the other, with curlers, is stacked like the sheaves of wheat.

"Bob's mom and dad blame me for the whole thing. They say that if I had been a decent wife and provided for Bob at home, he would not have had to go off and find gratification elsewhere. They went so far to say we should get an immediate divorce. Bob should blame the whole thing on his frigid wife. Say he went to other men because they wouldn't ask him if he was married. They'd want to be anonymous."

Clara May asks, "What would William know about homosexual behavior?"

"Nothing, unless he's guilty. Can you imagine William Thompson going into the library and asking for a book on homosexuality?"

"Did Bob agree?" asks Judy.

"Of course not. Bob told them he would not agree to any such foolish story, and told his Dad he was off his rocker for suggesting it. William threatened to cut Bob out of his will if he didn't give up his ways. Bob's response was, 'Go ahead, you've wanted to disown me ever since I refused to go into business with you, so just get it over with'. At least my husband has balls, even if it's some other man massaging them. I think massaging them. You know I really don't know what they do, but I can imagine."

Clara May takes this opportunity to dig deep for the dirt. "What *did* drive Bob to other men? Is there a problem with the two of you in bed?"

I hear the sudden intake of breath from the other woman as they stare wide-eyed at Clara May. I don't mind and answer her question. "To tell you the truth, I don't know what drove Bob to have sex with other men. I thought we had a great sex life. It's not that Bob and I were prudes in the bedroom -- you could hardly call our sex ordinary or vanilla, at least that's what I read in the magazines."

Despite my efforts to remain calm, I become very animated, waving my hands and making provocative gestures. "We tried every position imaginable. We tried anal sex, on me not him. Bob likes oral sex, so I oblige and find it fun to turn him on. He also seems to enjoy oral sex with me. So by all that, you'd think everything was fine. Bob wants sex more frequently than me, but I rarely refuse. He could usually talk me into something."

The ladies raise their eyebrows, but not a one refuses to listen. Clara May looks around the room smiling and nods her head at me. She says, "Go ahead, Mary. You're doing fine. We're not judging. We just want to hear your side of the story."

Not judging, I doubt that. The phones will be ringing as soon as these old broads get home. Clara May will be the first. Despite this, I continue. "Oh, I admit I've looked at other men, fantasized about their naked bodies, wondered what it would be like to have sex with them." I can't believe I'm talking about my sex life in public to a bunch of blue haired women, but I feel better talking, so I continue. "When I suspected Bob was having sex on the side, I followed through on these fantasies. This guy at the country club, Peter, kept hitting on me. He's a good 10 years my junior, which immediately is a turn on. You think Bob could get a younger man? I always try to keep myself in good shape, playing golf and tennis. Bob was out of town at a conference and the kids were at his parent's house for a sleep over. I was free. Of course, we couldn't go to my house. It's too close to his parents."

The women in the shop are like old turkeys, the fat on their necks wobbling, or those geese they force-feed for foie gras, waiting with their mouths stuck wide open. None of them have ever liked me and now they want to feel sorry for me. This town is better off because of what I've done, and they know it.

The only one able to form a question is Clara May. "I suspected an affair, but your car was never somewhere it didn't belong."

"Clara May, I never thought there would be something in this town you didn't know. It gives me a sense of achievement." I continue, "Peter lives in the country a few miles out of town, a perfect rendezvous spot. I parked my car in my garage, turned a few lights on upstairs like I was in the bedroom, and then left through the back door. I met him at his car a block the other direction from Bob's parents. Sex with Peter is not any better than sex with Bob. Maybe the lesbians have it better. I've continued with the affair because of the intrigue, the danger of being caught, as well as someone 10 years younger wanting me. Each time Bob has to be out of town, I let the kids go to their grandparents and we meet."

Again Clara May speaks, "Good job, but didn't Bob suspect? Were you afraid of being found out?"

"I did worry at first, but the delight of getting away with it under Bob's nose *and* all of Dewers spurred me on. There was a gnawing feeling in my gut that there was something else causing me to continue. I didn't think it was Bob, but I started keeping track of our love-making and it was very rare."

This time Peggy is able to ask, "Did Bob know about this, or suspect?"

"I have never told him about the affair, and I don't think he knows. If there really was a problem with our sex life, I was not aware of it. According to Bob, it was about this time that the gay sex ring started. Perhaps the sexual desire for my husband decreased then. Did Bob notice, is that what drove him to other men? The only thing I'm certain of now is that Bob had an affair with several men, and I have no intention of continuing in this marriage."

I know the word of my confession will spread faster than a wildfire in the dry stubble of a wheat field, and the smoke will engulf this sleepy town. The gossip mill will distort the truth. People will choke on the smoke-filled rhetoric, and some eyes will sting from the anguish caused by it all. I'm not looking for pity. I won't lose friends. They'll all want to be close to me so they can get the latest gossip. The best I can hope for is a little support.

"Okay now, any more questions? The floor is open."

It may be a trite phrase, but the group looks like deer caught in the headlights, not knowing whether to run away covering their ears and eyes never to hear or see such tales and to repeat them again. But, I bet that is not the case. I'm sure all of them are eager to run back into their private woods to tell the story to anyone who'll listen. It will be something like this: *You won't believe what I just saw and what Mary Thompson told us at the beauty parlor.* Of course each will add their twist to the story. It's like no two apple pies taste the same because each person has their own secret ingredient they add to give it their personal touch, their signature.

Clara May is first with another question. "What about the kids, what have you told them?"

"I told them their dad has some legal problems, but I haven't told them what they are. They wouldn't understand. There hasn't been a 'birds and bees' talk yet. Besides, Bob is an attorney, and though he's teaching, he does occasionally go to court. Seeing him go there is not out of the ordinary for the kids."

Clara May again, "Now, Mary, you know other kids at school will bully, tease, and make them feel bad."

"I know. I've told them to just walk away, don't respond, and don't fight. It's all I can do. If they weren't being teased about this, it would be the color of their hair, or the pants they're wearing. I tell them it's all the same. Ignore it."

Fiddling with the comb, and twirling her scissors like a baton, Judy is visibly anxious. She's probably wondering if the shop will ever be safe again. After all, these chairs are our confession booths. No, I think her shop will still be a safe haven and probably increase business. We have to confess our secret desires, dreams, and dreads to someone.

Judy composes herself and asks, "Don't you feel shame, abused? Do you feel it was your fault? Do you put all the blame on Bob?"

"No I don't feel …" The door opens and Bob's mom enters. I forgot this is her standing appointment day.

Chapter 19

Clara May on Rose Thompson

Rose's maiden name is Snodgrass. No matter how you say it, no matter where you place the emphasis, it doesn't elicit even a hint of elegance or money. Frieda says, "It conjures up a pipe smoking, tobacco chewing woman ringing chicken necks and slopping pigs."

I'd been talking to Frieda about how upset Rose is over hearing her son was having a gay affair. "Rose is afraid it will reflect badly on her as a mother."

Frieda twists her mouth as she thinks then puts down her coffee before speaking. "In what way?"

I answer, "Isn't it always the mother's fault?"

"Since I am a mother, and you never were, Clara May, I think I can best understand this. A mother always feels she's at fault for what happens to her children, especially her sons."

"So you're an expert in child psychiatry. Go on, Dr. Frieda, or should it be Dr. Freud?"

"Honestly, you think no one should know more than you, but in this case you're wrong. I know how mothers feel."

"Well, continue on then," I say.

"Thank you, Clara May. Moms have a closer bond with sons. I'm the first woman my son knew. He came to me when he cut his finger. I was the one he turned to when he was bullied at school, not his father. No other woman, or even a father, is as good. I could never do anything right for my daughter. Her father was her knight."

"I see. This is all your personal wisdom?"

"It could be," says Frieda, "but I read an article in *Cosmopolitan* and then another in *Reader's Digest*. Rose is furious with Mary and it fits the picture they paint of a daughter-in-law's relationship with her husband's mother."

"And she doesn't have a right to be self-righteous. It's no secret she married for money. Before Rose hooked William, she was a poor farmer's daughter. I doubt she chewed tobacco, but I bet she slopped the hogs a few times."

Frieda agrees. "Rose's ticket to the city and away from the farm was William and his family money."

"She's losing her place as the grand Dame of Dewers. Mary is trying to take over, and Rose resents it. This affair gives her a chance to drag her daughter-in-law through the mud."

Frieda points out. "She needs to be careful or she'll end up wallowing there with her daughter-in-law. Rose could ruin the reputations of William, her son, and herself."

"You'd think this was Queen Elizabeth and her royal family trying to keep them in line."

Frieda puts her coffee cup on the table, rises, and then curtseys. "Don't they know that you, Clara May, are the queen of Dewers and you're not abdicating? You plan to die holding the title."

I wave my hand in a royal wave. "I am. I am. I'll never step down."

Chapter 20

Rose Thompson

Sitting in my sewing room, cutting loose threads, and ironing, I think, *What cute costumes -- a hobo and a fairy princess, even if I did make them myself.* I don't consider it an imposition. I love to sew, but you'd think Mary could learn; after all, they are her kids. I hope Mary doesn't forget today is Halloween. She thinks she's such the social butterfly, gets herself involved in every committee she can wiggle her way into, wants to be some high faluting socialite. It's why she married Bob. I warned him about her -- the social climber -- but Bob could not see past her curves, her perky breasts, and that short skirt she wore as a cheerleader. I told him one day those shapely curves would become bulges, and those perky breasts will sag, but he wouldn't listen. I'd be surprised if she remembers to bring the kids for their costumes, let alone trick-or-treating.

Bob had his choice of any of the girls in high school. He was on the football team, a member of the student council, and, after college, headed to be the next President of the bank, and then he married her. I'm surprised she let him go to law school because it meant she had to work and get those pretty little hands of hers dirty. It was Mary who talked Bob into teaching law rather than working with his father in the bank. What can you expect from a working class family? She'd like to have the life suitable of a royal family, so maybe I should call her princess and make a dress for her like my granddaughter.

When I married William, we expected a modest life. He was not supposed to inherit the bank -- his older brother was, that is, until he was killed in the service. He was in the Infantry, a Captain, didn't see much fighting until he was part of the D-Day invasion. He was killed on the beach and his body was never returned. William couldn't go to the war because of a heart murmur. He was selling insurance and I was working in the local ammunition factory as a secretary. He was proud of me doing what I could for the war effort. William was always self-conscious about not being able to enlist.

I know my husband thinks Bob should have enlisted in the Vietnam War, but I resisted. It was the only time I stood up to him. I was not going to have my only living son coming home to me in a body bag. I already gave one son, and my husband gave a brother. That should be enough for our country. I won the argument although I lost the battle. Since he didn't go, he was free to wed Mary.

As I finger the silk of my granddaughter's princess dress, I think of my silk wedding dress, unassuming white with a bit of lace at the bodice. Because of the depression, money was short. My parents owned the hardware store in town. Father was kind-hearted and gave a lot of credit for which he was never repaid. I made the dress myself but splurged on the white shoes. The wedding was simple, two sets of parents, some aunts and uncles, and a few friends. The ceremony was in my parent's house. We didn't take a honeymoon because there was no money. How different it was for Bob. Mary insisted on a big church wedding with a full dinner reception at the country club. Her family didn't belong to the country club, so we had to sponsor it.

The wind interrupts my dreams. It sounds like it's getting cold out. This Victorian house is old and talks when the wind blows. I walk to the living room and look out the bay window. The sky is grey with heavy clouds, and snow blows around in the wind. Glancing from the window to the grandfather clock in the hall, I notice it's time to get ready for my hair appointment. I almost forgot this is my regular day for a wash and set. It's a treat I give myself now that we can afford it.

What should I wear? It looks as if it's going to be cold today. It's a good thing I took my winter clothes down from the attic last week and got my mink out of storage. I'll wear the mink today with my brown hat and white gloves. I like myself in hats, I think they make me look younger, the gloves, well they're elegant and besides, it's cold, and the mink, because I can. I want to look nice and feel good about myself today, at least on the outside. I am not feeling good about myself on the inside.

Today is the day Bob is in court. I can't wait for this ordeal to be over. It's so difficult to go out. I can't sit and visit with my friends. Everyone is afraid to ask how I am doing; they avoid the subject of Bob's arrest as if it was polio and talking about it would paralyze them on the spot. It's worse than polio. You can't die thinking about polio, but I could just die every time I think of the scandal. There's a vaccine for polio but nothing for bad judgment. My bridge club has become intolerable. A normally talkative table is now quiet except for the bidding. We love to gossip. Anyone and anything is fair game, from the garden to who is the worst dressed. Now I am lucky to know who died, who's pregnant. Everyone is afraid of offending me. I don't care anymore if I'm offended. I need to hear what people are saying. I need to talk to someone.

Bob and Mary still give the impression of being happy. They're always seen together in public and Bob looks especially good at her side when she's chairing one of her functions. He's always at her tennis matches. Mary enjoys going to the university functions with him, and they have season tickets to both the basketball and football season. They and their friends go out often, enjoying lunch or dinner together. William and I babysit the kids. He seemed to be having a normal life, a typical marriage, despite the affair. I don't understand it. I don't believe for minute that they are doing okay.

I know after a few years of marriage that sex is often far from your mind, or at least mine and my friends'. My husband looks at other women when he thinks I don't notice. I see him. I know what he's doing, but if it gives him pleasure, I'm content to let it be. If he was having an affair I don't think it would bother me too much. It would keep him happy and I'd be free of that part of marriage. But his affair would have to be out of this town. Anything done here would make it back to my friends before he got home from The Square, or at least it would have before this whole deal with Bob. I don't know what men find so exciting about sex. Oh yes, it does feel good most of the time, but it's so, I don't know, so personal, so intimate. Maybe my Catholic friends have it right, that sex should only be for having babies.

I can understand straying from your wife to have an affair with another woman, but with another man? Well, that's just not right. It's not normal. I've told Bob exactly what I think of homosexual acts. What do they do? No, I don't want to know, I don't even want to imagine what might be going on. I told him he was going to go to hell for his actions if he didn't repent, pray, and ask God for forgiveness. The meeting when his father and I found out was the worst day of my life. We didn't find out from Bob. Mary asked one day if she could come over and talk to us alone. William and I couldn't imagine what was happening. We thought maybe she had cancer, or Bob was sick. Never in our wildest dreams did we think she'd be telling us about a sexual affair our son was having and that he'd been arrested. She wanted us to know before the news hit the streets, didn't want us to hear it from our friends or read it in the newspaper.

My heart was racing so fast I thought I was having an attack. I couldn't breathe. My chest was tight. I must have turned white, because Mary asked me if I was okay, did I need some water. What I needed was to see my son and hear the words from his mouth, that and bourbon on the rocks, any alcohol. She told us there had been a ring of men having sex in the restrooms of the courthouse. People had complained and the sheriff caught them in the act. All the men were brought in on public indecency charges. Because they were all local, they were released without bail.

How did Bob even know about such things? I didn't teach him, or let alone have books that would have told him. I don't think his father would have. William hardly talked about regular sex to his children. With every inch of my soul I wanted to blame Mary, but at the time, I could form no words, or at least ones I could say out loud. But you can be sure, I was blaming her, and to this day, I'm not sure she wasn't involved. And now they both act so normal in public. Honestly.

How could I have let my guard down and thought all was well with those two? She had to have everything. I wouldn't be surprised if she asked another man into the marriage. I've seen the way she looks at other men at the country club. I thought those things only went on in big cities or in the soap operas.

Not my son, it couldn't be him. We're family. He's above such desires. When I caught my breath, I thought of the Pastor. What would he say? What would my friends say? I told Mary I wouldn't talk about this with her until I had spoken to my son. That dummy of a husband of mine, he just stood there with his mouth open. I said, "William, shut your mouth. Open the door, and start the car. I need to go for a ride, get out of this house and go anywhere, as long it's away from here. I don't care where. Take me wherever you want. Drive."

Once I got in the car I lit into my husband. It had to be his fault. I certainly was not to blame. I accused him of ignoring his son, not giving him a good sex education, and any other issue I could think of that could even remotely be his fault. Bill stopped the car in the middle of road, looked straight at me and asked me if I was finished. I told him I was, but reserved the right to continue later. His comment hit me to the core. My husband says, "If a guy is a homosexual it's due to having an overbearing attentive mother." I took my purse and began beating him with it. I told him to take it back; it couldn't be my fault. I saw to it Bob had been baptized. He had godparents. I made sure he went to Sunday school. I attended every parent-teacher association meeting. I was the one who made sure his homework was done and checked for mistakes.

What did William do as a father? Nothing. He did nothing, except go off to play golf with his buddies and when he did take his son it was to act as his personal caddy. He wanted his son there so he could brag. My son was on the Senior Varsity Football team. The good ol' boy network, a lot of good it has done. It was his idea to make sure Bob went to law school so he could brag, not because it was something Bob wanted. My husband practically ignored his son, except when it was convenient to have him around.

Do you know what he did after I was done talking? He grabbed my purse, looked me in the eye and said, "You just proved my point about being a mother hen." He told me, "You've tied a mighty tight knot to him with your apron strings."

I turned away and just stared out the window. I thought about getting out of the car and walking home, but I was concerned about what I'd say if anyone saw me. It was a day not unlike today -- late fall, chilly. I even think it was the first snow of the year. I can't believe all this was last year.

I hear the hallway clock chime and realize I've got to leave for my hair appointment. On the way to the beauty parlor I avoid The Square. I'm sure there will be reporters at all the exits of the courthouse. They dare not miss the gossip of the century. *Criminal prosecution destroys a founding family of the county.* Nothing has been this exciting since Abraham Lincoln's visit. They'll be looking for anyone to interview or capture their reaction in a photo. What better image for the newspaper front page than a grieving mother circling The Square without enough nerve to enter the courthouse?

I want to attend the hearing, but my son said no, to stay away. He doesn't want my histrionics. I reluctantly agreed but now that it's the day of the hearing, I have a need to be there. I'm feeling guilty about my earlier brazen remarks. My words didn't speak the truth of my heart, which is incapable of withholding love. Bob's presence never left me. I can still feel him in my womb. What else can my heart do but ache at the loss?

Heavens! Without thinking I've pulled onto The Square. There's no one waiting at the courthouse steps. Where are the reporters? Doesn't anyone else care? Maybe they're in the courthouse?

There's a crowd in front of Spurgeons, but they're all looking at the Halloween window and won't notice me. I quickly exit onto Main Street without being seen. I think.

I can't wait to get to the solace of the beauty parlor. I will literally be able to let my hair down. Since Judith opened the shop, I've gone every week to get my hair done. I hope she's not too busy today. The older women are not a problem - - get them under a dryer and you could give the code to launch a nuclear warhead. They would never hear it. As I round the corner to the shop, I notice more cars than usual in the parking area and my first response is to drive back home. If I were seen leaving after driving by, it would be as bad as going in. All the chairs, except for those at the washbasin, face the window, and they would see that I have chickened out. I pull into a parking spot, and my mouth feels like cotton. My hands are sweating beneath the white gloves, and my hand is trembling so much I'm not sure I can open the door.

Once out of the car, still holding on to the handle for support, I take a deep breath. My legs don't want to move. I force them to move, step-by-step, closer to the door. I'm resolved to keep my regular schedule. I keep repeating to myself, *I'm not the one accused. I'm not the one accused. I'm not the one accused.* Finally, at the entrance, my hands still trembling, I grasp the door, pulling it open. With a phony smile and wide-open bright eyes, I greet the other customers, but they don't notice me. They're all huddled around Mary. As they hear the door, and turn to face me, all the efforts I made to conceal my anxiety fades.

My smile becomes a scowl. My vision blurs. Tears make it seem as if I'm driving in the rain without windshield wipers. Alien women, with bizarre heads of curlers, bobby pins, and wet stringy hair, in choreographic slow motion fan out to reveal the featured attraction sitting on her throne. A drier's hood forms a backdrop for a crown of peroxide bubbles. It's Princess Mary. Suddenly mid sentence, "and Bob …" She notices the women have parted and I am the only one listening.

"Mary, go on. Don't let me stop you. I'd like to hear your story."

Mary is smiling and greets me as if I were visiting her for Sunday dinner. "Rosy, you look very smart today. Good thing you got the fur coat out of storage."

My friends call me Rosy and I tolerate it because the nickname was given to me in high school. I don't like it when Mary calls me Rosy. She's not one of my contemporaries and she's certainly not a friend. I wouldn't expect to be called Mrs. Thompson, but Rose shows respect. I wouldn't dare to call her by the nicknames she was given in school. It was, *Mary, Mary quite contrary, how do the boys in your garden grow?*

Nothing is happening in the shop: dryers are switched off and sitting empty. Judy is holding a strand of hair between the fingers of one hand, while the other hand hangs poised mid-air with open scissors. She is the first to salvage some sense of composure. "Good afternoon, Rose. Take off your gloves and hat. Hang your coat up. I'll be with you in a minute. The coffee's fresh. Pour yourself a cup and take a seat."

I'm not going to let this opportunity pass. As the other ladies abandon Mary and her story, there are plenty of chairs next to hers where she's waiting for the peroxide to make her a blond. "Mary, I've been wanting to talk to you about Bob, the trial, and your side of the story. Since it appears you have already opened that can of worms, we might as well have our discussion in public."

Mary does not lose her composure. She sits erect, her shoulders rolled back as if she is attempting to make her body appear larger. Her eyes make contact with mine and do not look away.

I will not let her get the upper hand. Somewhere I find the courage to be calm. I walk to the coat rack, slowly remove my right glove, the left glove, take off my coat, hang it on a hanger, remove the pins from hat, and place the hat on the shelf above my coat. My hands have stopped shaking. I'm ready for Mary.

When I turn to take a seat, I practically run into Clara May. Her hair has tight pin curls not yet combed out, and she is still wearing a white plastic smock tied around her neck. As is her knack, she shows no signs of the tension that hangs in the room like fog. "I'm sorry, Rose. I didn't mean to bump into you. I was just going for a fresh cup of coffee. Can I get you one?"

I could use something to hold in my hands. It will keep them occupied. I'm not sure I can control the urge to slap Mary across the face. "Thanks, Clara May. That would be nice."

Clara May asks, "Cream or sugar?"

I respond, "No, black is fine."

I wait until Clara May comes back with the coffee, and then take a seat to Mary's right. Except for Clara May, the rest of the ladies in the shop have become statues. Just like Lot's wife, they've turned into pillars of immobile salt which is on the verge of crumbling. They can't resist the temptation to watch what they think will be the destruction of Mary or myself. I speak, "Go on with your story, Mary."

Mary falters, ever so slightly, in her confident stance. Her breathing becomes shallower. She begins wringing her hands. Wrinkles appear in her forehead, and her eyebrows have a slight downward turn in the center. However, she is confident in her speech. "Well, Rosy, I was just telling the girls that I felt betrayed, alone when I discovered Bob was having an affair."

I break in. "Mary, please don't call me Rosy. Only my closest friends call me that."

Mary's hands have a slight tremor. "Sorry, Rose. I didn't know that. Bob's affair was a surprise to me but I did suspect something. He wasn't as responsive in our lovemaking."

She has opened the door for me and I will not let her shut it before I have my say. "Was this before or after you started your affair with the tennis coach?"

As if they all sucked a bitter lemon at once, on cue, the ladies in the room recoil and fall out of their immobile state. Mary returns her eyes to mine as she speaks. "I'm not sure when Bob started his romp with the men, but I suspect it was well before we were married. As for when the current affair started, I don't know. Rest assured, it was Bob's inattention that drove me to seek comfort elsewhere."

I respond, "There must have been some reason for Bob to stray the way he did. He's a Christian man, football star, outstanding teacher."

Mary finishes her coffee in one long gulp and licks her lips. As she begins talking, her neck and face flush. "As if that makes a difference. Are you trying to convince yourself or me? Your son is a homosexual. He has sex with men ... in public! And you want to defend him, call him an outstanding Christian?"

"No matter what Bob has done, you're not innocent, either. You're an adulteress," I say.

An alarm goes off somewhere in the shop, and Judy, ever the beautician, speaks. "Sorry to interrupt, Mary, but it's time to wash out your hair."

Mary goes to the washbasin with Judy. I watch as she places her head in the curve of the basin and wish I had a sword to chop it off. Clara May interrupts my thoughts. "I brought in some nice lemon pound cake. Would you like some with your coffee?"

Chapter 21

Clara May on Washington Street Bar:

Evening of Bob's Court Date

This morning over coffee I told Frieda, "I bet we can find the boys at the Washington Inn tonight."

Frieda said, "I'd be there too if I was in their shoes, and I'd probably get drunk."

I pointed out to Frieda, "I don't think that will ever happen. You're not exactly the person to get involved in a sex affair. Now, drinking is another thing."

If you're from the Dewers area and park on Washington Street at night there's only one thing you're doing: drinking. The reason for drinking is as varied as a person's life, but whatever troubles you, whatever you're celebrating and alcohol is involved, you're either at Washington Street Inn or the Elk's Lodge. Squeaky's is more for everyday drinking.

Not that I'm complaining -- Frieda and I often go to the Elks. I've only walked by the Washington Street Inn. I leave it for those who need solitude. I have no need for privacy. My life is an open book. Besides, no one should expect privacy in this town.

The Elks lodge is like going to the barbershop or beauty parlor. They're all gossip centers. You shouldn't go to any of them and discuss your problems unless you want the whole town to know and chime in. If you want isolation, if you want to drown your sorrows and have the tears remain where they fall, then the Washington Inn is the place.

When Frieda and I drove home from our early dinner, Danny's truck was not in the driveway and I didn't see it on The Square. If he's working, it should have been parked on The Square. I could use some information but it looks like I'm not going to get it from Danny.

Frieda and I settle into the living room when suddenly I say, "Frieda, we're going back in town. I want to see if the boys are at the bar. I'll even buy you a Dairy Queen when we're done."

Frieda is always up for a Dairy Queen, so of course she says yes. We grab our coats and head out to the car. The night sky is cloudless, exposing all the stars. If they can be beautiful exposing themselves, I see no reason that Dewers can't do likewise. On the way back into town, I notice Danny's truck is still gone. A note to him will have to do for now. "I'm going to stop at Danny's house for a moment to leave him a note. He'll have a story to tell. I'll have him come over for a hot breakfast tomorrow."

On our drive to The Square, James' red Camaro passes us. It has to be him driving because he doesn't let anyone else drive that car, not even his wife. Frieda and I wave, not expecting any response.

Frieda comments, "Do you know he gave that car a name?

"I suppose it's something like red hot mama."

"Not even close. He calls it 'ata boy'. Ata boy!" says Frieda. "I ask you what kind of name is that. No, don't answer that. I don't need your opinion. I reckon we know where he's going."

I guess he forgot there'd be a lot of people on The Square for Halloween because he makes a quick exit. I turn to Frieda with a suggestion. "I'm sure he's going to Washington Street, but let's follow him and see."

Washington Street is deserted except for a few cars. Frieda spots James' car first. "He's parked by the Elks. Anyone who sees the car will think he's at the lodge."

Then I see him walking. "Definitely not at the Elks. He's headed to the Inn."

"Let's honk and scare him. He thinks no one sees him."

"Frieda, that's cruel. Let him be for the night." We see some kids running by on the other side of the street with rolls of toilet paper. I tell Frieda, "I bet they're after the Principal's house again." His house is around the corner on Maple Street.

Frieda rolls down her window to yell. I think she's going to scold them, but she surprises me. "Go for it guys. I hope you've got some soap for the windows, too."

Smiling, she rolls up the window. I couldn't let this go by. "Got a little mischief in you, do you?"

Frieda looks at me sternly. "You can't say you don't remember our episodes as kids."

I spot other cars. "Frieda, look. There's Thomas' blue truck, Danny's truck, Bob's is across the street, and I bet Gary walked. Oh, to be a bit of sawdust on the floor soaking up the conversation in there tonight. James is looking over his shoulder to make sure no one sees him going in."

Frieda asked me, "You think Bob's going to report on the trial."

My response, "No, Frieda, they're exchanging cake recipes."

Chapter 22

Washington Street Inn

My car's at the Elks so if it's seen, people will think I'm there. I shouldn't have gotten a red car; it's too easy to spot. As I open the door, I can already feel the comfort of the bar. My neck feels less stiff. I stop grinding my teeth. My drooping shoulders become more upright. The smell of stale beer, sawdust, sweat, smoke, and something like dirty feet ease me into a sense of relief. I can't tell if the light is dim, or whether it's the haze of smoke. Stopping a minute for my eyes to adjust, I notice a large man sitting at the end of bar. He turns his head to look at me while flicking cigarette ashes. He tumbles to the floor.

The bartender looks up to greet me, says, "Hi, James," then comes from behind the bar and looks at the man attempting to get up. After determining that there doesn't appear to be any injury, he inquires just to be sure. "Doug, are you okay?"

Dazed and shaking his head, the man continues to try and get up with no success. He finally notices the bartender, "What the hell am I doing down here?" Doug swings his arms madly in an attempt to part the air in front of him so there is room to get up. In a stubborn demanding voice like he's a boss addressing a group of workers, he replies, "Get the hell away from me. I'm fine."

Other people in the bar are taking notice and coming over to offer their help. "All of you, whatcha looking at? So you wanta see a man down on his luck. Here he is. That's me. Take a look. Hell, take a picture. That's it, turn your fucking backs."

Those who had come to help return to their drinks and their own sorrows, glad it's not them on the floor. Doug's wife caught him playing around with the babysitter and kicked him out of the house. With three kids, his wife gets most of his paycheck. Doug now lives in the flophouse across the street.

I try not to look at Doug and order when the bartender gets back. "Yeah, I'd like a Budweiser on tap."

Doug has managed to stay on the stool but is slumped over the bar mumbling. "Fucking wife, fucking bitch. Fuck women."

I notice his pants are wet. Good God, he's peed his pants.

"That's it stare, you bastard."

What have I become? Is that me, a loser?

Doug manages to wave his glass before spilling half the beer. "Have a drink guys."

As I'm handing the bartender cash, a hand touches my shoulder. I turn to see Bob in his suit and tie. After the event with Doug, he looks out of place. His refined voice doesn't belong in this bar. "James, we thought you might show up."

I responded, "I'm glad that's you. I thought you might be one of my customers."

Bob started laughing and waving his arm to take in the bar, "It's all yours. No one but us lowly folk in the corner will notice you're here. And I'm sure no one else wants to talk to you. If nothing else, they're afraid you'll sell them a new car."

I put a dollar on the counter and grab my beer, "Who in this bar is willing to talk to you and me? Folks will think they're a part of the sex ring."

Bob stops walking and turns to me, "Who do you think would be here tonight, Perry Mason? The gang is over there in the corner."

Bob seems a little too cheerful. He leads me through the smoke haze to a corner table where all the remainder of the gang is drinking: Thomas, Gary, and Danny. Gary holds up his martini for a toast while the others follow. "To The Square Affair Five. May we long be the infamy of Dewers."

Bob adds, "May we stay out of prison."

I add, "And out of mental hospitals."

A cry of "hear, hear" goes up. Glasses and bottles rise, and we all drink.

Bob looks at each of us directly and then surveys the group, "What a sorry bunch of men you are. There's not a hint of a smile on any face. The lights in this smoke are brighter than your eyes. All of you look as if you're at a funeral for a lost friend."

Thomas puts down his beer, crushes his cigarette in the ashtray, and then rests his chin between thumb and index finger. "Well, aren't we?"

Bob moves to stand over Thomas. "Aren't we what?"

Thomas rubs his forehead between thumb and fingers before looking up at Bob, "Aren't we at a damn funeral? We might as well be dead. It doesn't matter what the court has to say. We're finished in this town: at church, with our friends, with our families. We're finished. All that's left is the burying."

Danny is sitting across the table from Thomas. He looks into Danny's eyes. "I'm not going to anybody's funeral, real or imagined. I won't give up my business. Dewers may be petty, judgmental, and hung up on sin, but they're my family. It's the only home I know. I'm here to stay. Clara May told me yesterday she didn't care what I'd done, unless I'd murdered someone, and she knew that wasn't so."

Gary is leaning back in his wooden chair blowing smoke rings between sips of his vodka martini. He leans forward looking at the other four. "For Christ's sake, we don't even know what happened to Bob in court. No one has come into my agency demanding to cancel his insurance. Squeaky's was packed last night. The only eulogy we should write is for the restrooms. The city closed both the men's and women's. We'll have to pee at Sears. Now that's a passing that I could mourn."

I have nothing to add to the conversation, at least not until I hear what Bob has to say. He takes a long drink of his beer, turns a chair around, and sits facing the back. "It's not all bad. No one wants a trial, especially the State's Attorney. He's up for re-election next year. Regardless of the outcome of the trial, the publicity can't be controlled. No one knows the public opinion stance."

I commented, "I think I know where Pastor Jenkins stands on the issue."

Gary was quick to chime in, "On the side of sin. The devil made them do it. Do I hear an amen?"

Bob gives Gary an evil eye to which Gary raises his glass. I think Gary is hiding his fear because he knows this town can be evil. Being a clown is how he copes. Bob resumes his summary. "Other than Pastor Jenkins, we're not sure of the general public's feelings. We're only sure of what's been printed in *The Journal*, and they've mostly kept to reporting just the facts."

Thomas, looking worried, comments. "Letters to the editor haven't been supportive. They'd like to run us out of town."

Danny breaks in. "Yeah, the fact is that public sex is still illegal. We weren't behind closed doors. We were in the courthouse restroom."

"Letters to the editor are mostly written by disgruntled people. Sodomy may be legal in the privacy of your bedroom, but no sex is legal in public." Bob continues, "That fact is not in question. There's no denying we did it. They have us. The sheriff's deputy is an eyewitness. Our goals are: pay no fine, stay out of jail, stay out of a mental hospital, get our records expunged."

Thomas looks confused, "Expunged? What's that?"

Bob puts on his teaching hat. "Sorry to get technical. It's a hazard of the profession. Expunged is when there's no trace of your record. It's usually after you serve a sentence or court appointed probation. Nothing remains on your record. Not even the arrest. There is no record."

I'm worried about the publicity. "What about the newspaper articles, the original arrest story?"

Gary seems to be distant from the rest of us, almost cynical. "Tell us, Bob. What about the newspapers?"

Taking a deep breath before speaking, Bob addresses Gary first. "Gary, we don't need any snide remarks from you. It doesn't help us. We're all aware that Dewers is not your hometown, but it's our town. Even if we decided to move, there's an effect on our friends and family."

Gary pushes back his chair and stands face to face with Bob. "Do not accuse me of being snide. I may be brisk, even rude at times. Yes, my family and friends know I'm a homosexual, but Dewers doesn't, my clients don't. I'm in this with you, with all of you. Just like the rest of you, I can't walk away. A Chicago weekend will not solve this problem. My nerves are on edge, the same as all of you."

Bob looks at all of us before talking. "Gary, I'm sorry. I know it's just, well … just your take on things. God, how I know it's just you. It's what we all love about you. No, there's no erasing a news story; we'll all have to deal with that. How we do it is up to us. There's no right answer."

I want to get us back on the trial and away from emotions. "Bob, what did the State's Attorney say? What did the judge say?"

"Thanks for getting me back on track. The State's Attorney said if I would change my plea to guilty, he would recommend probation with a request to expunge the record at the probation's successful completion. There would probably only be a fine."

Thomas still looks grim. "We all pleaded not guilty at the initial hearing. Now we plead guilty? Isn't that saying we lied?"

Bob answers, "Technically Thomas, you're right. But it's a common tactic used in law. Everyone is assumed innocent until proven guilty. You can be proven guilty through a trial, by a judge, or by your confession. You have the right to change your plea. It's a way for everyone to avoid a trial."

Gary has finished his drink and has motioned the bartender to bring him a coffee. "No more drinking tonight. It sounds as if that's what we're looking for, except probation. What does that entail?"

Bob looks at his empty beer. "I'm having another." He waves his bottle at the bartender. "Probation means you have to keep your ass clean for the time the court imposes -- usually a year -- and maybe community work. That is no bathroom sex. No arrests for any crime. I wouldn't even chance a traffic ticket. Don't give the probation officer anything to use against you."

It's Danny's turn to question. "Is it a done deal if the State's Attorney and I agree to change the plea?"

"No. The judge has to approve the deal, and in most cases they do. There doesn't seem to be pressure from any source to do anything but approve." Bob sits down with a sigh. "I'm certain the plea deals will keep us out of jail, away from a mental hospital. We'll probably have to pay a small fine. Now, let's talk about us. How we're feeling. Who can we count on? Who's against us? My wife is ready to explode. She went to the beauty parlor today and I'd bet she spilled the beans, told her side of the story. And before you say anything, I know her side of the story includes an affair. Turns out neither one of us were hiding our secrets too well."

I look at Bob. "I'm glad that's out in the open. I've known about it for a while and wondered why you didn't know. Sue's affair may make your problems a little easier on your parents. There's nothing worse than a daughter-in-law's infidelity to a son. A mother cannot tolerate any woman cuckolding her boy."

Bob ignores James' remark. "We may get off without jail, but getting off without Dewers' punishment is another thing. In time they'll forget, but we'll have to rebuild our reputations, our lives."

Through laughter Gary responds, "What about a man cuckolding the mother's boy?"

Bob gives Gary the finger and the gloom is broken for the moment. We all start laughing. "You'd think we're the Women's Church Circle." A number of frowning faces turn to look at us. "They're jealous. Their lives have no laughter. They spend time drinking in this grimy bar thinking if alcohol cannot bring them joy it will at least let them forget why there's no laughter." We all raise glasses in a toast to them. I give the toast. "May we continue to have friends to laugh with."

As our laughter dies, the melancholy mood returns.

Thomas is the first to speak. "But we're only laughing so we don't end up like them. Hell, I'm already halfway there."

Soon, we'll all leave the laughter behind to be swept up with the sawdust floor along with the cigarette butts and spilt alcohol. I ask, "Have any of you been thrown out of your house? Obviously that doesn't apply to Gary or Danny. As for me, I'm still sleeping with my wife. I said sleeping, not having sex."

Thomas responds, "I haven't been thrown out of the house. I am sleeping with Sue, but I don't think she wants me with her. She has wanted to talk, but I don't know what to say. Maybe after the trial thing is over I'll know. I feel too guilty, too confused right now to talk to her. I've thought about what I would say if my sexual affair were discovered. I rehearsed the excuses in my mind. I've had nightmares about what would happen. Now that I've been laid open the excuses are, I don't know, not important. Excuses don't mean anything when you've made your family suffer. I'm not about to talk to my parents until Sue and I can talk."

Thomas' words penetrate to the heart of what I'm feeling. "I couldn't agree more. Judy and I may be sleeping together, but we've talked little about why I did what I did. Neither have we discussed where we go from here. I think she would be happy to turn the other cheek attempting to be ignorant of any future affairs I might have. I think she heard far too much about sinful behavior from her father, the good Reverend."

Bob has been listening intently to Thomas and me. The three of us have the most at stake. We all could lose our wives and our kids. Finally he speaks, "I for one am glad this has come out. I've not been happy with Mary for a while, and I don't mean just the sex. I've known she was having an affair for over a year. I never mentioned it to her because in my mind it gave me permission to go have sex in the restroom and occasionally with Gary. I haven't had the balls to end the marriage. This gives me an easy out. I worry most about what she'll say to the kids. And even though Dad and I have had our problems, I worry about him. He lost one son and now he'll think he's lost the other. Dewers will recover with time, but as for me, I'd be happy to get out of town."

Danny looks at his watch and says, "Men, it's getting late. We'd better get home to our wives -- or in my case my cat -- or people will be thinking we're at it again."

I don't think anyone wanted to leave, but everyone knew they had to face their other lives. There's a lot of shoulder patting and firm handshakes. I long to hug these men that know so much about me but also know that this is not the time or place for such public show of affection.

Chapter 23

Clara May on Gary and Bob

I'm driving Frieda home from Halloween on The Square when she makes a prediction. "I bet you Bob leaves Mary and moves in with Gary."

"Are you going to continue to play the role of a psychic with that witch's hat on?" I ask.

Frieda poses with that ridiculous hat and asks, "Are you jealous because I might know more than you?"

"Jealous, no. I've told you most everything you know, and what I haven't told you is not worth telling, but if you must know I agree with you."

"Was that so hard to admit I might be right?" Frieda asks.

"Yes, it was. I won't deny it. Tell me, why do you think Bob will leave Mary."

Frieda responds, "Bob may want to leave, but he won't initiate the separation. Mary will ask him to leave and demand a divorce."

"But doesn't it leave her open to be accused of adultery herself?" I inquire.

Frieda has thought this through and has an answer. "All Mary ever wanted was the money and the family name. She's got the family name and the prestige by marrying Bob. A divorce may tarnish it but not take it away. She'll get money in the divorce. Courts always side with the scorned wife."

"I wouldn't be so sure about that Frieda. The Thompson family has a lot of power in this town and they're all lawyers."

Frieda responds, "Whatever happens, it looks as if it will be a messy divorce."

"I'm sure Bob would be happier with Gary. They've been close friends since college, more than close friends," I say.

Frieda cocks her head slightly and looks worried. "It's always the kids who suffer. I hope there won't be a battle over custody."

"I don't think either of them would put the kids through it. I'm sure Bob won't and Mary won't risk ruining her image."

Frieda says in a sing-song voice that makes me want to slap her, "Even though the restrooms are closed, I guess Bob will be visiting other parts of the courthouse soon."

Chapter 24

Gary

I don't feel like myself anymore. After what's happened today, I'm definitely not the Gary I was a year ago. No longer feeling cocky or full of myself, there's not even any bullshit left in me. I tried leaving this uncertain life behind in the bar, drop it like a burned out cigarette, but each time I crushed out that cigarette, it came back to my mouth.

I said my goodbyes to the boys, leave with that cigarette dangling and walk to my apartment. The Square is almost deserted. As my father was fond of saying, "They roll up the sidewalks at dark in that town."

There's some activity after dark, but not much. Bars and filling stations stay open late. Stores on The Square are just closing, having been open late for the trick-or-treaters. They'll keep their lights on tonight so the Halloween paintings can be seen.

I walk The Square to take my mind off today. Some of the art is very good. The creators have a possible future in art, and some are not so good. This is one of the things I missed growing up in Chicago. Sure we had block parties and summer outings, but they didn't give me a cozy feeling. The parties were more an excuse for the parents to drink and act silly. Kids were a second thought. Often we roamed the streets free -- no organized activity for us. I like knowing the parents and some of the kids who did the paintings. Town folk leave the Halloween Square party laughing, kids in hand. It's more fun than I remembered in my youth. But then again, having no kids, it was not a part of my life. Will it be now?

I arrive home, unlock the door, and climb the stairs to my empty apartment. No matter how much stress the others are feeling, they have wives and families to offer support. Tonight they'll be talking at kitchen tables, in front of a television, or in bed. They have something, somebody else that defines who they are. I'm not a father, not a husband, there's only the insurance business. Gary, the insurance man: it sounds like some fly by night Bible salesman or someone selling encyclopedias door-to-door.

I throw open the window and scream to The Square below, "Hi, I'm Gary, a homosexual insurance agent. I can insure your life. All you have to do is die to collect it." The wintry wind catches those words, tosses them to the trees, which bat them back into my face. The sting of the slap hurts, not because I said it, but because no one heard it. There's emptiness on The Square. The goblins, the cowboys, the princesses that roamed earlier have all gone home with parents to inspect their treats. A few pranksters circle in cars. They're too busy looking for tricks to hear me. Soon they'll leave in search of trees to toilet paper, windows to soap, or possibly some farmer's outhouse to tip over.

As I watch, The Square becomes deserted, even of them. I'm left in the emptiness of my apartment staring at the emptiness outside my open window. The kitchen table has empty chairs. The living room is empty except for the couch and chair. A television remains black, silent, an empty screen. The bedroom is empty. No one sleeps under the covers waiting for me. The apartment is silent. I'm alone. I'm lonely. I wish Clara May would call. Her voice could crack the ice of this empty solitude.

Wet snow sprinkles the courthouse limestone like it's crying, its tears glittering in the moonlight. We five were once its gallant men, crusading in shining armor of defiance. We now have fallen from our white horses with tarnished breastplates, fighting an unwanted war. Humpty Dumpty has fallen from the courthouse wall, and our shields no longer protect us. Are there any horses, any men who dare put us together again?

Suddenly I notice I'm not alone. A spider has woven a web in my pane. What are you going to catch so late in the season? Flies are gone for the winter, and because of the early chill those tasty insects have hidden, left, or died. What savory treat are you seeking? Seems as if we both will starve this winter, looking at The Square. Shall we be friends in our distress, relieve our emptiness? Will your web remain empty? Have I woven a web that will remain empty? Will you be glad you've chosen to live in my pane next spring, or will you resent the choice? Perhaps you'll crawl off to where the insects have hidden.

Is Bob glad he met me? Is he cursing fate for our chance meeting? Myself, I don't believe in fate. We're not predestined to anything but death. I know I'm a homosexual man. I've known since high school and probably sooner, if I had known what to call it then. I've dated women, and I like the company of women. I don't want to have sex with a woman. What does that mean to me now that everyone knows? I might as well be standing naked next to that statue of Lincoln. "Fooled myself some of the time, but I guess never all the people all the time." Now, I'm just the fool.

Who did Bob fool? He still wrestles with his demon. We've never talked directly about his sexual desires but, given his past actions, I would guess he's had questions for a long time. With or without me, Bob has no choice now but to answer those questions. There are at least three other men in town tonight asking the same question, and I'm sure there are more, given the scandal's publicity.

The spider moves to the center of his web, catching my attention again. So can anyone answer our question? As I'm watching the spider, I see Bob approaching my door. He wouldn't be at my door late at night, uninvited, unless something happened at home. I hurry down the steps and unbolt the lock. Bob's earlier neat appearance is in disarray: His tie is undone. A dark beard is showing. His usual perfectly combed hair is messy. In one hand he holds a briefcase and in the other a suitcase. Every part of his appearance cries for help. "Bob, come in. Get off the street."

I lock the door and wave Bob up the stairs. Not until we're seated on the living room couch does he talk. His speech is rapid, vomiting the words in the hope that getting rid of them will ease his distress. "After meeting Mary and the kids on The Square, we drove home in separate cars. I arrived home after Mary and found my suitcase packed, sitting by the front door. She's upstairs putting the kids to bed. I needed a confrontation to clear my guilt. If she voiced her loathing and admitted it was her choice for me to leave, I could have some relief of my guilt. I wanted her to admit her affair. She needed to shoulder some of the blame. I would not leave without talking to her, and I wasn't going to make it easy for her."

I interrupt. "Do you want a drink?"

Bob shakes his head no, "No …Yes. I'm going to need something to help me sleep. Give me a scotch on the rocks."

I pull out my fine Irish single malt and pour a glass for each of us. Walking back to the couch, I wonder if it's wise to sit next to him. If there ever was a time Bob needed a loving touch, this is it. No matter what might have occurred in the past, whether or not it was my fault, whatever the trial outcome, I have this moment and I'm not going to let it pass. Maybe this is who I am. Maybe I want a relationship, someone I can care for. I sit on the couch next to Bob and hand him the scotch. "Do you want to talk, or do you just need a place to sleep?"

I feel helpless at this point. I'm one of the king's men trying to put Humpty together again, and I don't have a blueprint. I haven't put myself together yet. I have no skill for this. I know how he fell. Why he fell is uncertain, but I have my theories. I need to hear what Bob has to say. Bob looks into my eyes searching. He must have found what he's looking for, because I see myself reflected through his eyes, eyes that are hard to read but beginning to tear. He places his head on my shoulder and cries. I hesitate before putting my arm around him but this is not a time to be timid. It's a time to be honest. And to be honest, I love this man. I have loved him since college.

With my arm around his shoulder and his head on mine, his crying stops. Bob tells his story. "Mary had figured out my scheme a year ago and was waiting for the right time to pounce.

She's so hung up on money and prestige. She said that she's known for a while what you've been up to. She has known all along that you're a homosexual. As a Delta Kappa Sorority girl, she has contacts in Chicago. They're everywhere. Mary thinks my behavior only gives the appearance of something new. She knows I was playing around in college and went to bars with you on those Chicago weekends. She asks if our whole marriage has been a lie. She wants to know why I married her if I knew I liked men.

"I don't know why I married her, but I had to give some response. I told her I didn't know what I wanted then, and I'm not any closer to knowing tonight. She was ... is a lovely woman. She admired my career goals, thought I was brave for not following in my father's footsteps. I told her that I had sex with men in college, but I didn't think of myself as a homosexual. I was a horny young man, and this was an easy way to get my rocks off."

Bob picks up his scotch, twirls the ice cubes, and looks at it as if all the answers to his problems were imprisoned inside the thawing ice cube. "Mary got up pacing, chain smoking, lighting one cigarette off the other until she was almost through the pack. She paused to light another cigarette. She asked, 'You didn't know? You sucked men's cocks in a restroom where the whole town could see, and you didn't know? I was working hard to maintain the name of your family in this community while you were having sex. I was at Wednesday church meetings while you and your gang of five were drinking at Squeaky's and you didn't know? You said you were at faculty meetings. Were they in the restroom or Gary's apartment? Wherever you were, I was at PTA meetings and school functions alone.'"

I want to comment but look into Bob's eyes, which are fire, and know I shouldn't. Bob continues. "I asked Mary if all this time she had been innocent? First she used my family name, my father, my mother, and me to become "queen bee" of Dewers. We had elaborate Christmas parties and barbeques in the summer. We had to be in the country club. Why, I asked her, if she was to get closer to the tennis instructor? Was it to have excuses to be with him? Did they have sex in the locker rooms there? Maybe I wasn't the only one in restrooms. I wanted to know when her affair started. I told her not to look so surprised, and not to deny it. The entire town knew what she was up to.

"Mary would not back down, even with this revelation. She was the scorned wife and would prove it. She responded, wanting to know what she was supposed to do since nothing was happening in bed at home. She was adamant that there was no more denial in her. She couldn't look the other way anymore. She couldn't sit at the dinner table and look at me without wanting to throw food in my face. She couldn't bear to have me in the same bed with her, let alone touch her. She wanted me out tonight. She pointed to my packed bags at the door, and inquired if she should send the remainder of my things to your place. She wants a divorce, and says I'll have nothing when she's finished because she plans to drag my nasty ass through court. She thinks no judge will deny her request when he hears about my behavior. She wants sole custody of the kids."

Bob's voice is beginning to quiver and I can see tears forming in his eyes again. "I was not going to cry in front of her. I would not give her that satisfaction, but she's right. Psychiatrists still consider us deviant, sick, and unable to be cured. I'll lose my position at the university. I can see the headlines: *Fag professor fired for fear of infecting the morality of his students.* Though my heart was not in it, I attempted reconciliation. 'Can't we talk? Can't we work something out?' I pleaded with Mary to allow joint custody. I don't want to be shut out. I want to see my kids."

Bob stops a moment to dab his eyes with the napkin under his drink. He sighs deeply to stop his tears and then continues, "She'd have none of it. I imagined this scene had been playing out in her head for months. She said I should have thought of that before opening the restroom door. She told me there is no forgiveness. Gary, she talked to my mother today at the hairdresser and says Mom agrees, which explains why she chose tonight to kick me out. I won't believe my own mother wants me to leave. Doesn't she want me to see the kids?"

Bob's crying grows more intense. I hold him tight. I hold on so I don't fall. I hold on in fear. I hold on in relief that the lies are over. I hold on in anticipation that the future will be better. I hold on because I love him. I can do without Dewers, but I can't do without Bob.

Bob sits up straight and takes a drink of his scotch, "Gary, I'm afraid: afraid of losing all contact with my familiar world, afraid of losing what has been me for so many years. I'm afraid that I'm a freak of creation: a bearded lady in the circus, a man born with two heads on one body, a side show where people gawk, they point fingers and thank God it's not them."

I respond, "You've been reading too much and thinking the worst will happen. Not everyone thinks we're freaks. There are people working in medicine who don't agree that homosexuality is a deviant behavior. I'm sure there are even people in Dewers on our side. We've got Clara May and Frieda for sure."

Bob looked at me holding up an index finger, "But it won't help us now."

I continued. "I think it will. If there's some question in the medical community about us and the cause of our ... our desires, then no one can speak with absolute authority in the courts. I also have the Mike Wallace report on homosexuality running through my mind. I'm thinking, my God, that's me. That's my friends. They can't be right. It's not how it is."

Bob grows excited and points his index finger at me as if I was an expert witness on the stand. "But it is how it is. Isn't it? People think I can stop doing this if I want to. They think it's my father's fault because he was not man enough. He didn't stand up to my mother. They think I seek men to become the man my father wasn't. They blame my mother because she was too protective of me. None of it's true. You know my dad. Do you think he'd let a woman control him? Changing isn't like going on a diet to lose weight. I can will myself to stop eating. I can't will myself to stop liking men. How the hell do priests remain celibate? How can I get through probation if it means not having sex with men? It's not going to happen. It just isn't!"

As Bob walks to the window, I follow and we both look at The Square and courthouse. Bob turns his head to me. "I'm sad for the lost years of joy I could have had. I'm anxious because all that's familiar to me is fading into darkness, and the deeper I go into that darkness there's nothing, nothing but black. I can't see any light. There's nothing but the darkness of an uncertain future. At this moment the only light I see is in your eyes, but I worry if it's light enough to see us through the darkness."

Bob turns again to stare into the night and I turn to the spider. Seems as if I've caught mine without a web, at least not one of my making. Bob became tangled in his own spinning. My task is to catch him when the web fails and he falls.

Chapter 25

Clara May on Judy and James Turnbull

Frieda and I have decided to return to The Square after our Dairy Queen. We like seeing the decorated windows and watching the kids trick-or-treating in their costumes. Frieda asks, "Hey, why don't we go as a couple of witches. We could be the witches of Dewers. I think I've got some old costumes from my working days at the high school. Let's stop by my house and have a look."

"Are you out of your mind? Enough people in town already think we're old bitties, crazy and lame elderly women who are out of touch with the world, yet think they know something relevant and feel compelled to share it with us."

"If they already think it, then what's the problem?" Frieda asks.

"The problem is I don't want to do it and I'm driving. We're not stopping at your house."

"Have it your way, spoiled sport. We'll stand out like a sore thumb if we're not in costume," Frieda says.

"There's no disguising us. I've taught most of the kids and their parents and you know the ones I didn't."

Frieda digs in her purse and pulls out a black witch's hat. "Have it your way, but I'm wearing this."

"Good thing you don't have your broom. I'm sure you're above the weight limit for takeoff."

Frieda scrunches her eyes and face in a scowl. "I'll get you, my little pretty."

"Why don't you use some magic and gaze into a crystal ball? May you can tell me what's happening to the married couples after Bob's hearing today. Make yourself useful so I don't feel like your chauffer." I say.

"Oh, I have no need for a crystal ball. Frieda sees all."

"Well then, tell me about Judy and James."

Frieda moves her hands left and right in a rhythmic swaying, conjures up some hocus pocus. "Judy is worried about James."

I'd close my eyes not to see but I'm driving, so I shake my head in disgust. "Great insight, Frieda the witch."

"I'm not done. Visions take time to materialize. James is torn, and he wants to keep the marriage together. Judy is worried about the kids. I still see them wearing wedding rings."

"Thank you for those words of wisdom. Now change your focus and find me a parking space on The Square. It looks as if all the town has come for the Halloween festivities."

Frieda immediately yells. "There, quick! Turn in before someone else gets it."

"I may have to rethink your powers."

Chapter 26

Judy and Thomas Turnbull

Judy went straight home after school and is waiting for me as I come in from the bar. She asks, "Is that you James?"

I walk into the living room. She is seated on the couch reading the newspaper. "Yes, I'm home."

I can't read Judy's expression. She could be angry or concerned. Her eyebrows are arched and her forehead is wrinkled. I think she's more concerned than angry. At least that's my hope. "I was worried about you. Where have you been?"

"I met the boys at the Washington Inn. We wanted to talk to Bob about the trial."

The wrinkles in Judy's forehead deepen and she frowns. "I might have known you'd be there. Can't you find out what's going on without meeting the others? What's wrong with the phone? I know you need support. She pauses as if she needs to gather her thoughts. "Doesn't mine count, or is it not good enough for you? I thought the attorney told you not to be seen with the others."

She was in a good mood when she left this morning, but now she sounds angry. There's no warmth in her voice. She's sitting erect with both feet on the floor. She looks like a policeman ready to give a ticket for some violation. I answer, "Yes, your support counts, but what the state's attorney and judge said today should be important to both of us."

I'm not sure what has changed in Judy, but she's different. She seems angry tonight. I sit on the couch next to her. She notices me attempting to take her hand in mine and makes a point of deafeningly folding the newspaper that's been in her lap and places it on the coffee table. Her hands are shaking. I want to reach out and hold them so they'll stop, but she interlaces her fingers and places both hands in her lap. She turns to look at me. There's ice in her eyes. I'm surprised the tears haven't frozen on her face. It looks so cold. "Why wouldn't I want to know what happened at the hearing? No one talks to me anymore." Judy picks up the paper, folds and unfolds it again, then those cold eyes stare at me. "There were a lot of parents at school today for the Halloween party and it was like I was a real wicked witch that could cast a spell by just recognizing my existence. The kids were the only ones talking to me. When the party was over, parents yanked their children and escaped. I hope you're going to tell me it's over."

I proceeded to tell Judy about the plan to change our plea to guilty, pay a fine, and to be on probation for a year. There was no sign of warming in her face. I think she was hoping it was all over.

"And you'll have no record, right?" she asks.

"Yes, the record will be expunged, but there's still the newspaper account." I say.

Judy holds up her hands to either side of her face, palms facing me, in a gesture I don't really understand. Is she pushing me away? "You should have thought of that consequence before. Can't undo what's out there now, can you?" Judy gets up and paces, as a teacher would when giving a lecture to her students. She sounds like she's chastising one of them for throwing a spit ball or not handing in their homework. "And what are you going to do about saving the business? What about us in the community? When can we eat at the diner without people staring at us?" She stops pacing and stands in front of me pointing her index finger. "When do people stop looking at me with pity in their eyes?"

I've resigned myself to what the community knows. I'm almost fatalistic about what effect it will have on me. Judy and I talked about the affair when it first hit. It didn't seem to bother her that much then. She was trying not to be judgmental like her father, the good Reverend. How could I be so dumb? I've been more worried about the business than my marriage. Why didn't I think about Judy? To hell with whether the people of Dewers will still buy cars from me. Will Judy be there? My record may be erased on paper, but it still gets a grade on Judy's card.

Judy continues, "It's not all *que sera, sera*. We can't wish away the ill will of the town. Your behavior has brought the people of this town into a new reality and they don't want to be there. They don't want us there -- me or you." At this point she stops pacing, takes a deep breath, blows it out through pursed lips, then sits back on the couch. She takes one of the green throw pillows and holds it in her lap. She looks like a child holding their Teddy bear. "A plea bargain will not erase that journey like it will erase your record. What have you five got to offer the town? At least Moses offered manna to his followers when he forced them into the desert. They were given the Ten Commandments. They were rewarded with food and the support of God if they followed His rules."

I can't read Judy on this. Her lips have turned slightly down, not quite a frown and she's biting her upper lip. Is she's angry with me for not coming home? Does she want some kind of public apology to the town? I'm becoming frustrated, and I'm terse in my reply. "Yes, Dewers is in a different place than where they were a year ago, but what do you expect me to offer them?"

Judy takes another deep breath that seems to melt some of the ice in her eyes, but her expression is still stern. "I may not have always agreed with my dad, but his sermons, his morality, taught me a basic principle. Dad said that when you drag a soul through the temptations of evil, the lure of Satan, there must be something other than hellfire and damnation on the other side. There has to be some enticement to change." Her eyes soften and start to sparkle. I think tears are forming. I'm not sure if they are for us or if she is remembering fond memories of her childhood. "For Dad it was the promise of a life spent with Christ, with God. He would tell his parishioners that having endured evil and Satan, they have the mighty sword of God to protect and guide them. My point is, there needs to be some reward for the journey, for me and for the town. What's in this for me?"

The town? It should be this town's ability to see beyond their narrow, bigoted view of the world. I, for one, know there is no assurance of a static world. What the hell do I say to Judy? She wants some answers now, but I don't think I have any.

Judy doesn't wait for an answer. Her speech is rapid. She spits the words at me. "What is *your* road back to acceptance for me, for the community, for your customers? How do *you* restore your credibility and how do we return to a normal life?" The emphasis is on we. "We cannot pretend either one of us is the same. I can't speak for you, but I know this affair has changed me, changed our relationship."

An apology is all I know to say. "I admit I've not thought as much about you as I should have. I'm sorry."

Judy puts her hand on my knee. Though her words are no less angry. "You're sorry. Is that all you've got to say? You think that will solve all of this? Say you're sorry and everything will be okay? I'm worried about the business. I'm worried for you. Your father's answer to stress was drinking and gambling. I don't want that to be your reward. I'm not ready to give you up to either of those, but I will if that's all you can say."

"Do you think I would make the same mistake as my father?"

Judy puts both hands to her forehead and with her mouth slightly open, she thinks. She then removes her hands and clutches her left first in the palm or her right hand. "I don't know. I'm concerned. This affair has created a lot of anxiety in me. I don't know if I should walk out the door and never look back. Should I send you out the door? Will you turn to alcohol? I don't know, and I don't think you do either. You like to drink. You went to a bar tonight. Can you keep that under control?"

"I'm not my father. I think I've proven that."

Judy puts the throw pillow back on the couch. She gestures with her left hand, pushing it toward me, palm up. "Have you? Isn't your sex an addiction? I don't think you've been under this much stress before. If it doesn't unsettle you, it unsettles me."

"I'm telling you I won't. Have I failed in our twenty-five years of marriage?"

Judy's deep breath is followed by a long sigh. "I didn't know you were having an affair, and I wonder what else I don't know. What else do you do on those trips for car shows? What do you and your friends do in the hotel in the evenings? I'm sure there was some sex involved. Was there also drinking?" Judy grips my hand in hers and looks directly into my eyes. It's not a sign of affection but a warning. It sounds like her father preaching. " I'm wondering if I really know who you are."

"I admit there was sex at the shows. There always seemed to be other men interested. Not other dealers, I know better than that." Judy rolls her eyes then looks away from me. She gazes at the mantel clock. "They were businessmen staying in the hotel, and sometimes it was local men looking for sex. I may have had one or two beers, but that was the extent of it. I worked hard to undo the damage my father did to the business. How can I convince you I won't make the same mistakes he did?"

Judy is not prone to crying, but as she turns back to face me, tears are forming in her eyes. She picks up the pillow again and grips it. "I don't know that. You can't deny that this affair won't affect business. Your dad didn't think his drinking and gambling were causing any damage." Judy slams the pillow on the couch between the two of us. "I'm not sure you can promise me anything right now. I want what we were. I want you as mine. I ... I ... want us to be a normal couple again. I don't want to wonder what you're doing when business is slow. I don't want to picture you in a hotel restroom looking for sex. I don't want to picture you at a bar drinking." At this point she pauses and looks directly into my eyes. "I can't picture myself without you. I want the heaven Dad promised his parishioners and me. I don't want to be in this hell. I don't want Dad to be right about you."

I don't want her dad to be right about me either. I didn't want to be in those restrooms thinking of being caught, thinking of having to be here explaining myself. I respond, "I need to go to the dealership meetings and the shows if I'm to stay in business. I can't stay home. As for during slow business days, there's not a place to go anymore. The restrooms are closed."

"What kind of an answer is that? The courthouse restrooms are closed. Do you think I don't know that there are other places: rest stops, department store restrooms, bigger cities nearby?

"At least there's AA for alcoholics." Judy dabs at her eyes with the tissue, tents her hands across her lips and looks up as if in prayer. "I'm willing to work this out. I don't want to live alone. I don't want to lose you, but, if this doesn't stop, I'm gone."

I'm thinking of Judy's earlier discussion. What does she get for going through this affair? We're not there yet, but maybe a closer relationship is what we get. I grab another tissue from the box and wave it like a flag. "Truce, I surrender. Right now I cannot see any redemption for me except being truthful. And truth is all I can offer Dewers. But for you I can add respect, admiration, and love. Yes, I think, we'll need counseling. We'll also need help with what to tell the kids."

With sarcasm, Judy says, "We all deserve the truth. Truth may redeem you, if you really tell the truth. Do you even know what that is yet? You haven't shown me that you do."

Chapter 27

Clara May on Thomas and Sue

"Are you getting out of the car with that hat on, Frieda?"

"I certainly am. That's what I brought it for. Of course you won't need any disguise. Ask any high school graduate -- they'll tell you they already know you're a witch."

"Unless you want to walk home, I suggest you button up your lip."

Frieda tightly closes her mouth and uses her hand like she's locking it shut, but before she can complete it she notices Thomas and has to speak. "Clara May look. Over there, isn't that Thomas with his wife, Sue?"

I follow Frieda's pointing finger. "It is. I'm glad he has the gumption to come out and be with his wife and kids. I just hope he didn't drink too much at the bar."

"I doubt Sue would let him stay with her and kids if he had. Besides, his parents are there, too. His dad will not put up with Thomas being drunk in public."

We walk The Square looking at the decorated windows and watch the kids trick-or-treating at the stores. I almost knock over Pastor Jenkins, who is gawking at an adorable princess. "Watch where you're going, Clara May. You almost knocked me over."

I am not in the mood for Pastor Jenkins tonight. I look over at Frieda and roll my eyes. She gives me a downward glance that says, *behave yourself.* "Why Pastor Jenkins, how nice it is to see you out and about. I thought you might be protesting such a pagan affair as Halloween."

"You of all people should know Clara May, Halloween stands for All Hallows' Eve, the night before All Souls' Day. Did you know souling was the root of trick-or-treating?"

"No, I didn't, but I'm sure you'll tell me."

Pastor Jenkins continues as if he never heard me. "Poor people, often children, went door-to-door on All Saints'/All Souls' Day collecting soul cakes. It was a means of praying for souls in purgatory. It was believed souls of the departed wandered the earth until All Saints' Day. All Hallows' Eve provided one last chance for the dead to gain vengeance on their enemies before moving to the next world. In order to avoid being recognized by any soul that might be seeking such vengeance, people wore masks or costumes as a disguise so no one would know their true identities."

I turn to Frieda who is shaking her head no. I guess we should have stopped for that costume. Maybe the Pastor would not have recognized me and I could have avoided a sermon. "Maybe you could work that into a sermon. It would be a welcome reprieve from the subject of sinful sex." Pastor Jenkins purses his lips and lets out a long breath. His narrow split eyes tell me he's not pleased with my comment.

"Clara May, you better hope someone gathers soul cakes for you when you're gone," says Pastor Jenkins.

"I don't think it's me that'll need them Pastor. Now if you'll excuse me, I've got to catch up with sinful Thomas before the devil grabs him and takes him to the depths of hell. You think I should bake up a batch of soul cakes and bring them to church next week? I'm sure you could give me the recipe. You could bless them before I pass them out. I'll bake some for you, when it's your time."

Pastor Jenkins turns sharply and stomps away like a kid who has not gotten his way. Frieda has turned her back to us looking at a decorated window. I can hear her muffled snickers. "It's okay to come out now, witch Frieda."

Frieda is laughing. "I guess you don't need me to put a spell on Pastor Jenkins. You did a pretty good job of doing that yourself."

"I'll be baking no soul cakes for him. That's for sure."

"That's not very Christian," says Frieda.

"Neither is he," I reply. "Hurry up. Waddle a little faster. I want to catch up with Thomas to see if we can hear anything."

"You're not going to ask him questions about the affair in front of his family, I hope."

"I'm hungry for information Frieda, but I'm not cruel," I say.

"Could have fooled me with Pastor Jenkins."

We catch up with Thomas and Sue in front of Montgomery Ward. They are holding hands as if they are the ideal married couple. The kids are pulling candy out of their buckets, showing it to their grandparents, and begging their mom and dad to let them eat it. We'll get no tidbits from them tonight. I reckon there will be some discussion tonight after the kids fall into a sugar-induced sleep coma.

Chapter 28

Thomas and Sue

I make it to The Square in time and find Sue and the kids in front of Montgomery Ward. I was hoping to be alone with them, but Mom and Dad are there. Jimmy and Jane see me and come running. Both speak, "Dad, Dad, you made it! Wanna see my candy? Do you like our costumes? Isn't this fun?"

"You both look great. Got any chocolate for me in your buckets?"

Jimmy digs into his candy and comes up with a small Hershey chocolate bar. "Just one, okay? The rest are for me."

"Let me see that bucket. How many you got in there?"

Jimmy holds the bucket of candy close to his chest covering it with his free hand. Jane looks at Jimmy and says, "You're selfish. You've got lots of candy."

"No, I don't," Jimmy responds. "You're selfish. You haven't given Dad anything."

Jane reaches in her bucket and gives me a Tootsie Roll. "Is this okay?"

"Anything you give me is okay."

Sue starts to kiss me on the cheek and then stops. She looks me in the eye and gently shakes her head back and forth while rolling her eyes. "Kids, why don't you take Grandma and Grandpa inside. Do some trick-or-treating. I hear they have good stuff here. I saw it this afternoon when I was in town."

Mom takes them by the hand and leads them in, but not before giving me one of her looks -- the one that says, *I know where you've been.* Dad follows but doesn't look at me.

Sue takes my hand, but I think it's for show. God forbid someone should see us fighting. There is no tenderness in the touch. Does this mean she's working up the nerve to ask me to leave? She asks, "Where did you go? I thought you were coming to the house first for supper so we could drive up together. You just left."

Sue wants to upset me, wants all the people on The Square tonight to know I'm not a good husband. Well, I think they already know. I tell her, "I don't want to have this discussion here, Sue."

Sue starts with the accusations anyway. Her index finger is outstretched. Her arm turns in small circles, and then she jabs a finger at my chest. "I smell it on your breath. You were at the bar again. It's got to stop. Don't you think of us? Don't you think the town knows when you're not with us?"

Sue won't stop badgering me about drinking. She thinks I've become an alcoholic. I haven't. I don't see where it interferes with my farming. She tells me I should be at home, not in a bar. What does she expect? It's the only escape I get. I comment, "I said I don't want to talk about it here."

Sue won't stop. "Well I do, and I am. You can't get angry here and storm off. There are too many people watching. Look, Clara May is over there with Frieda. They'll be sure to notice."

I look. Clara May and Frieda both wave. "Sue, they're harmless. They keep the rest of the town honest."

"Exactly my point. You won't get angry in front of them. They couldn't deny it when people commented on it."

The kids exit Montgomery Ward with my parents, so the conversation abruptly ends. My mom speaks, "It's nice to see you could make it. I thought you were going to try and finish the field, but I saw you quit early and drive off."

About this time I'm wishing I had stayed in the bar. I shoot Mom a look with squinted eyes and a firm tight mouth that says enough. "I needed to find out what happened today."

I'm sure Mom wants to create a scene. I tell Sue to take the kids into Woolworths and I go lean on the hood of a parked car to finish my smoke. As I expected, Mom takes advantage of them being gone and walks over to me. "What were you doing at the bar? You should have been home with your kids. What you needed was to support your wife. What you didn't need was another beer."

First Sue and now my mother, a record: I get two lectures on the evils of drinking in one night. "How do you even know I had a beer?"

Mom sighs and lets out a long exaggerated breath. "When do you not think you need a beer? I know where you go when you leave. Where else do you guys meet but in a bar?"

I take another drag on the cigarette and blow out the smoke before I speak. "Would you have us meet here on The Square in front of the kids, their parents?"

Dad walks over to the car, pulls out a Camel cigarette and offers one to Mom. He lights hers and then speaks. "Tonight is for the kids. We're not having this discussion here."

Mom takes a deep drag, releases the smoke like a steam engine climbing a hill, and then, looking at Dad, she speaks. "That's it, stand up for him. Honestly, you men."

Dad takes the cigarette out of his mouth, pointing it at Mom. "Enough Dorothy. Do you understand? Enough." He then turns to me. "This night is for you, Sue, and the kids. Your mom and I are going home. Talk to Sue tonight. Don't let it fester."

Dad takes Mom's elbow and leads her to their car. That will the last I hear from Mom for a few days. She can only go so far before Dad reels her in. He'll keep close watch over her for a while.

The kids come out of Woolworths all smiles. Jane is the first to notice Mom and Dad are gone. "Where's Grandma and Grandpa?"

"They were tired and went home. Said you could show them your candy tomorrow, if there's any left by then."

Jimmy's eyes grew wide. "You mean we can eat it all tonight?"

Sue speaks, "No, young man, no. You're not eating it all tonight. Remember when you had too much ice cream and threw up all night?"

"Oh, yeah. I forgot, but I'm older now."

"So, what's left guys? What haven't you done yet?"

Jenny starts jumping up and down. "We've got to go to the courthouse lawn. They've got apple bobbing and a scary house."

I notice Sue visibly shivers when she hears the word courthouse. I take her hand and give it a firm grasp. She pushes it away. Reluctantly, she goes to the courthouse lawn. While the kids are bobbing for apples, we talk. "Sue, you can't avoid the courthouse. You come to The Square to shop. We have to file taxes here. It's a part of this community. The only way you won't see it is if we move. I'm in no position for a move, and I don't think you are either."

Sue stands with her back to the courthouse. "I can't look at it without thinking of what went on there. I see you ... doing ... doing ... whatever it is you do with men."

I see Bob with his kids at the haunted house and wave. Did anyone notice? What a way to draw attention to ourselves. Damn it, I can't even wave at a friend without feeling guilty, without wondering what other people are thinking. My thoughts are interrupted. Jimmy and Jane return, each with an apple. "Are you two ready to go home? Looks like your buckets are full."

Jimmy replies, "Okay, Dad. I'm kind of tired."

Jane has to get her dig. "Spoiled sport."

"No, I'm not. Tell her I'm not, Mom."

Sue says, "You're both tired and we're going home. I don't want to hear any more from either one of you."

Jimmy starts whining. "I don't want to ride with you. Why can't I ride with Dad in the truck?"

Sue looks at me and mouths the words, "Don't you say a thing." She then turns to Jimmy. "Because I said so, that's why."

I walk them to Sue's car. Once the kids are inside, I speak to Sue. "What's the matter with Jimmy riding home with me?"

Sue shakes her head back and forth and then she exhales loudly. "Do you really need to ask? I don't want either one of them riding with you when you've been drinking!"

I don't argue. It's not worth it. It would only upset the kids. I welcome the few minutes of solitude. Sue always thinks I've had too much to drink. There will be an argument with her when we get home. I try to think of what to say, what she'll say. Nothing comes.

When I get home, Sue has parked the car in the garage. Jane is standing at the kitchen door pouting because she wanted to stay longer and Jimmy is asleep in the back seat of the car. I carry Jimmy into the house behind Sue and Jane. Jimmy wakes up and wants a bedtime story. "You and Jane get into your pj's and I'll tell you a ghost story."

I make it short, partially because they're sleepy, but mostly because I want to talk to Sue. Once they are both in bed with their doors closed, I go to our bedroom where Sue is already undressed and in bed. "Sue, we need to talk. Tonight."

Sue spits out the words. "Go ahead. You talk. I'll listen. That's what you do best. You're all talk, all apologies, saying 'I'll be better.' When are those better times coming?"

I light another cigarette, inhale deeply, and try to be calm. Both of us speaking in anger will go nowhere. We're like two bulls butting each other or dogs peeing to mark their territory. "There's no use talking about the bar. You know I was there. Bob says there will probably be a small fine and probation if we plead guilty."

Sue grabs the covers, throws them to the end of bed, and then turns and sits up. She's wearing red flannel pajamas. What happened to negligées? "You are guilty. How could you say otherwise? And stop looking at what I'm wearing. The last thing on my mind is wearing some sexy something to bed."

I would like to see her in something other than flannel, but I'm not going to say anything. I back up and sit on the bench at her dressing table. "Yes, I'm guilty. I'm guilty of being unsure of myself. I'm guilty of wanting to go into the Navy, to see the world, to have some time away from Dewers. I'm guilty of wanting to stay in the Navy, never marrying you, never coming home again." I pull out a Camel from my pack, put it between my lips to light, but instead take it out and wave it at Sue. "I'm guilty of a sexual desire greater than yours, guilty of finding satisfaction in ways not everyone agrees with. I'm guilty of cheating on you." I notice I've been waving the cigarette at Sue, place it back in my mouth, and light it.

Sue sits up in bed. I can see wrinkles around her eyes and fine lines at the corner of her mouth. Have I done this to her? I don't remember seeing them before. She speaks. "What makes you think I'm not interested in sex? Let me see. I wash your clothes. I wash the kid's clothes. I cook food for all of you. I clean the house. Did you ever think I'm too tired?" Sue gets up close. I can feel her breath as she speaks. "And I'm a fool for thinking you'd be anymore than what you are. I stayed home because I believe you wanted to come back to me." She stands up and looks out into the dark through the window.

She speaks without looking at me. "I let you have your wanderlust and it left me in the cold. Am I going to be a bigger fool for staying with you?"

As much as I want to be with the kids, ending it now would be an easy way out but I can't say that. I'm not ready to face life without Sue. My response is, "I hope not."

Sue turns from the window to face me. "I've never been further than Chicago. I'm a country girl. I've no desire to be anything else. I know nothing of the world you found in the Navy. Maybe one day I'll want to know, but right now, I'm comfortable in Dewers." Sue sits on the edge of the bed, scratches her scalp, and then rests her head in her fingertips as she rubs her eyes. "If you need to go, go. The kids and I will get along fine. I know I can get a job. My parents will let me move back home."

Crushing my cigarette in the ashtray, I stand to face her. "You've never had any interest in being alone. Since high school you wanted to get married. I thought your graduation goal was to find a man to be your husband."

"Yes, to find a *man* to be a *husband*, with an emphasis on man and husband." Sue's voice rises. "Recently you haven't been either one. A husband forsakes all others. He loves, honors, and cherishes his wife. A man has integrity. Can you say yes to any one of these?"

"Ah ... I guess I can't at this moment." I pause. "I did once. I had good intentions when I spoke those vows. I liked the freedom in the Navy, but I didn't like myself much. I thought coming home to you would change that and it did, for a while."

Sue uses her thumbs to rub her temples, looks down with closed eyes, and then speaks. "And then what happened, Thomas? Were you using me to see if you could become who you wanted to be? Or were you using me to avoid who you wanted to be? Which is it Thomas? I'm tired of living your lie. Do you even know it's a lie?"

It's my turn to look into the night. I think I'd like to be hidden in the dark -- anywhere but here -- but I know that's not true. I've wanted this conversation since I came home from the Navy. "Up until the day I was arrested, I felt I was playing at living. It was as if I was in a game of make-believe and I couldn't escape. I didn't enlist in the Navy because I wanted to be a sailor but because I wanted to leave Dewers. I left the Navy not because I wanted to come back to Dewers but because I didn't like the man I was becoming." I walk to the bed, sit, and face Sue. "I married you because I thought I loved you and that's what you do when you live here. And I married you because being a loving husband was the man I wanted to be. He was the role I was playing. I wanted anonymous sex, not because I wanted men, but because I'm not sure marriage is what I want anymore."

Sue goes to the closet and gets a pillow and blanket. She gives it to me. "I'm not playing house with you. I know I want a man who wants me, and unless you're that man you don't sleep with me."

"I want to be that man. I'm just not sure how to get there."

"You get there by being truthful. You recognize you're escaping through alcohol. I can't do that for you. You have to want it. The change has to come from you."

Just a few minutes earlier I was standing over Sue. She was looking up to me from the bed. Now I'm on the bed looking up at Sue. I feel inadequate, small. "But I do want it. The arrest woke me up from my dream world. I know I want a family. I want a wife. I want to be proud of who I am. I want you to satisfy me sexually. I want to feel comfortable in your arms but I'm not there yet."

Sue puts the pillow and blanket in my lap and then speaks. "I want a man who wants me and no one else. When you're that man, you can bring your pillow and blanket back to this bed."

"What do we tell the kids? Won't they know I'm not sleeping with you?"

"No, they won't. You're going to sleep on the couch. I'll make sure you're awake early. They won't see you've been sleeping on the couch. There's no use upsetting them any more than this affair has already. And if they find out, make up a story. That is your specialty. Isn't it?"

"Will you go to counseling with me if the court orders it?" I ask.

"Truth Thomas, truth -- you'll have to tell a counselor the truth. Your fairy tale world is over. Come join us in the real world. None of us gets everything we want."

Chapter 29

Danny and Clara May

I can't remember getting into my truck. I can't remember going through town. I can't remember turning off the highway to my house. Good thing my name is on the mailbox, otherwise I might not have known the house

Once inside the back porch, Tiger realizes I'm home and wants out. As soon as I unlock the back door, she rushes out and wraps herself around my feet and legs a few times before scurrying off to the yard. I grab the broom and sweep the snow from the steps and before I'm done Tiger's back. "Cold isn't it? Let's go in then where it's warmer."

When I open the door again, Tiger rushes in to find her favorite spot over the living room heat vent. By the time I get there, she's happily rolled into a furry ball with a contented purr. "You've got it good, Tiger. You know that? I don't track your whereabouts when you go out to roam. You don't ask me questions about where I've been. You just want your ears rubbed, your tummy patted, and of course, a full food bowl."

Tiger uncurls enough to look at me with her green eyes and gives me a big yawn as if saying, "Yeah, yeah, so what?"

"Tiger, don't get up. I forgot to check on the mail." At the mailbox, I find the daily paper along with an envelope from Clara May. After returning to the house, I flip through the paper to see if there is anything about the trial. Since the paper is rarely over 10 pages, this only takes a moment. Good, there is nothing today.

Now, what is it that Clara May has to say? Inside the envelope she has written me a note. Her handwriting is beautiful -- learned I'm sure by many hours in grade school drawing circles and lines. *Danny, I'm sure by this time you've talked with Bob and know the outcome of his trial. If you want to talk, come by in the morning and I'll make some biscuits with gravy.* I'm glad Clara May offered. I need to talk to someone not involved in the trial. I'll go in the morning, but right now I need to sleep.

I wake to a chilly house and a bright day. After making a pot of coffee, I turn up the thermostat and let Tiger out. The light snowfall is still pristine on the grass and trees. I'm reminded of the song, "Over the river and through the woods to Grandmother's house we go." I'm at Grandma's house so there is no need to travel, but unfortunately Grandma is not here. Clara May is a good substitute. I pour myself a cup of coffee and head to the hallway to call her.

"Morning, Clara May. Are you up? ... No, I knew you'd be, but it's always polite to ask ... I was late getting home. It was probably around 7 or 8 p.m. ... I went to the Washington Street Bar to talk with Bob and the boys ... yes, you're right it's a good place for no one to see us ... I'd love some of your homemade biscuits. I'll be over in about a half hour."

After letting Tiger in, I take a quick shower and change into my work clothes because I probably won't get back home before going in to the bar this afternoon. Clara May and I have a lot to talk about.

Clara May's house is only about a mile down the road. She lives in the farmhouse her father built, a large Victorian, and as most houses of that period, it faces the road. A hitching post remains at the edge of the road, a reminder of the days when visitors would come with horse and buggy, tie up the horses at a hitching post, and then follow the brick walk to the front door. Cars don't park on the side of the road but go into the side driveway and park near the back door. Elegant front hallways are rarely used anymore.

As I park the truck, I imagine Clara May with her eight brothers and sisters running in the large yard chasing fireflies, greeting visitors as they tie up their buggy, or sitting on the front porch swing eating watermelon, and seeing who can spit seeds the farthest. Her father built an addition to the house to accommodate the growing family. In the wooded area behind the house is a family cemetery where her mom, dad, brothers, and sisters are buried. Clara May is the last and is now alone in the rambling house. In the winter she closes off the upstairs and sleeps in a small bedroom downstairs. I see her pulling the kitchen lace curtain aside now and waving at me.

I walk along the stone path to her back porch and notice that her well-maintained flowerbeds have not survived this cold snap. Proud gold and red mums that once stood erect are now drooping as if tired and ready to retreat. The remnants of her vegetables are weeping. The tomatoes have borne fruit and are canned. I would imagine the green ones that hung on until the end are pickling in brine somewhere in her kitchen.

As I reached the screened in back porch, Clara May is there in a flowered apron with ruffles to open the door. "Come on in. Coffee is on the stove and biscuits are in the oven."

Most likely her coffee has been on the side of the old cast iron cook stove since early morning. Clara May said it was just in her nature to get up with the chickens. Growing up on the farm you get up when it's light and you go to bed when it's dark. The kitchen is warm, smells of coffee and bread. Just as always, the coffee's on the side of the stove in a blue speckled enamel coffee pot. There's a coffee mug sitting atop the water well of the cook stove. "I take it you've got this cup warming up for me. I'll just pour myself a cup of coffee."

Clara May's busy at the other end of the stove frying some thick slab bacon in a black cast iron skillet older than she is. "That cup's yours. Same one I give to you all the time. I know you don't like my fancy china because you have to get up too often to refill the cup. Go have a seat at the table yonder while I finish the bacon."

Some things never change. The coffee's strong. It's been slowly evaporating on the back of the stove. Clara May occasionally adds water to it from the stove's water well, but it still needs sugar and cream. "Got any cream out?"

"Sugar's on the table. Cream's still in the Frigidaire. Help yourself. It's in the small white cow pitcher."

Her kitchen has never been modernized except for an electric stove and running water. She still brings water in from the well pump stand for drinking. She says the stuff that's piped into the house tastes funny. Clara May still has a pantry where she keeps her supplies and where the Frigidaire is located. The pantry is full of canned vegetables from her garden: green beans, stewed tomatoes, tomato juice, corn, pickles, and as I expected, a crock of green tomatoes in brine. I grab the cream, go back into the kitchen, and sit.

The kitchen table is covered with an oilcloth that has colorful turkeys and cornucopias. With one side of the round drop leaf table down it's pushed up against the wall, leaving room to seat three. "Sure smells good in here."

Clara May finishes taking out the bacon and sets the pan on the cook stove shelf before coming to the table with her coffee. She pulls out the chair next to me and has a seat. "I'm thinking about now you're needing to talk. I didn't see your truck at the bar and it wasn't at your house when I came home from the beauty parlor. I figured you were at the Washington Street Bar talking with the others."

There's very little that escapes Clara May's attention. You would think living out here in the country would make keeping up with goings on difficult, but it doesn't. "You must have eyes and ears all over this county."

"My heavens, Danny -- just the county? You underestimate me."

My face was feeling red because her smile was breaking into laughter. "I didn't want to call you a busy body or snoop."

Clara May puffs out her chest and holds her head high. "If the skillet is black don't say it's red. By now you should know Bob's wife let loose at the beauty parlor yesterday. I reckon the strain has gotten to her. Though I never thought she was screwed together too tight. There's only one thing I didn't expect or didn't already know. Did you know she's planning on asking Bob for a divorce? She says the marriage has all been a lie. And guess who comes into the parlor as she's telling her story? Bob's mom, Rose. She came in. Sat down next to Mary and told her they had to talk."

"Lightning could not shock me more. I was sure Mary would stick with Bob forever. He has the money and his family has the prestige. I guess she'll play the scorned wife."

"And she will. Enough about Bob and Mary, how are *you* doing?"

I'm not sure what Clara May knows or wants to know. Where do I begin? It's embarrassing talking about your sex life with an elderly woman. Even if that woman does drink gin and tonics with you. "What do you know, and what do you want to know?"

Clara May doesn't look embarrassed, and she's never been shy. "I know what's in the newspaper. You and the four other guys were having sex in the courthouse restroom. I'm told there may be others involved but they're not being charged due to lack of evidence. I know Mary was having an affair while Bob was having his affair."

I say, "I know. Bob talked about it last night at the bar. It was no surprise to him or any of the rest of us."

Clara May gets up to remove the biscuits from the oven. She places them on the stove then moves the skillet over and adds flour and milk to make gravy. "While I'm making the gravy, why don't you tell me your side of the story?"

I walk over to the stove for some more coffee and back to the table. After a sip and a deep breath, I begin. "I need to give you some background. You've known me since birth, but I don't think you know everything."

"Honey, I know more than you think, but go ahead."

Did people know I was weird all along? Was it that obvious? "In school I never felt a part of the boy's world. When the guys were old enough to talk about girls, I wasn't sure what to say. Dad gave me no advice and Mom did what Dad said. I had a few girlfriends because guys who didn't date were thought of as funny or faggy. The girls didn't excite me, or shall I say, didn't give me a boner … sorry."

Clara May looks over her glasses as she carries the biscuits and gravy to the table. "It's okay. I may be old, but I know a thing or two about men."

I smile and go on. "I thought I was just a late bloomer. Then a kid at school gave me a muscle magazine. He told me this was how he wanted his body to look. He thought he'd have more interest in girls if he looked like the men in the book. All they had on were shorts, and their large muscles glistened. He said he had another and let me take the book home. After I went to bed, I looked at it under the covers with a flashlight. I'd get a boner and masturbate. I wasn't sure what this meant. I only knew it made me horny to look at the pictures. And I knew if Dad found it I'd be in trouble, but you know that story."

Clara May first puts plates and food on the table, and then she sits down before speaking. There's no sign of judgment or anger in her eyes, but they're wide open in anticipation. "That was an ugly scene with your dad. Your granddad and I used to talk about it over an evening drink. Your granddad knew you were different. He thought you'd figure it out on your own."

An image of Granddad passes in front of me. He's sitting in front of the fire with his pipe and I'm on the couch. We're discussing life plans and dating comes up. "Danny, if you don't want to get married, don't let anyone push you into it. There's lots of men who don't take a liking to marriage." At the time, I wasn't sure what he was getting at. Now I know.

I return my attention to Clara May. "One day while looking for books in the library, I wondered into the adult section and came across a book on homosexual behavior. I don't remember what it was, but it described in detail my feelings. It explained what guys did together. I went back often."

Clara May drops her fork before speaking. "But where were you to find a place in Dewers to act on your new knowledge?"

"Yes. Dewers isn't exactly Chicago or New York City. I thought about going to Chicago to see if I could find anything, but how could I explain that to Granddad?"

Clara May says, "In my youth when I went to dance in Chicago a man being with a man wasn't a big thing. They didn't flaunt it in your face, but you knew it was happening. The cold war and McCarthy's witch-hunts caused havoc. We haven't been the same since. All of a sudden anyone who didn't seem to fit in was a Commie, some pervert to be destroyed. Your granddad knew you were anxious to find yourself. He just wasn't sure what it was you were trying to find, and he thought it best if you found it on your own."

"I didn't know what I was trying to find either, that is until a year ago. I was in town early to buy some new pants and needed to use the restroom, so I went over to the courthouse. There were three stalls. The center was occupied, so I took the one nearest the urinals. After I sat on the toilet, I noticed the guy next to me tapping his foot. Initially I ignored him. He tapped again, and then passed me a note under the stall. If you want a blowjob show your hard-on. This was intriguing. I'd fantasized about this but never in my wildest dreams thought it possible in Dewers. Next he placed his hand under the partition and motioned me to show. I was erect. My stomach was doing cartwheels. My heart rate was off the wall. I was beyond frightened but well into intoxication. There was no turning back. I knelt on the cold concrete floor and did as he asked.

"My ejaculation was quick. The man in the next stall rose then and left."

Clara May tilts her head from side to side and looks at me. What's she up to? I can't take it if she's judgmental. Finally she speaks. "Well, well, I'm losing the knack. I don't know everything that goes on in Dewers. A little hotsy-totsy in the restroom. You know though, doing it in a public restroom is not the smartest thing you ever did? That's worse than getting caught toilet papering the principal's house, but I think you already know that."

I'm thinking, *Hell, yes, I know.* "So, am I ruined here?"

Clara May takes the plates to the sink while answering. "So, you're gay. I don't see anything wrong with that. Others may, but I don't. One thing on your side, you own a bar. No one expects a bar owner to have moral perfection. Will the town get over it? Yes, in time. Things in this town are harder to stop than a freight train. It will eventually go away but probably never forgotten. You, young man, your job is to keep your nose clean. I don't mean you shouldn't continue to have sex. Don't do it in public."

Clara May stops a minute to finish her coffee. She continues. "You haven't said anything about how you feel. A lot's gone on and you've got to be feeling something."

We're interrupted by Clara May's phone, which gives me time to collect my thoughts. During this whole time since being arrested I had not thought much about how I felt. I have been worried about how the town felt, would the men have to get a divorce, would people still come to the bar.

Clara May returns and after sitting, looks at me. I don't know where the words come from, but I start talking. "I think I should feel shame like the rest of the town, but I don't. I don't feel guilty for the sex. I'm angry with myself for carrying on in the restroom. I should have found a safe place. I'm afraid of where I go from here.

"It's like I'm not living in the same world as everyone else. I'm not worried about prisons and psychiatric hospitals. I know what to expect there and there's eventually an end to them. From this point on, I'm afraid of life. I don't know what's going to happen now that everyone knows what I've been hiding."

Clara May's eyes widen, her face cringes, and crinkle lines appear on her forehead. "Goodness gracious, you're not thinking about suicide are you?"

I wish it were that easy. The sin of suicide is one teaching of Dad's that stuck. "No, I'm confused, but not thinking about killing myself. Ever since Granddad took me in I've known what the future held for me. Now it's muddier than the creek down the road. I know I've been longing for the affection of another man, not a woman. But where do I get that affection? All I've known are the restrooms. And worse yet, I like restroom sex. I don't want to stop it."

There is still worry apparent in the crinkles on her forehead when Clara May speaks. "I wouldn't tell that to the prosecutor or judge. They want to hear some remorse and want to think you're willing to stop."

She doesn't know how true that statement is. I respond, "I don't know if I can lie. I seem to have no control over that behavior. I'm always looking for an excuse to go the restroom, not just the courthouse, but also others. Any public restroom is fair game: in department stores, in gas stations, in rest stops on the highway, in bars. I fantasize about men in restrooms, anyone that's attached to an erect dick."

Clara May is not fazed. Her eyes are still riveted on me. "Do you think it would be different if you met a man to have an affair with? Would you like to be with a man where there is no need for secrecy? I could always tend bar for you so you could get away."

Clara May, tending bar? I couldn't help but smile. "That would be some good gossip."

"This town needs to get over itself. Back in the 40s, Blanch Gibson had a bar on Main Street and I attracted quite a crowd bartending on Saturday night."

That lightens my mood. "I may take you up on that offer."

Clara May's head is resting on her left hand and she uses her index finger to tap her cheek as she speaks. "I think you should ask Gary about going to Chicago with him. He could introduce you to someone, or at least show you where to go to meet other men. A little time out of this town could do you some good, as long as you stay out of restrooms. Public sex is illegal in Chicago, too."

That's a good idea, and I don't know why I hadn't thought of it. Glancing at the kitchen clock I notice it is time to get to the bar. "Thanks for being here for me. I've got to get to town and open the bar."

As I rise to leave, Clara May stands up, holds out her arms, and gives me a hug with a kiss on the cheek. She gives me some final advice, "Stay away from your dad for awhile. You don't need his form of Christianity. He's basically a good man and I think he will come around in time."

Chapter 30

Clara May on Pastor Jenkins

When it comes to Pastor Jenkins, Frieda and I have agreed to disagree. Over coffee after church the other day, she brought up the subject. "Clara May, why are you so hard on Pastor Jenkins? He's just doing his job, calling people to task when they stray. I don't agree with him, but he has a right to interpret things his way. The church is not exactly liberal."

Frieda has beady, squinted eyes and the hint of a pout when she thinks she's right. I told her, "Get the self-righteous smug off your face. Ministers should be tending their flock, forgiving them, welcoming them with the grace of God."

I told her to drop it there, because this discussion will go nowhere in changing either of our opinions. But in true Frieda behavior, she doesn't let it go. "He's just keeping us to the Bible teachings. Following the rules set down by God."

"So I guess then you believe the Bible to be the exact word of God?"

"No, I believe they're God-inspired."

"Let me see. You've never taken God's name in vain? You've never coveted something someone else has? I know you want my grandmother's teapot. Paul says women should be quiet, not to speak in church affairs. What about adultery? Where are the good Pastor's sermons on these topics?"

Frieda asks, "Why do you keep coming to church if you dislike him so much?"

"I want to see what his latest rant is. I want to be sitting in the pews when he looks out over the congregation and have him wonder what I might be up to next. He needs to know someone is paying attention to his sermons and finding them falling short."

"Honestly, Clara May, if you feel that way, why not go to the Universalist church down the street?"

"They're way too far in the other direction. All churches have their faults. I might as well stay with one I know. I don't want to deal with some other minister's problems."

Frieda shakes her head and sighs. "Honestly, Goldie Locks, I'm not sure what you're looking for."

"I don't either, but I'll know when I find it."

Chapter 31

Pastor Jenkins: Dorothy and Joe Turnball

Living across the road from Thomas and Sue initially seemed like a good idea. We could be close to our son and his wife as well as help with the kids; but since this affair, it has become stressful – for them *and* us. Dorothy, my wife, is constantly checking on Thomas's whereabouts. She bugs him about his drinking and every time he leaves the house alone, she's sure he's headed to bar and hitting the bottle. And as for me, it was hard giving up most of my farming to Thomas. I want to tell him when he should plant, when it's best to harvest, and when's the best time to sell crops. I know alcohol won't solve his problems, but Thomas will have to come to the conclusion himself. I want to be a supportive father, but I don't want Thomas to think I'm trying to tell him what to do.

As we pull out of our driveway on the way to church, I glance across the road to see if our son and daughter-in-law are also leaving for church. I tell Dorothy, "Looks like they're not going again. A lot of good your prayer list is doing. How long are you keeping them on it?"

"How long am I going to have to keep them on it? I won't let anyone take them off until I'm satisfied." Dorothy sighs deeply, causing the veil on her black hat to flutter."They haven't been to church since this whole thing started. Why should it be any different today? I wish they'd let us take the kids to Sunday school. And just so you know, I plan to keep them on the prayer list. How do you know it hasn't helped?"

I light a cigarette, roll the window down a bit and inhale deeply, hold the smoke in my lungs to get the maximum effect and then respond to my wife. "He's a grown man. If he wants God's help, I reckon he can ask for it. We did what we could so he'd have a good upbringing. Untie the apron strings. They're getting frayed. What he does now he does on his own. But the kids, you're right. I don't want them thinking anything that makes them feel good is okay. There are limits."

Dorothy opens her purse and takes out one of her cigarettes. She reaches for the cigarette lighter and pushes it in. She fidgets with her cigarette between her fingers, rocking it back and forth, until the lighter finally pops. She lights it, inhales, and through squinted eyes, watches the exhaled smoke drift out the window wing. "We've got to talk to them about the kids. I want to know what they know, what they've been told. I'm sure it's being talked about on the playground. One of Jane's best friends is Mary Beth's daughter Joy, and you know Mary Beth can't keep her mouth shut. I'm sure she's tried to get her daughter to pump information out of Jane. I heard the police went to all the schools and talked with the kids about the dangers of sexual predators, specifically men and young boys."

I notice there are long ashes on my cigarette and flick them out the window. "Aren't our grandkids too young to get that talk in grade school? Someone should say something, though. You know what I hate most about this, Dorothy?"

Dorothy seems agitated, still bouncing the now lit cigarette between her fingers. "There's a lot to hate about the affair. I for one don't know where to start."

I cut in. "I don't know who to blame, but I'll start with how it bothers me. The only place or event where men can gather as a group these days is church. There are only so many men's Bible studies I can go to. We're suspect if we go fishing as a group. Poker night is a bust. No one wants to go. It was suggested we include a woman so it would look better. I'm not having a woman in my poker club." Mark asked me the other day when was this whole business going to be done. He was tired of the suspicion of being with a group of men. I think he might have been blaming me for his forced isolation. I turn back to Dorothy, "To hell with it all." With those words I sling my cigarette out the window and roll it up. The conversation is over.

Dorothy knows not to break this forced silence. She finishes her cigarette, crushes it in the ashtray, and then looks out the car window at the empty fields.

We slip into our pew just as Mabel is finishing the prelude with a flourish. The near late arrival is planned. We have no intention of being denied the right to attend worship, but we don't have to arrive early and be subjected to pity stares or questions that try to get us to talk about the affair.

Dorothy is annoyed and whispers to me, "I don't like coming in late. I want to hear what people are saying."

"Well, I don't. Come by yourself if you want to come early."

Dorothy studies the bulletin. I think she wants to make sure no one took Thomas off the prayer list. She comments to no one in particular, "They're still there."

I frown at Dorothy, squinting my eyes. I hold up my right index finger. "Hush. Pastor Jenkins is starting."

As pastor Jenkins walks to the pulpit, the congregation stands. "Let us pray. In the name of God, who loves us, we open our hearts. In the name of Jesus Christ, who gathers us and redeems us, we open our minds. In the name of the Holy Spirit, who enlivens us, we open our doors to the God who dwells among us. Now let us sing hymn 687, *A Mighty Fortress Is Our God.*"

This is my first opportunity to look around the church and it's almost full this morning. Perhaps it's because most of the crops are in. Perhaps they're all looking for a piece of gossip. "Dorothy, why do you think the church is so full this morning?"

Dorothy leans to whisper in my ear. I can smell the lingering cigarette smoke along with her Avon perfume, Elusive. "To show their righteous indignation, as they should. We're here to pray for forgiveness and to pray that Thomas sees the way of his sin."

"You think so. I don't need to be forgiven. I didn't have the affair." I want to laugh, and then again, I want to scream. I want to say, *Here we are. Here are the parents that you think went wrong. There she is, Dorothy, the domineering mother who castrated her son because of her inattentive husband. Here I am -- the son of a bitch father and husband. You know -- the one who couldn't bond with his son, couldn't pass on his masculinity. Go ahead stare; that's it stare at us. We've all read the Time article, heard the report on television. Every set in Dewers was probably tuned to the Mike Wallace report.*

As the singing stops, I'm brought back to the worship and Pastor Jenkins. "Let us now have a reading of the Psalms."

Deacon Jim rises from his chair and approaches the lectern,

"The 31stPsalm:
To the Chief Musician.
In You, O LORD, I put my trust;
Let me never be ashamed;
Deliver me in Your righteousness.
Bow down Your ear to me,
Deliver me speedily;
Be my rock of refuge,
A fortress of defense to save me.
For You are my rock and my fortress;
Therefore, for Your name's sake,
Lead me and guide me ..."

I begin to lose track of time, partly because Jim's voice puts me to sleep and partly because I'm not in the mood to pay attention. I notice William and Rose Thompson. They used to sit in the front pew. They're now in the back with us. He gives me a nod and I nod back. Sitting in the very last pew are Clara May and Frieda. They always sit there so they can watch the parishioners. Clara May waves a gloved hand. I acknowledge her with a wave of my index finger. Frieda starts pointing and Clara May pats Frieda's hand.

Wait. What did I just hear Jim read?

"For I hear the slander of many..."

Hell yes, I hear the slander of most of the people sitting in these pews. Maybe there's something in this Psalm I should hear.

"Deliver me from the hand of my enemies,
And from those who persecute me.
Make Your face shine upon Your servant;
Save me for Your mercies' sake.
Do not let me be ashamed, O LORD, for I have called upon You;
Let the wicked be ashamed ..."

With a clenched fist and furrowed forehead, I look at Dorothy. She whispers, "What's wrong?"

I attempt to keep my voice low. "What's wrong? I have a feeling this whole service is going to be about the affair, about us." Then in a voice too loud, "That's what's wrong!"

Several heads turn and look at us. There are a few shushes. Clara May looks at us, puts an index finger to mouth, and shakes her head no. Thankfully, Jim descends from the altar and takes a seat with his wife in the first pew. Mabel cranks up the organ for the choir. When that's finished, Mark approaches the lectern for the Old Testament reading from the book of Leviticus,

"Leviticus 18:20-30. *"Thou shalt not lie with mankind, as with womankind: it is abomination. Neither shalt thou lie with any beast to defile thyself therewith: neither shall any woman stand before a beast to lie down thereto: it is confusion. Defile not ye yourselves in any of these things: for in all these the nations are defiled which I cast out before you: And the land is defiled: therefore I do visit the iniquity thereof upon it, and the land itself vomiteth out her inhabitants.*

And just how is my land defiled? The land would be fine if Thomas kept his mind on it. He spends too much time at the bar. Hell! I don't like the way this church service is headed.

Ye shall therefore keep my statutes and my judgments, and shall not commit any of these abominations; neither any of your own nation, nor any stranger that sojourneth among you: (For all these abominations have the men of the land done, which were before you, and the land is defiled); that the land spew not you out also, when ye defile it, as it spewed out the nations that were before you. For whosoever shall commit any of these abominations, even the souls that commit them shall be cut off from among their people.

I'd say the community has done a good job of shutting us out with referring to the Bible. It's not that people don't talk to us. They do, but they are not concerned about our welfare. They want information on the trial, on the men's lives. There must be somewhere in the Bible where it says thou shalt not gossip.

Therefore shall ye keep mine ordinance, that ye commit not any one of these abominable customs, which were committed before you, and that ye defile not yourselves therein: I am the LORD your God."

I lean over to Dorothy, "This is going to be a stern sermon from Jenkins today."

She puts her index finger to pursed lips, quietly shushes me, and then whispers, "Don't get people looking at us again."

Pastor Jenkins rises to read passages from the New Testament.

"1 Corinthians 6:9-10, *Know ye not that the unrighteous shall not inherit the kingdom of God? Be not deceived: neither fornicators, nor idolaters, nor adulterers, nor effeminate, nor abusers of themselves with mankind, nor thieves, nor covetous, nor drunkards, nor revilers, nor extortioners, shall inherit the kingdom of God."*

"1 John 3.8-10. *He that committeth sin is of the devil; for the devil sinneth from the beginning. For this purpose the Son of God was manifested, that he might destroy the works of the devil. Whosoever is born of God doth not commit sin; for his seed remaineth in him: and he cannot sin, because he is born of God. In this the children of God are manifest, and the children of the devil: whosoever doeth not righteousness is not of God, neither he that loveth not his brother."*

Pastor Jenkins must have searched the Bible to find every passage to suit his sermon today. How many other evil behaviors are there in the Bible that he chooses to ignore? I'm sure Clara May has already asked him that question. I'll have to talk to her.

Pastor Jenkins places the Bible on the altar, walks to the pulpit and grips the sides. He looks as if he must hold on for dear life or the wooden pulpit will be lifted up and thrown at the congregation in a Godly wrath.

"To quote a line from the movie, *Music Man*, 'We've got trouble right here in River City.'

With these words he points an index finger at the congregation, stabbing then wagging. "Yes, we've trouble right here ... in this town! Right here. Not someone else's town. Not another city. Right here. We cannot sit quietly by, stick our heads in the sand, and let whatever happens happen. It's in our town! We've got to respond to the world we live in. That is the mandate that comes to us as people of God. And this issue couldn't be more to the forefront than it is today.

"Events of the past few months have troubled me deeply. I have quietly listened to the gossip around town. I have read the papers with their scathing editorials. I've prayed for the men involved. I've prayed for the wives of the men. I've prayed for the families, their children, their parents. These are all fine, outstanding citizens of our community. I wake in the morning and think of them. I eat lunch thinking of them. I cannot sleep thinking of them."

Yeah, well do you think I don't? I think: Was I a good father? Did Dorothy and I do something wrong? What will become of him if he goes to jail? What will happen to my farm? I wake mornings thinking of these men, of my son. I wake in the middle of the night thinking of them. Dorothy and I avoid The Square. We shop in other towns. We don't want to hear the gossip, have people stare at us. Jenkins is now talking like he's a victim because he didn't do enough. Pious old fool! Does he think he's at fault?

"I worry about the moral fiber of our children. What should we tell them? What should you tell your children? There are no innocent ears left in our town, young or old, only innocent minds. We have trouble here, now, under our noses, in our own town. This is not some big city problem. We can't blame it on Chicago, New York, Los Angeles, San Francisco, St. Louis. We can't say our boys brought it back from the service. We've grown it right here in our home.

"We've grown it as surely as we grow wheat, corn, and soybeans. The question is - what will the harvest be? Will we be penitent? Do you, any of you, have a sense of guilt? I know I do".

Guilt! Do I have guilt? Yes I have guilt. I don't know why Thomas did what he did, but I still think I'm partly to blame. Dorothy feels guilty. She and I should be on that prayer list. Who's helping us through this?

He continues. "As the church of Jesus Christ, we cannot sit on the sidelines and do nothing while those in our community are destined for damnation. I cannot hide in my office behind a Bible and wish it would all go away. We cannot sit inside our churches singing pretty hymns, reciting comfortable prayers, familiar creeds, eating at our dinner parties, drinking coffee, having pancake breakfasts, dunking for apples on Halloween, patting ourselves on the back for being good Christians, being thankful for our neatly tied bundle of faith. This must be mowed down as surely as you mow your grass. Rake the dead and decaying leaves from your lawn. Clean up our own back yard."

I don't want to, but my eyes search the congregation to see reactions. Some people have their heads bowed as if in prayer, but I'd like to think they're embarrassment. They can't believe the words they're hearing. They know all these guys. Maybe Dorothy and I have been wrong in not talking to our friends, the neighbors.

Pastor Jenkins is not done yet. "Homosexuality is not just a preference, preferring strawberry jam to grape jelly. An affair in a public restroom, where children go, is not like playing pool in the bar with the boys. It's not a night of poker at the Elks Club. Homosexuality is a sin. It is a sin in the eyes of God, in the words of God. There is only one conclusion: homosexuality is less than God's best for his creation. It is less than God's best for us. And if our lives are less than God's design for us, it's sin. Hear God's word, his voice. It is not ambiguous or unclear. It is sin. It is all our sin if we do nothing.

"God says very clearly in Leviticus, verse 22, after he talks about a lot of different kinds of relationships, he says in verse 22: *'You shall not lie with a male as one lies with a female. It is an abomination'*.

"Anyone who has heard of the cities of Sodom and Gomorrah knows that they were notorious hotbeds of homosexuality. Genesis 19:5-8 says, *and they called to Lot and said to him, 'Where are the men who came to you tonight? Bring them out to us that we may have relations with them.' But Lot went out to them at the doorway, and shut the door behind him, and said, 'Please, my brothers, do not act wickedly'.*

"Even the New Testament clearly states exactly the same thing in Jude 7: *Just as Sodom and Gomorrah and the cities around them, since they in the same way as these indulged in gross immorality and went after strange flesh, are exhibited as an example, in undergoing the punishment of eternal fire.*

"Paul in his first letter to Timothy says that the word of God is not, I repeat is not, ambiguous when it comes to homosexuality. It is wrong. It is a sin. It is against God's will. In the very beginning of the Bible, the first few pages of Genesis tells us: *So God created man in his own image, in the image of God created he him; male and female created he them. And God blessed them, and God said unto them, Be fruitful, and multiply, and replenish the earth, and subdue it: and have dominion over the fish of the sea, and over the fowl of the air, and over every living thing that moveth upon the earth.*

"God did not create another man to be with Adam. Let me repeat. He did not create man and man. He created man and woman, Adam and Eve. God told them to be fruitful and multiply. Can two men be fruitful, can they multiply? No they can't. It requires a man and a woman to multiply, to replenish the earth. This is God's intent. This is God's will. How many times must it be said? When you turn away from God, when you disobey his will, you are committing sin. Big S big I big N, sin!

I'm ready to crawl under the pew in front of me and hide, but another part of me wants to stand up and scream. What about the words of Jesus concerning the prostitute? *Let he who is without sin cast the first stone.* What about that passage, Pastor Jenkins? I saw you looking at the new Corvettes in the showroom. You go to the Ladies' Circle and listen to their gossip.

"Remember our reading today from Paul to the people at Corinth. *Know ye not that the unrighteous shall not inherit the kingdom of God? Be not deceived: neither fornicators, nor idolaters, nor adulterers, nor effeminate, nor abusers of themselves with mankind, nor thieves, nor covetous, nor drunkards, nor revilers, nor extortioners, shall inherit the kingdom of God.*"

"My fellow Christians, here is the question. Just what should you do about the sin of others? There are a number of responses: You might turn the other cheek. You could forgive them and urge them to repent. Should you just stay away from them least they taint you. Or do you have some responsibility? Should you worry about your own sin? All of these answers and more occur in the Bible.

"Let's go back to 1 Corinthians 5:1-2. *It is reported commonly that there is fornication among you, and such fornication as is not so much as named among the Gentiles, that one should have his father's wife. And ye are puffed up, and have not rather mourned, that he that hath done this deed might be taken away from among you.*

"If any one of this congregation brings to the church a bad reputation because of their public sins, they should be asked to leave and not return until the problem is solved. If you or I do nothing about a public sinner it says that sin does not matter to us. Public sins do have an effect on us."

I wonder if the good Pastor has thought about the money. If those people leave so do their pledges, so do their good works.

He's not done yet. "Remember we are a community of believers in Christ. And I as the head of you, the believers, have a greater responsibility. Paul states this responsibility in his letter to Timothy 3:2-5. *A bishop then must be blameless, the husband of one wife, vigilant, sober, of good behaviour, given to hospitality, apt to teach; Not given to wine, no striker, not greedy of filthy lucre; but patient, not a brawler, not covetous; One that ruleth well his own house, having his children in subjection with all gravity; (For if a man know not how to rule his own house, how shall he take care of the church of God?)*

"So you see, none of us can sit and do nothing. We must hold the men accountable and urge them to repent, to return to the rules of God, the love of God, the fellowship of this congregation. If you repent and turn around, there is forgiveness. However, even if a person believes that homosexuality is a sin based upon this scripture, the next verse does say that homosexuals can inherit the kingdom if they come to the Lord, Jesus Christ."

1 Corinthians 6:11. *And such were some of you: but ye are washed, but ye are sanctified, but ye are justified in the name of the Lord Jesus, and by the Spirit of our God.*

"Our Lord Jesus has paid the price for your sins. You can become a member of the fold but you must do it through Christ, our Lord. Only through him can you be washed clean, can you be sanctified. I beg of you, my fellow Christians, as a congregation, help these sinners to see God, to follow Christ, and to turn away from their sins. Help them to return to their families, to their wives."

"Remember, *Ye are justified in the name of the Lord Jesus, and by the Spirit of our God.*

"God calls us to rebel against sin, to hate sin. But God calls us to love the sinner. Bring the sinners home. Let us again raise our heads proud before God and say we have stamped out this sin, sent Satan back to his lair."

"Yes, we have trouble right here in River City. But the trumpets of God shall lead us on and we shall follow him into a glorious time. Let us pray.

"Dear God, heavenly Father, Your name is great. Your wisdom is to be praised. You have given us Your word in Holy Scripture. You have provided a moral code for us to follow. You have given us redemption through Your Son, Jesus Christ. You have provided us abundant grace in your love. Help us to help those afflicted with this sin of sexual immorality. Help us to bring these people to Your love, to the forgiveness of the crucified Christ. Be also with their families, their children, their wives, their parents, guide them, help them in bringing their loved ones back to Your love. Help us to help them. Help us to bring them to salvation. Let them know they can return to us. Let them see the right path of our redeemer, Christ the Lord. Dear God help our greater community outside this congregation to heal. Let them know Your love. Your Son is capable of great things. Dear God, Redeemer Christ, heal us all. Amen."

I'm sure my face is red because it feels hot. I turn to Dorothy. She's looking at her purse, head bowed. After that sermon, I feel as if all eyes in the congregation are on us even though we're sitting in the back pew. Pastor Jenkins might as well have asked us to stand up and take a bow.

I whisper, "Dorothy, let's go. God help me, I think he'll ask for an altar call. I know he will look right at us, expect us to go, to renew our faith. I'm not going to let that happen. I won't give him a chance."

Dorothy refuses to raise her head, but mumbles to me from beneath her veil as she fingers her black purse. "There's still the offering, the Lord's prayer. We'll be seen."

With the words just spoken, I'm not sure Pastor Jenkins would accept our money. Would he now take money from sinners, us, who've let this happen? Yes he would. He would consider it payment for our sins. He wouldn't go so far as to hurt the church coffers. "We're leaving, now. Say the Lord's Prayer in the car on the way home. It'll take your mind off my driving. Now go, before we're seen."

We don't make it to the car. Clara May has gotten up before us and she catches us in the narthex. "Joe, Dorothy, I want you to know not all the congregation agrees with Pastor Jenkins. I can speak for most of my bridge club and Frieda. We don't condone sex in public, but we don't believe your son is a sinner any more than all of us are sinners. Small town hearts are big and forgiving. You're right to leave early. See you later."

Both Clara May and Frieda hug us. Frieda has tears in her eyes. She looks at both of us. "This is not my kind of Christianity."

Conclusion

A year later and their probations are over. This affair has tarnished some lives but with support from the community and a memory that fades with the next newspaper headline, we survive. Now a war in Vietnam divides the community. Veterans say, *my country or die*, while their sons are not totally sold on the motto. We've forgotten our country's own shame in the destruction of Indians and their land. What about our fight for individual freedoms?

My neighbor on the opposite side of Danny has a son, Dennis, who is eligible for the draft. He tells me, "Miss Clara May, I can't go to the war. I don't believe in it, but I'm afraid to protest. I'd like to burn my draft card. Not only would I go to jail, but my dad, a WWII veteran, would disown me."

I turn to Frieda who's come over for morning coffee to get her opinion. "Now that all five have paid their fine and spent a year on probation without incident, do you think this war has overcome the affair in our community?"

Frieda prepares her tea with sugar and cream before answering. Her opinion is hardened, and her voice firm. "If a cake doesn't turn out well you can cover it over with icing and fancies, but underneath the cake is what it is, lousy."

"So you think nothing has changed, it just appears nice?"

Frieda responds, "I'm saying no one has forgotten the affair. They've hidden it from view, iced it over with smiles and platitudes. You can't forgive or accept a person as long as you find their behavior disgusting."

"So you're saying there's no redemption, no forgiveness because people can't see the act of sex with men as part of something normal?"

We both hold tight to our coffee cups. We ponder the question as if we are holding on to the accused, wrapping our hands around them. Frieda is the first to respond. "Yes, that's exactly what I'm saying. As long as Pastor Jenkins insists on the act as sinful, no one has a mind to accept it. But there's something else. We're a small community without much exposure to the outside world. We believe in motherhood, apple pie, and the American way. For most that is marriage, two children, and a house of your own."

"I see. So the very concept is hard to grasp when you're not exposed."

"Exactly. But it gets easier when it gets personal. The truth may hurt, but it won't kill you."

It's a warm, fall day, a true Indian summer. I suggest we go out on the porch. We sit in chairs and enjoy the warmth. "Frieda, did you see that the newspaper this Sunday ran their picture of Indian summer? It's the one where a man rests on a rake with a boy nearby while a pile of leaves burns and Indians dance in the smoke."

"Oh, I love that picture. It reminds of my dad raking leaves and us kids jumping into the pile. Life seemed innocent, but of course it wasn't. We were."

"When I see the picture I remember a poem by Henry Van Dyke. I especially like the last line where he talks about the burning campfires of the past.

Frieda smiles and we both gaze at the brown corn stalks in the field. Frieda puts her coffee cup on the table to speak, "That says what I've been trying to say."

"What's that?"

"The campfires of the past are burning. We can't will them away."

"My dad was a died-in-the-wool Republican and when Democrats were in control he was not a happy man. He was quoted once saying, 'A clean sweep over from Democratic to Republican – like cornbread to hot biscuits. Cornbread is good and you can enjoy it every day for a couple of weeks but the time comes when you get sick of it and want hot biscuits.' He appeared to change, but all along he wanted biscuits."

Frieda is laughing so hard she nearly spills her coffee. "I can see your dad saying that. And I know that he wanted biscuits every day. Your mom made them in the morning. You and I would grab one each after school, but she would always scold us. 'Don't you'uns eat all those biscuits. Save one for your grandpa's dinner.'"

"Frieda, don't choke on that tea. I'm not ready for life without you."

"I'm not planning on leaving you yet." Frieda stops laughing and can safely have a drink of tea before continuing. "What do you hear from Gary these days?"

"Well, he and Bob moved to Chicago after Bob's divorce."

"Yeah, go on."

"Bob got a job teaching at one of the universities. I think it's one of the law schools. Gary says Bob is in hog heaven. Happy to be out of the watchful eye of Dewers and his parents."

"Speaking of his parents, I hear say Bob's parents turned on Mary."

I was waiting to tell Frieda this story. "I don't think I told you what was behind that. It seems as if Mary was being a scorned wife in the divorce proceedings. She demanded Bob could never see the kids alone."

Frieda's eyebrows rise in a look of disbelief. "Why ever not? Bob has always been a good parent."

"Mary's attorney told the judge, 'You never know what he might be up to when the kids are there. They should not be exposed to that kind of behavior.' You can imagine how it hurt Bob but the surprise was how it infuriated his parents."

Frieda is all ears and can't wait for me to continue. "What did they do?"

"They threatened to help Bob sue her for custody based on the fact that she had been a Scarlet O'Hara herself."

"Did they?"

"Hold your horses, Frieda. I'm getting there. They didn't have to. Bob's attorney countered. He said they would comply with the request if Mary did, too. If Mary insisted, it would have come out in court about her affair. So Bob has custody on holidays, summer vacation, and one weekend a month. He comes and stays with his parents on his visitation weekend."

"He made up with his parents?" Frieda asks.

"Yes, but wait, Mary became greedy. Apparently she wasn't happy with the money settlement in the divorce. She and her parents went to Bob's parents and told them they had to convince Bob to pay her more in the settlement."

"This is juicy. What did they do?"

"They told Mary and her parents they were not getting involved. They told Mary that if she needed more money, she should get a job."

"And what did they say about Gary and Bob living together?"

"I talked to William at church the other day. He's accepting of the arrangement, but doesn't understand it. He told me he wanted to see his son and my grandkids more than he want to be a Puritan. He said Rose and he love their son. He said he talked to some of his friends who told us it was okay. He wants to be part of his son's world. They're even making a trip to Chicago next month. They'll be staying in Bob and Gary's apartment."

Frieda throws her head back as if horrorstruck. "What will Pastor Jenkins say? Do you think Bob and Gary will sleep in the same bed when they're there?"

"I don't know, Frieda. Do you want me to ask them to take pictures?"

"Would they? I'd love to see what their apartment looks like. Homosexuals are supposed to be good at decorating."

"Honestly, Frieda!"

"Well, they are. You still haven't talked about Gary."

"He says he misses our company and the friends he made in Dewers but is happy to be back in Chicago."

Frieda interrupts. "And his parents, what do they say?"

"They already knew Gary was homosexual, so he and Bob living together is not a problem. Gary says they wish he and Bob the best. When the kids come to Chicago, he takes them to see Gary's parents and they eat it up, both his parents and the kids."

"What about his business here? How's it doing?" Frieda asks.

"He said hiring Mary Turnbull was the best thing he could have done. Mary knows the community. She's familiar with farming and knows all the farmers. The farmers trust her judgment because she is one of them. And," I added, "she needed the job."

Frieda is anxious to speak and holds up her index finger to quiet me. "I talked to Thomas after church and he says he's okay, but he looks more fatalistic or resigned than okay. What do you think?"

"I think Thomas will always wonder if he made the right choice. As the saying goes, the grass always looks greener on the other side of the fence. I say don't covet the neighbor's cow because you think she produces more milk. You never know when she'll go dry. He loves farming and it is a lot easier and more profitable to work his father's land. Even with Sue working, he couldn't afford to buy the farm implements that he would need to start up on his own. He's staying put with Sue. They're going to couples sex therapy. It's a court order for the married couples. And before you ask, I don't know how the therapy is going. Even I don't ask some questions."

Frieda points to her now empty cup with pleading eyes. "How about some more tea, and haven't you got any sweets to go with it?"

I get up and take Frieda's cup. "As you wish, your majesty. How about a peanut butter cookie?"

"Make it two. All this news is making me hungry."

"Living makes you hungry, Frieda."

After getting more tea and the cookies, I return to the porch. Frieda is munching so I start talking. "My car is getting to cost too much in repairs so I went into the dealership the other day to look at new ones. James took me in hand."

Frieda stops eating long enough to respond, "I haven't heard much about him. Did he have anything to say?"

"You mean other than trying to sell me the most expensive car on the showroom floor?"

"Yes."

"He seemed eager to talk. We went into his office to look at prices but the topic quickly turned to their marriage."

Frieda has stopped eating and is all ears, "And ..."

"He said he was tired of people in the town avoiding him as if he had some infectious disease. He and Judy are still together. He says after raising two kids and over 25 years of marriage, he doesn't have the energy to start over."

"I'm not buying it," Frieda says. "He was married nearly 25 years when this whole affair started."

"It could have something to do with his recent diagnosis of prostate cancer."

"Prostate cancer!" Frieda says, "oh the poor man."

"Yes, prostate cancer. He is undergoing radiation therapy, and if that doesn't work, he'll need surgery. He told me he doesn't feel very sexy these days. Judy and he are trying to work through it all. He's more worried about how it will affect his kids."

Frieda says, "You and I know a lot about kids, and I would say most are very forgiving if you're truthful. He should let them do the worrying and take care of himself."

"Good advice, Dr. Frieda."

Frieda is finished with her tea, as I am with my coffee. We get up to take our cups back to the kitchen. As we're putting them into the sink she inquires, "Has Danny's dad come around yet?"

"No, and Danny doesn't think he ever will. But the good news is that Danny's mom has told his dad she intends on seeing Danny. His dad told her to see him if she wants, but he's not setting foot in Danny's house until he gives up his sinful ways. His mom drops by once or twice a week, usually with some homemade food. At least the affair has given his mom some guts to go against her husband."

"How's he doing with losing Bob and Gary to Chicago?" Frieda asks as she grabs another cookie.

"It's been good for him. They keep in touch and Danny takes a weekend off once a month to visit them in Chicago. If you'd get out at night more, you'd know I bartend for him on those weekends."

Frieda taps her upper lip with the end of her index finger. "Clara May, Pastor Jenkins is going to bar you from church."

With a hand on my hip, I try for my most defiant pose. "I hope he does. I fought back prohibition and I'll fight him. It will give me impetus to go to another church."

Frieda rolls her eyes ignoring my comment about church and asks, "Do you think Danny will ever move?"

"No. He loves the bar and his house. He told me the other day that as long as Bob and Gary let him visit Chicago, he's okay. He also said he was learning to be more independent when he visits Chicago. Then I asked him if he thought he'd ever bring someone home."

Frieda's eyebrows arch in a worried concern. "That would be a mistake. I'm not sure Dewers is ready."

"Dewers will never be ready. I told Danny when he's comfortable, do it."

Frieda goes to grab her coat. "I guess I won't need this."

"No, you won't. Enjoy the weather while you can."

"Bye, Clara May."

"See you in church Sunday?"

Pastor Jenkins is still there, but he's retiring soon and we are all too happy to see that happen. And that's where we stand today.

I almost forgot. I promised you lemon pound cake. Last weekend of the month I tend bar at Squeaky's. Drop by, have a drink, there will be some lemon pound cake for you.